# *Essence*

## LISA ANN O'KANE

*To my sister Shana,*
*for always believing I could do this*
*and for moving mountains*
*to make sure I did*

# PART ONE:

# GOLDEN GATE PARK

# CHAPTER ONE

I wish I could say I left because my brother died.

I wish the truth were as simple as me turning and running the moment Cedar ascended the worn altar steps. His face was drawn, and he clutched Brady's urn gingerly between his fingers. But the urn was all wrong – too small and too plain, not nearly vast enough to fit the joy and laughter and miracle that had been my baby brother's life.

So I should have left. I should have jumped from my meditation mat and burst through the peeling, tinted glass of Cedar's temple door. I should have dodged the crumbling sidewalk cracks and barricades, and I should have dashed from the Haight-Ashbury District and never, ever looked back.

But I didn't.

Of course I didn't. My mother would have never forgiven a display like that.

Instead, I sat stock-still during Brady's memorial, eyes focused and legs folded with everybody else. I bowed my head when

Cedar read Brady's transgressions, and I repeated the mantra with just the right emphasis: not too fervent, and not too lax.

*"Neutrality is the key to longevity."*

I nodded to Cedar before leaving, and I followed my mother and Aunt Marie away from the converted Victorian homes that served as our temple headquarters. We walked through the barricades on Ashbury Street, past the Jesus freaks and lingering protesters with megaphones.

We didn't discuss the protesters – that day or any day. Instead, we skirted the condemned entrance to Golden Gate Park and took three left turns to make sure we weren't being followed. Aunt Marie nodded when the coast was clear, and then we entered the quiet home we shared on Fifth Avenue without another word.

I took a shower and said my evening prayers as usual, but the truth is, our mantra had begun to sound hollow that day. The protesters' words lingered in my thoughts even when their demonstrations dissipated, and they cast questions and doubt onto the very foundations of my faith.

Brady was only six when the universe took him. And he *was* neutral. Mostly. As neutral as any six year-old could be, separated from his family and starting kinder classes at the temple for the first time in his life.

So what if he had nightmares and cried to be held sometimes? So what if he held hands with his classmates when no one was looking?

Did he really deserve to die for it?

The presence of these questions frightened me even more than my fear Cedar would discover them. They filled the crevices of my mind even during my most solemn moments of reflection, and no amount of self-deprivation or meditation could curb them.

I tried increasing my fasting periods – dropping from two meals per day to one, and then finally skipping meals entirely until the hollowness in my gut became a raging fever that kept me bedridden for nearly a week. Then I tried increasing the length of my meditation sessions – arriving at the temple at dawn and lying prone on my mat until the masters shooed me out to begin morning lessons.

Still, my questions wouldn't cease. They followed me everywhere, and they distracted and poisoned my neutrality until they were finally noticed by Cedar himself.

I was vacuuming the temple's reflection room after evening services when Aunt Marie entered without a knock. Her face seemed uncharacteristically anxious, and blue circles marred the half-moons below her eyes.

"Cedar wants to see you," she whispered. "Right away."

A stab of dread settled in my chest. Cedar *never* summoned us; he was too busy leading the Movement.

I unplugged the vacuum and turned. "Why?"

"I don't know. But I doubt it's good news, sweetheart."

We stood in silence for a moment, and then Marie began fussing – straightening the hem of my white meditation robe and smoothing the hair from my forehead. The fabric was stiff, thick and uncomfortable, and it was marred with sweat stains from the countless women who had worn it before me. Marie insisted on hand-washing it every time I was chosen to assist during services, but her extra attention only highlighted the fact that no amount of cleaning could safeguard it from the wear and tear of an entire temple of followers.

She shouldn't have cared what I looked like, anyway. Cedar preached against trivialities and displays of affection, but Marie seemed to relish these tiny acts of rebellion.

"You will be fine," she whispered as we slipped from the room. "Just remember to keep your head down."

We strode toward the staircase to Cedar's quarters, nodding silently to the Movement's other followers as they filed out of the temple for the evening. Cedar had converted every house on this block into classrooms and reflection rooms, but he chose to live upstairs in this one, in the converted loft/living room right above the main meditation sanctuary.

As we ascended the stairs, I glimpsed San Francisco's glass and steel high-rises through the dark glass windows. They shone in the distance, foreign and as incomprehensible as stars.

"Do you think he noticed when I fell behind on the quilts?"

"Probably." Marie's wool skirt swooshed as she followed me. "But maybe not. I tried to sew extras for you..."

From somewhere outside, a car alarm blared. We both started, and she smiled ruefully. "The quilts are trinkets, anyway. Centrist souvenirs. No one out there takes them seriously."

We arrived at the top of the stairs, and I realized Cedar's door was propped open at the end of the hall. Behind its thin wooden frame, my mother waited. Her pale hair – usually long and flowing – was chopped in a jagged line above her shoulders. She knelt in plain clothes beside the altar at Cedar's feet, and her eyes looked hardened and weary. Her lips were pressed in a thin line, and she seemed much older than her thirty-four years.

Before I could say anything, she motioned for me to enter.

Cedar's space was the most luxurious in the temple, but it was still sparse by Outsider standards. The walls were unadorned, and a simple bed sat in the room's back corner. A low altar opened just past the entrance, and it was decorated with candles, incense and tokens. Some were Buddhist, some were Centrist and all were arranged around the mantel's centerpiece – an open book framed and protected by glass. Its pages were affected by ash and debris, but its words were still legible. *The Four Noble Truths.*

I had only been invited inside Cedar's quarters a handful of times, but I still knew the significance of the book. Everybody did. It was the basis of everything we believed in, the beginning of the entire Centrist Movement. If it had fallen open to any other page during the Great Quake of '20, if it had been burned or crushed beneath the beam that held Cedar pinned for seven days, he may have never had his Essence vision. None of us would even be here.

Cedar nodded as I entered the room. Heat surged to my cheeks, and my eyes immediately dropped to the floor.

It wasn't that Cedar was particularly handsome. He was rather normal-looking, with graying copper hair, a square jaw and a scar that stretched diagonally across the bridge of his nose. Still dressed in his forest green meditation master robe, he vaguely resembled the twentieth-century cartoon Brady and I had dug up while organizing earthquake supplies last fall. "The Jolly Green Giant", the can had said, and we had both clasped our hands over our mouths to prevent anyone from hearing our eruption of giggles.

It wasn't Cedar's appearance that made me self-conscious. It was his *presence* – the way light filled his eyes and pulled everyone to him like a magnet. It was the way the earth seemed to shiver a little every time he spoke, the way his words flowed like a current. They filled us and guided us and imparted us with so much wisdom that I felt like a shadow in comparison.

"Welcome, Sister Autumn. Sister Laurel and I have been waiting for you."

I couldn't help it; I blushed at the sound of my name. Cedar knew who I was – of course he knew who I was – but it was still startling to hear the word spoken aloud. He usually had so many more important things to think about.

I kept my eyes locked on the floor. "Good evening, sir."

"Do you know why I called you here?"

"No, sir."

"Please, have a seat."

He motioned to the floor, where Aunt Marie had already taken her place beside my mother. I slipped into a seat beside them, and Marie pressed her shin against mine. The warmth comforted me a little, but I felt a tightening in the pit of my stomach when I glimpsed the pruning shears resting on Cedar's window ledge.

He followed my gaze. Instead of addressing the shears, he took a step sideways to block my view of them. "Do you know why your brother died, Sister Autumn? Because he didn't follow the rules. Do *you* know the rules?"

"Yes, sir." Of course I did. Everyone knew the rules, including Brady: *You are born with a finite limit to your Essence, and once you use yours, it's gone. You're gone.*

But knowing and understanding are two different things, and no one would have ever suspected Brady had so little Essence to begin with. He had nightmares and cried when he was lonely, but most children would have survived such small transgressions without issue.

It wasn't until they were much older that their indulgences usually caught up with them. Maybe their hearts simply went out. Or maybe their Essence-drain manifested itself in a slow and painful death, like a disease; or a split-second ending, like a jet crash.

Because it was impossible to tell how much Essence your body stored to begin with, you never knew when you'd meet your ending.

*Neutrality is the key to longevity.*

*Too much happiness is just as dangerous as too much sadness.*

Cedar gazed at the book on his altar, and I dared a glimpse at his profile. "You must remember the Four Truths, Sister Autumn. Life means suffering. You must conserve your Essence by living neutrally, and you must honor the Buddhist and Centrist visions." He locked eyes with me. "Although it is unfortunate your brother's Essence wasn't stronger, you must remember he did this to himself. Every moment you grieve for him is a moment you will never get back."

I managed a weak nod. Cedar's words were harsh, but they were no harsher than the words I'd been repeating on a loop these past three months: *It's your fault, Autumn. You let him wander off by himself and choke to death. You weren't there for him when he needed you most.*

"I need you to give me the lion now," Cedar said.

Now, *these* words were unexpected. I wheeled to face my mother, and the panic that flashed in her eyes left no doubt who had turned me in.

Cedar waited with his hand extended. "Brady's lion," he repeated. "I know you carry it with you."

I hung my head and dug through the folds of my robe. Brady's lion – the tiny cotton doll I'd snuck to him when his nightmares started – rested just beneath my stole.

I shouldn't have even bought it. Cedar's distaste for material attachments was so well-known that the street vendor had spied the Centrist pendant around my neck and charged me at least double what it was worth. I had forked over nearly all of my weekly allotment for it – and I had gone without lunch for two days to make up for the expense – but how could I have ignored Brady's late-night sobbing?

Cedar plucked the little animal from my hands and dropped it on the windowsill. Reaching for the pruning shears, he passed them to my mother. "Thank you. And now, Sister Laurel, will you please assist me with her hair?"

"My hair?"

My mother pulled herself to her feet. "I notice the way you take care of it," she said. "I'm not being critical, because I'm the one who taught you. But with all that washing and brushing and styling... Well, it isn't a good practice for either of us to engage in. And in light of Brady's..." She opened and closed the shears before me, and the metal made a grating shriek. "Well, in light of everything that's happened, I think it's best if we reexamine our own indulgences. And we should start with the unhealthy relationships we have with our hair."

I knew I should take a breath and thank my mother for her concern. I knew I should be grateful, because deep down, I realized she was right.

I *loved* my hair. I loved its springy cinnamon curls and amber-gold highlights; I loved the way it framed my face and spilled down my back like a lion's mane. I loved the way it bounced when I walked, and I loved the distinction it gave me – setting me apart from the sea of secondhand dresses and suits that crowded the temple classes.

Worse, I realized, I liked the way boys looked at it. I liked their sideways glances and the way they sometimes seemed flustered around me. I liked being sixteen and pretty and different.

*I am the worst human being in the world.*

I nodded in resignation. I pried myself from the floor, slumping my shoulders and presenting my hair for my mother's inspection.

"That's better," she said, gathering my hair into a ponytail. "After everything that happened with Brady... We're just looking out for you."

I tried to say thank you, but a funny thing happened when I glimpsed my reflection in the dark glass of Cedar's window. I saw a girl with wide, frightened eyes and a golden-red halo, and I saw that halo extinguish the instant my mother's shears snipped the gathered hair at the base of my neck.

Looking at my reflection, I didn't see *anyone* anymore.

"There. Doesn't that feel better?" My mother extended the ponytail for me to see. Her face was serene – smiling and content – but my insides were anything but tranquil when I glimpsed the hair clutched between her fingers. It was dull, lifeless, the color of burnt earth and the texture of a dead squirrel.

That was *mine*.

I met Cedar's gaze over the bundle, and tears sprang to my eyes at the sheer injustice of it all. I gritted my teeth and tried to swallow those tears back, but it was too late.

Cedar's eyes hardened. "Sister Autumn, are you *crying*?"

I didn't know what to say. The walls suddenly felt like they were closing in on me, and the smell of incense became suffocating. Before I could stop myself, I blurted, "Brady didn't deserve any of this, and I don't, either."

My mother's jaw dropped, and the ponytail slipped from her hands. A cascade of twisted, cinnamon strands tumbled to the floor, and I turned and rushed from Cedar's quarters before I had time to change my mind.

# CHAPTER TWO

Fog swirled, thick as sludge, as I exited the temple and began running west on Haight Street. The wooden barricades were mostly gone now, but graffiti still marred the sidewalks where Outsiders sometimes protested. I surged past them, feeling the watchful gaze of the street's remaining Victorian homes as I lengthened my strides and began sprinting.

*I shouldn't be running like this,* I thought.

I shouldn't have been running at all, actually. It was one of the activities Cedar preached against in the interest of public safety. Aerobic activities not only affected oxygen levels and blood flow, but they also increased endorphins – which were the leading cause of Essence drain and death in teenagers and young adults.

If it was absolutely necessary, running should be approached with caution. Short breaks should be taken every ten feet or so, and movements should never be conducted in a state of heightened emotion. The conflicting hormones were powerful enough to kill you.

But tonight, I didn't care.

I was furious, and the sting of the pavement below my sandals drove me faster and harder than I'd ever moved before. My muscles burned and my breath came in gasps as I pushed through the shifting fog and began sprinting toward the crumbling, condemned entrance to Golden Gate Park.

The unfairness of Brady's passing stabbed me like a knife. I slowed to a trot and clutched my side in pain. Brady was so good. And light. And beautiful. He had only attended his Free Soul Ceremony eight months before; it wasn't his fault he hadn't quite gotten the hang of neutrality yet.

I took a breath and tried to run again, but the pain in my side didn't go away. Instead, it twisted somehow, and it jabbed the space below my ribcage until I felt my side knotting.

*What's happening to me?*

Fear sucked the air from my lungs as I dropped to my knees and clutched my ribs. Sweat rose on my temples, and I let myself sink sideways until I was lying on the ground. Cold seeped through the asphalt against my cheekbone, and my vision became blurred.

*Oh, no, I'm dying now, too.*

A mixture of terror and mortification filled me – *so Cedar wasn't kidding about this whole not-running thing?* – and then the pain intensified until my insides felt like they had turned into broken glass. *What am I supposed to do now?*

A vision of Brady flashed in my mind. Not the beautiful, rosy Brady of my memories, but the cold Brady, the stone Brady encapsulated inside that tiny urn. The artificial Brady, walled off behind a vessel, never to be seen or touched or held ever again.

*Did Brady feel like this right before he swallowed that cherry pit?*

I wheezed as fear began drumming in my ears. And then, a voice in my head: Get yourself together, Autumn.

The words took me back to the memorial, to the stoic grace on my mother's face as she observed me from her place beside the altar. We were supposed to file past Brady's urn – to demonstrate our detachment by not giving it so much as a sideways glance – but I stalled at the sight of it. My head pounded, and I braced myself against the altar to keep from collapsing.

"Take a moment to compose yourself," my mother had said. "You look like you're about to cry."

What could I say? I was about to cry. I knew I'd be shunned if anyone saw me, but what could I do? My baby brother was on an altar. My baby brother was dead.

"I'm serious, Autumn. Take a moment to get yourself together, or excuse yourself and go outside until you are under control." Her gaze shifted to the crowded sanctuary behind us. "I won't let you disgrace our family with your tears. Haven't we been through enough already?"

We had, but that didn't stop the grief from welling inside me. And now, lying on this crumbling trail, I felt those repressed cries finally running over.

*I'm going to die here. I'm going to die here just like Brady, and no one is ever going to find me.*

Golden Gate Park had nearly been destroyed during the Great Quake's shocks and aftershocks. The west side had been renovated and reopened, but this far east side had been condemned ten years ago. It stood vacant, overgrown and silent, and it had always reminded me of a cemetery.

It chilled me to imagine how many endorphins had probably been released on this very spot, and it chilled me even more to realize I had no idea where "this very spot" was.

The unfairness of the situation twisted my gut, and I felt my anger resurfacing. "Fine!" I shouted. "Take him, take me; I don't even care anymore!"

My words disappeared into the eucalyptus trees. The night was eerily silent for a moment, and then: "Doing all right over there, Red?"

The male voice startled me. I struggled to my knees and realized I was a lot farther into the park than I thought. I was a lot farther than I'd ever been, and this recognition sent a jolt of fear coursing through me.

I had veered north off Kezar Drive at some point, and the trail now wound through a moonlit stand of dripping green trees and rusty park benches. A sprawling sandstone mansion stood vacant and vandalized to my left, and a rotted, crumbling carousel lay silent to my right.

Through the fog bank beside the carousel, a match flared. A cigarette appeared in the mouth of a boy about my age, and he leaned forward until it caught. The tip flared for an instant, and it illuminated a long face, a strong jaw and a tapered expanse of smooth, tanned skin.

My stomach clenched. Cedar preached so strongly against cigarettes that I had rarely seen one up close before. Its lit tip was now the only clue that a person – an Outsider – stood waiting in the shadows for me.

"What do you want?" I didn't say what I wanted to say, which was: When will you people realize we're not interested in converting? When will you stop heckling us and just leave us alone?

"Name's Ryder." The boy shifted his cigarette from one hand to the other. "But here's a better question. Why is a Centrist running alone this late at night? In temple robes, no less? Kinda rebellious, don't you think?"

I narrowed my eyes. "What do you want?"

"Why? You got something you wanna give me?" Before my fear could escalate, Ryder laughed. "Only screwing with you, Red.

Hold on a sec; we don't often get visitors out here."

An antique lantern sprang to life in his hand. It was followed by two more, and I quickly realized Ryder wasn't alone out here. A hulking boy with thick brown hair and coiled shoulders leaned against the carousel beside him, and a willowy, elfish girl rested near one of the rotten wooden horses.

They were an outlandish sight. Ryder – with vintage camouflage pants and a mop of white-blond hair. The big guy – with a shell necklace and scuffed sneakers. The girl – by far the most bizarre – with dyed black hair, tall boots and a sweater that hung provocatively off one narrow shoulder.

All three wore matching metal wristbands, and I felt bewilderment surge in my chest at the sight of them. They didn't look like tourists, and they didn't look like the Outsiders that usually loitered outside our temple, condemning us to Hell or trying to convert us to Jesus.

The girl smiled and leapt from the carousel. The metal clasps on her boots jangled as she took a step toward me. "I'm Jett," she said. "And this is Cody. Sorry if we startled you."

Chipped, colored paint adorned her fingernails, and an assortment of bangles decorated her narrow wrists. Pale roots peeked beneath her choppy, black hair, and her smile was crowded with perfect teeth.

"I'm Autumn," I stammered.

The big guy, Cody, cleared his throat. "How's that pain in your side? It's called a stitch; happens when you don't stretch before you run. Try warming up next time."

*Next time?* I clutched my side and realized my pain had already disappeared.

"I love a good run," Jett said. "Especially when I feel frustrated or antsy. Sure beats staying bottled up, don't you think?"

"I've never… Well, this is the first time I've ever really…"

"Right." Ryder smiled and flicked his cigarette to the asphalt. Snubbing it with the heel of his boot, he said, "Gets the blood flowing; gets those hormones pumping a little too much. Detrimental to a long life, isn't that what you Centrists say?"

I stiffened. "Look, I've met enough Outsiders to know I'm not interested in converting. The Centrist way is the right way, and I don't care what you people think about it."

Ryder laughed. "We aren't here to convert you, Red. Aren't even real Outsiders. Grew up right inside that temple complex, just like you."

"Then what are you doing out here?"

"What are you doing out here?"

"I'm... running."

"Mm-hmm. Because?"

"Because... Well, because I'm kinda..."

"Pissed off?"

I struggled to my feet. "I shouldn't be talking to Outsiders like this. I need to go."

"Wait." Ryder approached, and I cursed myself for the nervous way his nearness affected my insides. *Watch it, Autumn.*

"Don't worry," he said. "I promise we're not here to lecture you for running. You just look like something's bothering you." He narrowed his eyes. "Wait, I know you. You're Autumn Grace, the girl outside the temple."

"What?"

"Your brother choked on something a few months back, didn't he? Centrist meditation masters wouldn't let the tourists resuscitate him."

I paled. I had done everything in my power to forget that day – the flashing cameras, the throngs of people, the meditation masters shoving aside the tourists and screaming, "Get back! It's the universe's way!"

Cedar maintained we had a religious exemption from Outsider interference, and Brady shouldn't have been talking to tourists in the first place. He certainly shouldn't have taken strange food from them. But still I had surged forward, hoping to fight the meditation masters and lead him to an Outsider who could save him. My struggles had been in vain.

Jett's face paled. "I recognize you now, too, Autumn. I'm so sorry for your loss."

Ryder and I made eye contact. For a moment, his bravado seemed to fade, and an emotion – sympathy? – flicked across his face. "I'm really sorry, Red. For everything."

No one spoke for a few moments, and then Cody finally cleared his throat. This seemed to jolt Ryder, and he snapped back to attention.

"Here's the thing that gets me," he continued. "Your brother was only five or six, right? So, my thought is, how much Essence could he have possibly drained in that short a time? I mean, really? He spent an entire lifetime's worth of Essence, and he didn't even do anything all that crazy? Doesn't that sound a little funny to you, Red?"

"What Ryder's trying to say, Autumn," Jett said, "is that sometimes, when someone as young as your brother dies... doesn't it ever make you wonder if maybe it wasn't his Essence giving out on him after all? What if it was just a freak thing, like an accident?"

I clutched the Centrist pendant around my neck, the one my mother told me to look to anytime I needed to refresh myself on the lessons of my Free Soul Ceremony. It was carved with our mantra – Neutrality is the key to longevity – and I repeated it to myself before answering, "There's no such thing as an accident. Accidents are just manifestations of Essence drain."

"I knew you'd say that," she said. "But just think about it.

Your brother was so young."

"And I've smoked a lot of cigarettes," Ryder said. "I've raised a lot of hell, and I've done pretty much everything in Cedar's warnings at least once. Doesn't it seem – if anyone was gonna die – it should have been someone like me instead?"

"Yeah, it does seem like that." I frowned. "But you didn't. Brady did, and I'm getting tired of talking to you about it."

"Wait." Ryder reached to stop me. "Don't misunderstand what I'm saying, Red. I'm sorry about what happened to your brother, and I'm certainly not bragging that I'm here and he's not. I'm just saying…" He leaned closer, and I inhaled the tangy odor of tobacco on his breath. "I'm just saying that sometimes we wonder if there's any truth to this Essence thing at all. What if the Centrists got it wrong?"

He began walking in a slow circle. "I mean, what if your Essence doesn't have anything to do with how old you are when you die?"

I shook my head. "Cedar found a direct link between emotions, auras and Essence drain. It's a fact; says so in The Four Noble Truths and all the Centrist texts."

"Yeah, but what if it's a made-up fact? What if Cedar is just trying to control you by telling you not to have fun?"

"You aren't supposed to feel anything," Cody said. "You can't be happy; can't be sad. You're just supposed to disregard the rest of the world and meditate until you turn into a zombie."

"We don't disregard the rest of the world," I snapped. "We know perfectly well what's going on out here."

"Do you?"

"Yeah. It's reckless, and it's dangerous. It's the very self-indulgence and excess that caused the Great Quake in the first place. We choose not to be part of it."

Ryder raised his eyebrows. "Just think about it," he said. "The

Quake was nearly twenty years ago; lots of stuff has happened out here since." He paused. "Haven't you ever wondered what the rest of the world is doing?"

I frowned. "You guys said you weren't here to convert me."

"We aren't. Not exactly." He tilted his head. "My friends and I live in the Sierras now, but we'll be here a couple more days. If what we're saying makes sense to you, we'd love to tell you more about what we're trying to do here."

"And what exactly are you trying to do here?"

He grinned, and dimples appeared at the corners of his cheeks. "Nothing much. Just finally spread some truth."

# CHAPTER THREE

I tried to forget about my meeting with Ryder and his friends.

I snuck back home and woke early for meditation the next day, and I pushed aside reminders of my outburst when my temple mates commented on my new shoulder-length haircut.

"I think it looks nice," my chore partner Juliet said as we dusted the classroom windows before lunch. I did my best to ignore the fleeting look of smugness that flashed in her eyes as she wiped the dust from her hands.

It was a bit harder to ignore my mother's disapproval at home. She did her best to stay neutral – as always – but her expression seemed extra guarded as we prepared dinner that night. I often caught her staring when she thought I wasn't looking.

The kitchen was dim, as always, and its soft overhead lights barely illuminated the sparse metal appliances and wooden cabinets. My mother stood chopping radishes in her blue cashier's uniform, and her newly cut hair was pulled back.

Aunt Marie stood fussing over a bowl of spinach and arugula at her side. The greens – castoffs from my mother's grocery store job – were past date, as usual, and the tips were slightly wilted and brown.

If she noticed, Marie hid her disappointment well. As she tossed the salad with fingers thick as sausages, she hummed softly to herself – a reckless habit that drove my mother crazy.

The women worked like bookends, and they leaned into each other slightly as they chopped canned tomatoes and beets. There was an easy solidarity to their movements – the quiet, neutral confidence that Cedar always preached about – and I felt guilt surge inside me in response.

"I'm sorry for leaving last night," I finally whispered. I wished I could squeeze in beside them like usual. "I acted rashly, and my decision was selfish."

My mother softened. "It worries me to see your aura so rippled, Autumn," she said, glancing backward and exhaling as if the tension felt heavy in her chest. "Now more than ever, I'm pleased to hear your emotions are under control again."

The guilt in my stomach twisted. "They are; I'm sorry for worrying you."

She nodded. Making fleeting eye contact with Aunt Marie, she added, "I have some news, then; I had hoped to tell you earlier. Cedar has invited Brother Thomas to join us for dinner tonight."

"Brother Thomas?" I felt my throat close. Mother hadn't received a visit from a meditation master for years, not since Brady's conception. The return of Brother Thomas – the master who had conceived me, too – could only mean one thing. "But Mother…"

"It's time, Autumn. It has been three months since Brady passed, and Cedar thinks I should try again. I'm almost thirty-five now; I can't waste time if I want to perform my duties and conceive two children."

"Mother, you can't be serious!"

The knife in her hand trembled. "Autumn," she said. "I understand Brady's death has affected you. It has certainly affected all of us. But I urge you to remember the lessons of your Free Soul Ceremony. Your Essence is precious, and every moment you dwell on Brady's passing is a moment you will never get back."

She paused. "You must understand I'm just trying to do what's best for our family. Since nothing we do has the power to bring back Brady, it will be better for all of us if we simply try to move on with our lives."

Tears sprang to my eyes again. This time, I didn't even attempt to hide them. "Move on? You honestly expect me to forget about Brady and move on with my life?"

My voice came out remarkably angry, and Aunt Marie reacted by steadying her sister. Her eye contact with me was pleading, but her voice was gentle when she said, "Sweetheart, please calm down. Your outburst is…"

"Your outburst is very distressing to both of us." My mother clutched a dish towel. "So I think it's best if you go to your bedroom early tonight. There are some sleeping pills left over from Brady's funeral in my cabinet; I will bring you a few as soon as we finish our dinner with Brother Thomas."

I clenched my fists. "But I don't want sleeping pills – just like I don't want to forget about Brady or move on with my life. He was my baby brother, and I'm tired of feeling like there's something wrong with me because I miss him!"

My mother scowled. "Autumn, please go to your room now."

"Fine!" I knew I was being reckless, but I didn't even care. I was already halfway up the stairs.

I lay fuming, facedown on my bed, for nearly an hour. Tears ran freely down my cheeks, and I let them fall, surprised by the feeling of relief.

I couldn't remember the last time I'd had an outburst like that. Maybe when I was five, just before my own Free Soul Ceremony. A scratched knee or a splinter or something; a childhood tantrum followed by a stern lecture from my mother.

"You will be a Free Soul in three weeks," she had said, clutching both my cheeks in her hands. "Do you know what that means, Autumn? It means we will go to the temple, and your Essence will be symbolically cut from mine. You won't be a baby anymore, so your outbursts will begin shortening your own life instead of mine. You don't want that, do you, sweetheart?"

I didn't. *I still don't, but what if Cedar is wrong about Essence drain?*

I felt like my foundation was crumbling, like everything I'd ever believed in was being called into question. *The Centrist way is the right way. Neutrality is the key to longevity. Too much happiness is just as dangerous as too much sadness.*

*But what if it isn't?*

I was so consumed by the question that I nearly missed the sound of my bedroom door creaking open. Aunt Marie's movements were tentative, and her expression seemed concerned. She cradled something small in her hands.

"I have something to give you, child."

I wiped the tears from my eyes. Into my palms, she dropped something soft and fuzzy. Brady's stuffed lion.

I opened my mouth, but she shook her head. "This never happened. Do you understand?"

"Aunt Marie, how did you–?"

"Fairly easy once the two of them got to talking last night." She squeezed my shoulder. "She's upset, too, you know. Doesn't like the idea of having another baby any more than you do."

"Then why is she doing it?"

"Because Cedar wants her to." She sank to the bed beside me. "She was only sixteen when she met him, you know. Cedar. Fell in love with every word he said. Joined his camp before there even was a Movement."

"I know."

She cleared her throat. "Yes, but you need to understand that our way of life isn't the only way. Your grandmother didn't even approve of this."

"My grandmother?" I felt myself reeling. No one ever spoke of my grandmother.

"Left the Bay Area soon after the Quake," Marie said. "Tried to take us with her, but your mother was already enchanted with Cedar's teachings by then. Wasn't long before she was pregnant with you."

"But..." The world took an unexpected spin. "Why did you stay? Why didn't you leave with her?"

She leaned sideways until our shoulders touched. "Sometimes, sweetheart, you have to decide where your loyalties lie. And mine lie with you and my little sister."

As she smoothed her pants and stood to go, she added, "I love your mother more than anyone in this world, but I don't always agree with her choices. And you are the only one who can decide what fits for you, because you are the one who has to live with that choice."

I was still holding the stuffed lion when a second pair of footsteps echoed up the wooden stairs. I started and shoved the doll beneath my pillow.

The second my mother entered, I knew something was wrong.

I mean, bad wrong.

Her jaw was set in a firm line, and she clutched a piece of paper in one hand and a bottle of painkillers in the other.

"Autumn," she said. "I brought you some medicine for your nerves, and I also brought you this." She extended the paper. It was crisp and official, with Caltrain Voucher printed carefully at the top.

I felt my stomach drop. "A train ticket? Why did you buy me a train ticket?"

"It's not just a train ticket." She pressed the paper into my hand. "It's a ticket to Los Gatos, to a Centrist meditation retreat run by Cedar's cousin Rayn."

"You can't be serious." My voice cracked. "I don't need to go to an Essence treatment center."

"It's not an Essence treatment center. It's a retreat. A good one, filled with space and peace and light, everything you need to get back in touch with your neutrality." She frowned and closed my fingers around the ticket. "Autumn, I'm only suggesting this because Cedar thinks it's the best decision. For all of us. You have been an emotional wreck ever since Brady died, and, frankly, I can't understand this recent explosion about your hair. You are becoming a danger, both to yourself and to this family, and I refuse to let you–"

"Oh, I see." I felt my temper rising. "You want to send me away, not because you care about my well-being, but because you don't want to have to deal with me anymore. Three months of sadness is just too much for Cedar, and we both know you'll always choose him over me. Isn't that right?"

"Autumn!" She stared at me in horror. "This is exactly why Cedar suggested Los Gatos in the first place." She backed away from me. "We can discuss this more tomorrow, but I'm going to ask you to get your temper under control. Your emotions are becoming dangerous, and I will not allow you to ruin everything we have given you."

She strode away, but my anger didn't cease. I was livid, but more than that, I was determined. I was not going to Los Gatos.

# CHAPTER FOUR

I'm not sure what I said in the note I left. I know I scribbled it haphazardly on the back of my train ticket, and I imagine it said something like "I left to find out if Brady's death was an accident. I'm not sure I believe in Essences anymore."

But that's just a guess. I was so panicked and infuriated that I honestly blacked out for a little while. It wasn't until I'd thrown a fistful of belongings into a backpack, squeezed out my window and started running back toward Golden Gate Park that I finally began to comprehend the reality of my situation.

*If I stay, Cedar may send me to Los Gatos. If I go…*
*What will happen?*

I slowed to a trot inside the park's entrance. I'd had a strange conversation with Ryder and his friends, but I didn't know who they were. I didn't know what they were doing, or what they stood for, or really anything about them – except that they wore showy clothes and smiled a lot and seemed unconcerned about the parameters of what was expected of them.

They mentioned going to a place called the Sierras in a couple of days. Wasn't that a mountain range? If I went with them, would I be able to return?

Was I even really invited?

I shifted my backpack and clutched the silver pendant around my neck. This excursion definitely wasn't a practice in neutrality. What if Cedar was right?

"This is stupid." I didn't realize I'd said the words aloud until I saw my breath mist in the night air. Golden Gate Park was silent, socked in once again with fog, and the air felt cold and electric as it swirled around my skin.

I peered toward the outline of the carousel in the distance. *How do I know they'll even still be there?*

I was playing with the idea of turning around when I felt the vibration of footsteps on the trail behind me. I spun to see the outline of a very tall, dark-haired person approaching me through the haze.

My heart dropped.

"Who's there?" The male voice on the other side of the fog was tremulous, even shakier than mine. "Is someone out there?"

I clenched my fists and attempted to disappear in the foliage.

"I can see your outline. Who are you? Are you with Ryder's group?"

I found myself stammering: "No. Um... not really. Well, I wanted..."

The figure approached. A break in the fog briefly revealed him as a lanky boy about my age, with a tangle of coal-colored hair and a drab, rumpled suit.

He relaxed when he saw me. "Hey, I know you. Autumn, right? What are you doing out here?"

His voice was warm, lilting, and he spoke with a degree of tenderness unusual to hear in a stranger's voice. It was unusual to hear in anyone's voice, actually, and it was so unexpected that I felt myself softening.

I squinted. "I'm sorry. I don't think I recognize…"

"I'm Javier." He extended his hand. "But everyone calls me Javi. I see you at morning meditation sometimes." He paused. "So, they got to you, too?"

"Yeah." I exhaled. "Found me in the park last night."

"Cornered me on my way home from afternoon lessons yesterday." He tugged at his Centrist pendant. "Think there's any truth to what they're saying about Essence drain?"

"I don't know. But… I really hope so."

He swallowed. "Yeah. Me too."

We began walking toward the carousel, and a knot of tension tightened in my chest. A few scattered raindrops dripped against the top of my head, and I felt a pang of longing for my bedroom's warm blankets. *What am I doing out here?*

It struck me that I didn't know Javi any more than I knew Ryder or Jett or Cody. This left my insides jumbled and unsteady. "I haven't really decided what I want to do yet, actually," I said. "I want to listen to what they have to say, but I'll probably go home if I don't like what I hear. I haven't made my mind up either way."

Javi glanced at me, no doubt appraising my backpack. "Yeah," he finally said. "I can definitely respect that."

A flashlight beam suddenly blasted me. Shielding my eyes and staggering backward, I groped blindly for a moment as Ryder's voice boomed through the darkness: "Red! Javi! You came back!"

Lanterns flared, and we were abruptly surrounded. Jett flitted forward and pulled me into a hug. "I was hoping you'd come back," she said. "Cody, what did I tell you?"

"Good to see you again, Autumn. Javi." Cody's voice was deep and genuine, and he lingered at the outskirts of the circle while Ryder strode back and forth between Javi and me.

His hair was damp from condensation, but his eyes were bright. "Wow, you guys already know each other? How fantastic is this?"

"No… we met on the way in," I stammered, glancing sideways at Javi.

Tall and affable, like a puppy that hadn't quite grown into himself yet, Javi appraised me through almond-shaped eyes the color of copper. His lips were curled in a tentative smile, and his skin was deeply tanned and smooth-looking. We made eye contact, and I quickly glanced at my feet.

"I want you guys to meet Amneet," Ryder continued, motioning to a small, olive-skinned girl with hair long and thick as a horse's mane. She wore a plain brown dress just like mine, and her eyes shifted back and forth as she sized us up.

"Amneet joined us this afternoon and, wow, it really is great to see all of you again." Ryder motioned toward the sandstone mansion nearby. "There. The Sharon Building. The rain's gonna really start coming down soon. Let's get inside, and then we'll tell you what we're all about."

Jett busied herself by tending the candles that crowded the turret's wide stone windows. We were seated in the one remaining wing of the mansion that still had glass in its windowpanes. Outside, the rain was pouring in sheets, and its chill infused the room with an eerie, expectant stillness.

"The first thing you probably want to know is who we are." Ryder pulled a handful of blankets from a pile in the corner and tossed them to the spot where Amneet, Javi and I sat on the floor.

He motioned and said, "There, get comfortable," before continuing, "So, Cody, Jett and I were raised right here in San Francisco. We grew up with the 'rules', we attended our own Free Soul Ceremonies… We even wore those terrible white temple robes, just like you guys." At this, he grinned over his shoulder. "Not that you don't look great in them, because I'm sure you totally do."

"Ryder's father was one of Cedar's very first followers," Jett said, waving an extinguished match and flitting to a seat on Cody's lap. It was an unexpected act of affection that made me blush and quickly look away. "Helped organize the movement, and even oversaw the purchase of all those buildings on Haight Street. Started as an apprentice under Cedar and then worked his way all the way up to meditation master."

"He was a good one, too," Ryder said, retrieving a flask of dark liquid from a box in the corner. He pulled the cork with his teeth and spat it to the floor. "Probably procreated about twenty kids in the name of the Movement over the course of the first few years, but then my mother had me, and everything changed."

Amneet snorted. "This isn't one of those 'love at first sight' deserter stories, is it? Because we've all heard those before, and I'm not impressed by people who are too weak to control their emotions."

Ryder chuckled. "Don't worry, Amneet. This isn't one of those stories." He took a swig of the liquid and passed it to Cody. "But everything did change when my mother had me, because he got attached. To both of us."

Jett motioned from her place on Cody's lap. "Cedar noticed, and it wasn't long before Ryder's father got reassigned. He was forbidden from spending time with Ryder or his mother, and when it was time for her to conceive her second child, another meditation master was given the task."

"My old man got upset," Ryder said. "Was generally pretty good at staying neutral, but when it came to my mother and me..."

He shook his head and sank to a seat on an empty windowsill.

"So, one night, he decides he's gonna protest his reassignment. Shows up at the temple late, figures Cedar's gonna be there somewhere, and guess what he finds? Way back in one of the meditation rooms – the small ones they use for students? – he finds Cedar all tangled up with not one, but two of his meditation masters. Male ones." He smirked. "Let's just say conception didn't seem to be on their list of priorities."

"No way," Amneet said. "There's no way Cedar would have ever…"

"Yeah? Then why did the meditation masters come after my father? Why did he find himself kicked out of the Movement the very next day?"

She snorted. "Because he was trespassing! Attempting to sneak into the temple without Cedar's permission!"

Irritation seemed to flash in Ryder's eyes for an instant. "Yeah, maybe," he said. "And that would make sense if they'd stopped at just kicking him out of the Movement. But they didn't. Soon he started noticing strange men following him everywhere he went, and then he started having near-death experiences – like the time someone shoved him toward the tracks just as a train pulled into the station."

He cleared his throat. "When it became clear Cedar was out to get him, my old man took the only option he had left. He appealed to my mother to skip town with him. When she refused, he took me and left without her."

"They headed down south first," Cody said. "Just outside LA, where Ryder's father decided to prove the Essence theory wrong once and for all. Spent the next few years investing his money, and studying as a medical doctor, and then he packed up Ryder and moved north to the Sierras. That's where he's been ever since."

My heart stuttered. Outsiders often claimed they'd disproved the Essence theory, but Cedar always countered by saying everyone is born with a different supply of Essence. No Outsider I'd ever heard of had taken the time to formulate a fully scientific approach.

"He's actually disproved the theories?"

Ryder sprang from his seat. "Red, we've been doing some incredible stuff out there. Groundbreaking stuff. Experiments that undoubtedly, unequivocally prove the Essence theory is bullshit – nothing but a Centrist scare tactic designed to control us."

Amneet frowned. "What kind of experiments? What are you doing out there?"

"I can't tell you, but I can show you. That's why we asked you guys here tonight."

"Our community is always on the look-out for intelligent, capable freethinkers," Cody said. "People who want to help us spread the truth."

"That's how they hooked us, anyway," Jett added, planting a kiss on Cody's cheek. "Two years ago, and we haven't looked back since. Have we, hon?"

Javi looked stunned. "You guys are allowed to… date? Isn't that–?"

"We're allowed to do anything we want," Ryder said. "Do those two look like they're worried about their Essences?"

"So, let me get this straight," Amneet said. "You expect us to believe your father saw Cedar engaging in sexual affairs with his meditation masters. You want us to leave our homes and join you – you're even telling us we can date if we go – but you won't tell us where you live or what kind of Essence experiments you're doing out there?"

"I've already told you where we live," Ryder corrected. "The Sierra Nevadas. It's a mountain range. But it wouldn't make sense for us to go around broadcasting our exact location to every stranger we pass on the street, now would it? Same goes for our experiments."

He leaned toward her, and I thought I detected his smirk when she squirmed and looked away. "Because we're not just out there plotting and planning," he said. "We're also helping people. Protecting them. Rehabilitating Centrists like you guys and helping you realize there's nothing wrong with allowing yourselves to feel things every once in a while."

He sauntered back to the center of the room. "And here's the thing. If you don't believe what we're saying – if you don't feel like it's a good fit for you – that's fine, too. We're not here to beg you. It's your life, and you gotta live it the way you feel is right. But…"

He motioned to our surroundings – to the crumbling, plaster walls and dusty, forgotten corners. "Don't forget, Amneet, that this place used to be a park. A real, live city park, where kids played and people laughed and no one was afraid they'd just drop dead at any moment."

He made eye contact with me. "Don't you ever wish you could just laugh, Red? And Javi, haven't you always wondered if there's something more out there?"

He flashed us a smile, and his face became serene. Knowing. Magnetic, and so filled with energy that I felt mesmerized by it.

"Well," he said. "We're here to tell you guys there is something more. And if you come with us, we'll prove it."

# CHAPTER FIVE

I felt myself paralyzed by uncertainty. *Leave? Like, really leave and go with them?*

I had never left the Bay Area in my entire life. Now, here, surrounded by strangers in the middle of the night... Was I actually considering this?

Amneet tossed her blanket to the floor and stood up. "That's it; I've heard enough. Your community sounds like some kind of cult, and you guys seem like recruiters." She paused with one narrow hand on the doorframe. "I don't know what you guys are trying to sell here, but I don't like what I'm hearing. I'm going home."

I shifted my gaze back to Ryder, expecting to see frustration or disappointment in his eyes. Instead, he simply shrugged. "Suit yourself," he said. "Be careful on your way out."

Anger creased Amneet's eyebrows, and I detected something in her stance I could hardly process. *Is she waiting for him to protest? Does she actually feel scorned by him?* The idea sounded strange, but somehow – in the curve of her stance, in the pursed line of her lips – it seemed to hit home.

Before I could make sense of the energy that seemed to pulse in her eyes, Ryder turned his back and reached for another cigarette. Within seconds, Amneet was gone.

Continuing as if she had never existed, he said, "Tell you guys what. Think on it. We aren't leaving until tomorrow morning, so you don't have to decide right now." He glanced toward the window. "Besides, the rain's about to let up, and we have some very important business to attend to in Sharon Meadows." He cocked his head. "You guys ever heard of a Slip 'n Slide?"

Javi and I cowered beneath a Monterey cypress while Ryder, Cody and Jett untangled something large and dark on the water-clogged grass before us. The rain had lessened to an intermittent drizzle, and the air smelled strongly of grass and eucalyptus leaves. Javi held a blanket over both our heads, and his body felt warm as it radiated heat beside me.

I felt unsettled. And nervous, yet privileged somehow, to be standing here under this blanket so close to a boy, smelling the scent of cooking spice that lingered, indistinct, on his skin. It wasn't even a particularly good smell. It was peppery and earthy, a shade shy of unpleasant, but it was Javi's smell. For some reason, the knowledge that I knew it made me feel like I'd been let in on some kind of secret.

Watch it, Autumn. Seriously. What are you doing right now?

"What do you think about all this?" Javi finally asked. He kept his eyes focused forward as Ryder straightened the corners of a large plastic tarp. "Think it's true?"

I swallowed. "I don't know. They certainly seem confident about it."

"Yeah. They do." A thoughtful expression crinkled his forehead. "I just… really want to get away from this place. So I'm not sure if that's clouding my judgment or not."

"Yeah. Me, too."

Something hummed between us – fluttery and expectant – before Ryder cried, "OK, we're ready for you guys! Do you want to try this or not?"

"Of course they don't want to try this," Jett said. Her unnaturally dark hair was plastered in wet rivulets against her forehead. "Not this time, anyway. But maybe next time. Guys, watch this. Slip 'n Slides are pretty much the most amazing inventions ever. We set them up all the time back home in the Sierras."

She took a few steps backward and began kicking out of her boots. They sloshed and protested, but soon she was barefoot. The sight of mud creeping between her toes was so strange that I found myself staring.

She unzipped her purple sweatshirt, and then she was only wearing a thin, lavender tank top – which quickly plastered itself to her small breasts. Then her pants were gone, and she was standing serene and long-legged in the middle of the park, in nothing more than her underwear.

My jaw dropped, and Javi's sharp inhale told me he was equally stunned by her lack of modesty. No, even more stunned, because his arms wavered, and the blanket in his hands dipped forward for a second. A cascade of water soaked my toes, but his forced breathing and suddenly flared nostrils told me he hadn't even noticed.

I ignored a stab of – something? – that surfaced when I glanced at him. And then Jett was running, leaping forward and diving headfirst across the plastic tarp.

Her long body was soon soaked with rainwater, and droplets ran down her legs as she threw her head back and laughed. "See? Told you it was awesome!"

I tried to ignore the curve of her thighs, the narrow scoop of her collarbone, and the hardness of her nipples as she smiled expectantly at Ryder and Cody. But the truth was, I felt paralyzed. And uncomfortable. And strangely stirred by the sight of so much skin.

*What was* wrong *with me?*

It was just a few moments before Ryder and Cody followed her lead. Kicking off their shoes, they pulled their shirts over their heads and tossed their pants to the lawn.

My heart nearly exploded. I had never seen an undressed boy before, and now two stood right in front of me, completely at ease and unruffled in nothing but tiny cotton undershorts.

They had all these muscles. Their chests were knotted, and their waists narrowed into tight stomachs and rows of blocky lines that led... well... downward... to a spot below their waistbands where I could clearly see the outlines of something. Something that made me want to cover my eyes and meditate for three weeks; something that made me feel dizzy and sweaty and unglued and uncomfortable.

I cleared my throat and looked down, and guilt surged inside me at the realization that I was definitely not practicing neutrality right now. *Watch it, Autumn. Seriously.*

Javi shifted beside me, obviously uncomfortable, and then Ryder and Cody were flying. They laughed like twin missiles as they streamed across the plastic and collided with a crash into Jett. There was mud everywhere, and I couldn't tell where one body ended and the others began. And then all three were up, racing toward the beginning of the slide again – laughing and pushing and shoving as they dove across the plastic a second, third and fourth time.

After the fifth time, Jett staggered over. Her breathing was heavy, and her tank top was smeared with long streaks of dark mud. Energy seemed to radiate from her, and her teeth gleamed unnaturally white as she leaned in and planted muddy kisses on both Javi's and my cheeks.

"I'm really glad I met you guys." Her breath was laced with the spicy, sweet scent of whatever had been in that flask. I tried not to jump when she touched me.

Ryder and Cody soon followed. They were both soaked and nearly unrecognizable, except for the wide grins that split both their faces.

"Wanna try, Red?" Ryder rushed forward and gripped my waist with two mud-covered hands.

I should have felt irritated by his proximity, by the familiar way he held me and by the mud that now smeared my dress with two identical pawprints. But I didn't.

I felt shocked, for sure. And a little bit terrified. But the truth is, it didn't even occur to me that I should push his hands from my sides. Instead, part of me actually wanted to lean into him. I had never been muddy before, and I had certainly never stood like this, staring into the eyes of a barely dressed boy in the middle of the night.

Ryder and his friends made me feel dangerous. And alive.

And they said they could prove the Essence theory wrong.

"I want to go to the Sierras with you."

I didn't realize I was thinking the words until they were already spoken.

# CHAPTER SIX

I woke with a start just before daybreak. My cheek was pressed against the cold tile of the mansion floor, and my blanket was skewed sideways – not quite covering me, but not quite not, either.

Javi slept a few feet from me. Dried mud coated his hair, and I could tell by his slightly open mouth and regular breathing that my gasp hadn't disturbed him. *Am I actually sleeping on the floor this close to a boy?*

I rolled onto my back and dragged a hand through my own mud-caked curls. They were tangled – knotted, really – and the muscles in my arms ached from the force of the Slip 'n Slide.

*Did last night really happen?*

I felt something strange well inside me. Shame? My dress – which I'd insisted on wearing despite Ryder and Jett's protests – was crinkly and stiff, and my arms and legs were smeared with beige spatters and grass.

The mansion was quiet, a jumble of blankets and muddy bodies. Jett and Cody were curled on my left, and Ryder was stretched like a cat on the window seat to my right. The cigarette clutched between his fingers had smoldered into an ash pile beside him, and his head was tipped slightly backward. The shadows below his cheekbones were particularly prominent in the morning light, and faint snores reverberated from his lips.

He was beautiful. They were all beautiful, but the reality of the evening was so foreign and pungent that it took me a moment to process.

I had slid through the mud and played with strangers on a Slip 'n Slide. I had laughed and run through a meadow in the middle of the night.

Although I had turned down the dark liquid in Ryder's flask, I had secretly relished the feeling of his hand against mine as he tried to pass me the bottle. "You're beautiful, Red," he had said, his breath infused with that lovely spiced sweetness. "You really are. You know that?"

I had pulled Javi down the Slip 'n Slide with me, and I had felt my cheeks color when his gaze lingered on my legs, when he wiped the mud from his forehead and whispered, "I'm really glad we're going through this together, Autumn."

It had all seemed so exciting, so real and invigorating that I hadn't even blinked when Jett and Cody started kissing. And the thought of sleeping on the floor in the middle of the mansion hadn't sounded strange. It had sounded daring, like I was really part of something.

A hard object pressed into my side. I rolled onto my back and dug through the folds of my skirt. Brady's lion, now damp and bedraggled, left mud stains in the palm of my hand.

*What have I done?*

I was struck by such a debilitating sadness that I nearly doubled over. *How can I be here, doing dangerous things with strangers, when Brady is in an urn somewhere? Why do I get to live and be reckless with my Essence when he barely did anything wrong in his whole life?*

I thought of Aunt Marie's words: Sometimes, sweetheart, you have to decide where your loyalties lie. And mine lie with you and my little sister.

After all that, had I actually considered abandoning my family?

*I truly am the worst person in the world.*

I pulled myself to my feet. Wiping the dirt clumps from my legs, I checked the sunrise and decided I probably had enough time to get home and get showered before morning meditation sessions began.

The train station was crowded, buzzing with Outsiders in dark suits and tourists with bright jackets and cameras. I stood with my back to the turnstiles, suitcases in hand and my hair still damp from my frenzied morning shower. My long trench coat was buttoned, and its hood was pulled low over my forehead to discourage inappropriate attention.

"There," my mother said, approaching from the ticket counter and passing me two plastic cards. "One stop in San Jose, and then on to Los Gatos. Cedar's brother will be waiting for you at the station." She pulled the hood from my eyes and smoothed my hair.

I swallowed and stared at the empty train tracks before us. My entire world felt like it was spinning out of control. *I really thought this Los Gatos thing was still open for discussion.*

"I am so pleased you've finally come around this morning," she said. "This retreat's combination of meditation and self-deprivation is decades ahead of its time, and you will feel so much better once you've been freed from the constraints of your anger and grief." She paused and touched the silver pendant around my neck. "Neutrality is the key to longevity, after all. Don't ever forget that."

I nodded, but for some reason, I didn't feel the need to repeat the mantra in agreement. My mother's words felt off this morning. Void in some way.

For once, I felt like I could almost see beneath the mantra – to the dark-paneled meditation room where Cedar and his followers had sat brainstorming its creation. Were they really concerned about their Essences, about the best way to express the gravity of the situation to their followers? Or were they just trying to figure out the smartest way to scare us into submission so they could dominate us?

I realized I didn't know the answer.

My mother was droning on about the private bedrooms, the spacious sanctuaries and the busy daily schedule, when two things happened nearly simultaneously. She narrowed her eyes with her hand poised above my ear, and I caught a glimpse of someone walking purposefully down the platform toward us.

"What is this?" My mother's eyes widened as she reached into the crevices of my ear lobe. Inspecting the muddy remnants I had somehow missed in my shower, she held her finger up for me to see. "Is this... dirt? Autumn Grace, why on earth do you have dirt in your ear?"

But I wasn't listening. I was watching the willowy figure march across the platform. She wore a long trench coat like me, but there was something defiant about the way she strode through the crowd. Although her face was mostly hidden beneath the folds of her hood, her jangling boots were unmistakable.

Jett.

"Autumn, are you listening to me?" I tried to focus on my mother, but my insides were suddenly so queasy I was having trouble concentrating. "Autumn Grace, what is wrong with you?"

"Be right back," I managed, brushing past her and walking forward to meet Jett.

Sadness filled Jett's expression as she closed the distance between us. "Why did you leave us, Autumn? You didn't even say goodbye."

"Jett... I'm sorry. I just..."

"Do you know how long it took me to track you down here?" She twisted her hands together. "We don't usually... We don't ever come after recruits when they leave us, but I had to know. Didn't you have fun with us? Didn't you like us?"

"I did. I do." I cast a worried glance over my shoulder. My mother's mouth hung open, and I knew it was only a matter of time before she ended what she deemed to be an overly emotional conversation.

"Listen, Jett, it's just..."

"Where are you going? You're not leaving because of us, are you?"

"No." I almost laughed. "No," I said again, this time more quietly. "Jett, I'm going to a Centrist retreat in Los Gatos. After everything that's happened with my brother, Cedar thinks..."

"Los Gatos?" Jett's eyes widened. "Autumn, you can't be serious. Do you know what they do to people at the Los Gatos retreat?"

"My mother..."

"Is clearly trying to turn you into a vegetable!" She grabbed my arm. "Autumn, I'm serious. It's like a prison camp. They barely feed you, and they make you sit in dark, empty rooms until you aren't even you anymore. You can't possibly go along with this."

From somewhere in the distance, a train whistle blared. I cast another glance at my mother. "Hurry along, Autumn," she called, struggling to keep her voice light. "It's time to tell your friend goodbye."

"Autumn." Jett clutched both my shoulders. "I'm serious. I've known people who've been sent to Los Gatos, and they've come back so screwed up you can't even recognize them."

"But... my brother..."

"Is exactly why you can't get on that train! Look, Autumn, I know you're messed up right now. I know your brother just died, but going to Los Gatos isn't going to bring Brady back."

The train's gleaming silver nose appeared in a blur, and the platform bustled with movement as everyone began jostling toward the tracks.

"Autumn, I'm serious." Now Jett's expression became pleading. "You owe it to yourself – and to your brother's memory – to ditch this train, get the hell out of here and do something with your life."

Passersby began shoving past us, and I felt my mother's grip tighten around my bicep as she clutched me from behind. "It's time to go, Autumn," she hissed, pulling me toward the train. "Tell your friend you'll see her when you return."

Jett's hand clasped mine. "Autumn," she said. "You may think we're wrong about Essences, but we just may be right. And your brother's death will be meaningless if you don't have the courage to find out."

PART TWO:

THE AHWAHNEE

# CHAPTER SEVEN

I'm not exactly sure what happened next.

I know I swung my arm and freed myself from my mother's grip somehow, and I know I glanced over my shoulder and said, "I'm not getting on that train," before Jett whooped in delight and pulled me away from the tracks. I left my suitcases behind, didn't even look back when we started running. And Jett's laughter was so wild and disobedient that I soon found myself laughing, too.

My muscles burned, and adrenaline flowed freely through me as we raced, hand in hand, toward the platform exit. Jett pulled her trench coat free, and the brown cloth billowed as she thrust it to the ground behind her.

Ryder, Cody and Javi waited outside. They stood beside a black SUV, and they bolted upright when they saw us. "What the hell, Jett!" Ryder's eyes widened. "This doesn't exactly fall under the 'don't draw attention to yourself' rule."

"Go, go, go!" Jett fought giggles as we raced down the stairs. "I'm serious; we need to get out of here now!"

Cody's eyes narrowed, and then he was at the wheel. The truck's engine roared to life, and Jett and I crashed into the back seat with Javi. Ryder vaulted into the front seat and pulled the door shut behind him. "Go!"

Cody jammed the accelerator. As the truck slid into high gear, Jett's frenzied giggles filled the air. She had collapsed, sweaty, against me, and my eye socket was crammed into Javi's right shoulder. My coat was tangled in a bundle around us, and the zipper was pressed too hard against my neck.

"I think I'm choking," I managed, and then we were all laughing.

It was a dizzying kind of laughter – the laughter that is born of close calls, adrenaline and danger. It was filled with friendship and camaraderie, with the mutual sense of relief that coats your insides when you realize you've come through something big together.

It was the first time I'd ever felt it, and part of me was scared by it. It felt reckless and defiant, and it filled the cab with a destructive energy that made me want to close my eyes, grasp my pendant and repeat the Centrist mantra over and over and over.

The energy was weightless, too – like the exhalation of a lifetime's worth of repressed emotions. I could practically taste the burning of our Essences, but the solidarity of our rebelliousness was delicious, as well.

I thought of the Slip 'n Slide, of the way I'd felt my entire body sing when I crashed through the mud and when I tangled myself in the blankets at the mansion. That feeling of really being part of something was back again.

And part of me prayed it would never end.

"I'm sorry I left this morning," I whispered once everyone had lapsed back into silence.

Our truck was racing over the new Bay Bridge, and the remains of Treasure Island lay overgrown and forgotten to our left. The vibrant emerald cliffs of Sausalito and Tiburon stretched like sleeping giants across the bay, and Oakland's steel and glass high-rises caught the sun's rays to our right.

"That's OK, Red," Ryder said, turning to make eye contact with me. "I just want to make sure you really want to be here." Before I could answer, he added, "That's why we have a policy never to chase recruits. We only want you if you really want to do this."

I couldn't help but notice his pointed pause, the way Jett shifted slightly at his words. "I do," I said quickly. "I'm sorry…"

"Her mother was sending her to the retreat in Los Gatos," Jett said. "She was supposed to leave this morning."

"No wonder you were screwed up," Cody said, and Ryder's face softened slightly.

"Yeah," he finally echoed. "It's no wonder. And you really want to be here, Red? You're absolutely sure?"

"I'm absolutely sure." I hated that look of hesitation in his eyes, the invisible distance that seemed to span the space between us.

He regarded me without speaking for a moment, and then he finally nodded and extended his hand for a truce. "Great. Welcome back, then."

The gentle slowing of the truck is what finally woke me from my nap. I hadn't realized I was sleeping, and I was horrified to find I'd slid into the crevice between Javi's shoulder and the seat back.

"Hey," he whispered as I lifted my head.

"I'm sorry," I stammered, wiping my hand across my chin. No drool. Whew. "How long have I been sleeping?"

"Maybe two hours." He smiled. "They blindfolded me for a bit once we passed Merced. We turned into the mountains at some point, and now…" He motioned to the dark stand of pines that crowded the winding asphalt road. "I'm not exactly sure where we are now."

"I've been asleep for two hours?" My disappointment was thinly veiled. My first trip out of the Bay Area, and I'd slept through most of it?

"Snored pretty good for a while, too," Ryder said, grinning back at me. "Impressive lungs, Red. Didn't know you had it in you."

"You didn't snore one bit, Autumn," Jett insisted. "Don't even listen to him." She was sitting cross-legged, and she seemed to be knitting some kind of brightly colored scarf. "Ryder, on the other hand… Don't let him fool you. You should hear that guy when he gets going."

"Are you guys ready for the fun part?" It was Cody, and he followed the question with a sharp tug on the steering wheel. The truck jerked hard to the left, and I was afraid it would tip as it barreled sideways off the road and crashed onto a rutted, hidden trail.

I may have screamed. I'm almost certain I shrieked, because Javi and I were thrown forward, and we smashed together as Jett whooped and cheered beside us. "Love this part!" she cried, dropping her knitting and bracing herself with her handrail.

The truck jerked through the pine trees, and it weaved and bottomed out as Cody attempted to avoid the very deepest ruts. Branches slapped against the windshield, and they screeched like knives against the metal doors.

"Don't worry," Ryder shouted over the chaos. "Just another mile or so. Road got beat to shit during the earthquake; we'll pop back out onto the asphalt once we pass the rockslides."

I nodded, but my gritted jaw made a real response impossible. I felt my teeth chattering in my skull, and I wondered how Jett could possibly laugh at a time like this.

"Checkpoint's just ahead," Cody announced, a few nail-biting, joint-crushing minutes later. "Almost there, guys."

I fought my nausea as the truck rounded a corner and crashed back onto asphalt. Up ahead, a wooden sign dangled from a stone structure by the roadside, its words completely obscured by a thick layer of moss. Just past the sign, a roadblock was set up with metal gates, sandbags and a sign that read, "Danger: Radon Gas Present in this Area. No Trespassing, by Order of the U. S. Department of Energy".

A duo of militaristic guards stood at our arrival. They were dressed in olive green camouflage, and their faces hardened into masks as Cody slowed to a stop and opened his window. My stomach knotted as I sized up their machine guns, the knives strapped to their thighs and the dark lenses of their sunglasses.

"No trespassing. Can't you read the sign?" one said, leaning forward. His scowl only lasted for a second. "Holy shit, guys, didn't even recognize you in this thing. Sorry bout that; welcome back!"

Cody shook hands with the guard, and Javi and I sat stupefied while Jett leaned forward and said, "Wow, Brian. They've got you on duty out here now?"

"Twice a week, once they get me trained," Brian replied with a grin. "Today's my second day." Sunglasses removed, I could see he was only a few years older than me, maybe in his early twenties. His eyelashes and eyebrows were so pale, they almost looked white.

"Congrats," Jett said brightly. "A big damn deal."

"Thanks." He locked eyes with me. "Hi, guys, I'm Brian. Welcome to Yosemite."

*Yosemite?* I reached forward to shake Brian's hand, and I felt my mind spin as I remembered the word from some forgotten history lesson.

Yosemite was a park. A national park. A big one back in its heyday, but shut down and abandoned after the Great Quake.

"Yosemite?" Javi clearly remembered the history lessons as well. His face pinched as Cody accelerated again. "Isn't this place dangerous? What about the radon gas?"

"Only gas we have to worry about here is Cody's farts," Ryder laughed. "Ain't that right, bro?"

I frowned. "There's no radon gas here? What about the history lessons?"

"Only halfway accurate. The government didn't know what to do with this place after the Quake hit," Jett said. "Roads were damaged beyond repair, radon gas was found in the redwood forests..."

"A few public hearings were held," Cody added, "but the National Park Service called it quits when Mammoth Mountain became an active volcano again."

"It never erupted, though, right?" Javi's lack of American history knowledge was apparent in the quaver in his voice.

"Right. And radon gas disperses fairly quickly. Hasn't been measured at dangerous levels here in years." Cody shrugged. "Doesn't matter, I guess. The damage had already been done. No government agency is ever going to approve the reopening of such a volatile place."

"My old man always thought the government gave up on Yosemite too soon," Ryder said. "So when we ditched LA and headed back north, this was a natural place for us to end up. We arrived in '31, and we've been here ever since."

"You've been living here for seven years? What about the Department of Energy?"

"Has no idea we're even here." He smiled and re-propped his feet on the dashboard. "When my old man stumbled onto this place, it really was deserted. We lay low for the first few months, but when it became clear no one was ever coming back..." He shrugged. "We rigged up that fake checkpoint about six months into our research. Capitalized on the already-public knowledge that this place is supposed to be toxic, and that's that. The Community's closed, and new members are only accepted through invitation."

"Which is why you were in San Francisco."

"Right." Ryder said the word matter-of-factly, without explanation or apology. "Monthly visits during the summer, a little less often during the off-season. We don't always pick up new recruits, but we always try."

I felt strangely let down by his words. Monthly visits during the summer? Nine or ten visits per year? Twenty, thirty, forty new recruits?

I surveyed my companions, and I felt hesitation creep into my bones. *Does Ryder tell every girl he meets she's beautiful? I wondered. Does Jett always peel off her sweater without a trace of modesty?* Were these people, my so-called new "friends", simply working off a script?

Ryder continued. "Nowadays, the Community has grown to about two hundred and fifty former Centrists. Mostly young folks. Farmers and artists and freethinkers... The absolute best of the best."

"And your father? You said he's doing Essence experiments out here?"

"In order to prove the Essence theory wrong, he's gotta have a mountain of evidence behind him. So a big part of what we do out here is participate in experiments. Monitor our heart rate and hormone levels while we perform a variety of activities. My old man compiles all this information into a database, and someday when he's finished..." He smiled proudly. "Someday, we'll present our evidence to Cedar's followers, and we'll save everyone from his tyranny."

"Participate in experiments?" I swallowed. I knew Ryder's father was doing research out here, but the idea that I'd be a test subject seemed somehow overwhelming.

"Yeah. Fun ones." Ryder's smile was genuine, but I couldn't help my shiver of apprehension. I leaned slightly into Javi, and I wanted nothing more than to glance sideways at him, to see if the expression on his face reflected any of my doubts.

But I didn't. It would have been too awkward. Ryder's attention was focused fully on me, and his smile widened when he said, "Trust me, Red. You're gonna love the stuff we get to do out here."

"Big Rocks, straight ahead." Cody motioned as our truck reached a clearing in the trees.

I crouched to peer through the windshield, and I instantly felt my breath catch in my lungs. Two massive walls of granite towered before us, and they formed a narrow opening to a valley so immense, it seemed to stretch forever. The canyons gleamed golden-gray in the afternoon sunlight, and they were so massive that their summits were blocked by the upper limits of the truck's windshield.

A waterfall cascaded to our right, and a wide, grassy meadow sprawled to our left. The valley smelled fresh, like pine needles and water, and I must have started sniffing the air, because Jett nudged me after a moment and giggled. "Smells good, doesn't it?"

"It's the Ponderosa pines," Cody explained as I slouched back in my seat. "I must have walked around with my nose stuck in their trunks for the first two weeks I was here."

"Very attractive, hon," Jett said. "Had all the girls fainting over you right away."

"Like you cared, anyway." Locking eyes with me in the rearview mirror, Cody said, "You should have seen her, Autumn. We grew up side by side in San Francisco, but she didn't even notice I was alive until we'd been here for more than a year. Too busy with other guys to give me the time of day."

"Whatever!" Jett punched Cody's arm as Ryder absently rolled another cigarette between his thumb and forefinger.

He continued. "Yosemite Valley was formed by the Merced River and by the movement of glaciers through this area about a million years ago. That's Bridalveil Falls over there on our right. And that cliff face on our left is El Capitan. Three thousand feet from base to summit, with more than a hundred established climbing routes and a perfect ledge for BASE jumping."

"El Cap is kind of a big deal around here," Jett said, rolling her eyes. "I call it Mount Testosterone."

"Oh, yeah? I seem to recall you chomping at the bit the first time I took you there," Ryder said, blowing smoke out the cracked window. "Couldn't wait to get a shot at it."

"I did a lot of stupid things back then," she snapped, and for the first time, I noticed tension simmering in the air between them.

"This place was discovered by explorers back in the 1850s," she continued, slipping into tour-guide mode. "After they captured the native tribes and burned their villages – in an epic display of brotherly love – they decided to make Yosemite a tourist attraction. Lodges were built, roads were laid out and this place became a national park. Who knows what it would look like now if the Great Quake hadn't hit?"

"You can still see the remains of some of the valley's landmarks," Cody said, pointing to a half-collapsed wooden structure on our right. "This used to be Yosemite Chapel, and that road to our right leads to what's left of Curry Village. Was a lodge and tent camp for the park's visitors."

"That's where my old man has his clinic set up nowadays," Ryder said, glancing down the road. "We check in there once a week to download our heart rates and hormone readings."

The truck veered left and crossed a bridge, and I glimpsed a bizarre cliff towering above the valley to our right. "What's that?" I asked, leaning across Jett.

"That," Ryder said, "is Half Dome. Grandfather of all of Yosemite Valley."

I was struck by the cliff's peculiar shape, by its sheer expanse of rock and its towering, rounded face. For the first time in my life, I felt awed, and speechless, and completely overwhelmed by the idea that something so beautiful had existed here this whole time, just beyond my reach.

I thought back to the city, to the afternoons my mother and I made small talk while preparing dinner. I thought of my nightly meditation exercises – the slow unruffling and smoothing of my aura's ripples as I released my pent-up emotions before bed.

*Neutrality is the key to longevity.*

An unfamiliar emotion welled in my eyes as I stared hard at this new world outside my window. I felt humbled. And amazed. And alive.

Every neuron in my body began singing, and suddenly, I didn't care if Ryder told every girl he met she was beautiful. I didn't care if Jett had been working off a script, and I didn't care if I was just one of the thirty or more recruits they brought to this place every year.

I was in Yosemite now.

And for the first time in a long time, I felt like I was home.

# CHAPTER EIGHT

The Ahwahnee Hotel was once Yosemite National Park's crowning jewel. Multistoried and constructed of river stones, it had once inspired the world's most affluent travelers to stop in and enjoy its amenities and sweeping views. Today, it served as the home base for all the Community's operations. It also housed more than two thirds of the valley's inhabitants.

That's what Ryder told us, anyway, as we pulled into a parking lot filled with shining trucks and rusted older vehicles. The hotel, half visible through the pines, looked massive and rustic, with stone pillars, exposed beams and wide-paneled windows that gleamed with dazzling reflections in the afternoon sunlight.

"Finally home," Jett said, leaping from the back seat. "Feels good, doesn't it!"

"It does." Ryder helped me to my feet and pulled a suitcase from the trunk. "What do you think of your new home, guys?"

"This place is incredible," Javi stammered. "Do we get to live in the hotel?"

"Not quite." Ryder smiled. "Newbies move into the tent cabins behind the hotel. From there, you get promoted to wood cabins, and then you move to a room inside the Ahwahnee if you're lucky and persistent."

"Lucky and persistent? But I thought the Community was closed. How do you get promoted if no one leaves?"

"Oh, people leave," Ryder said, taking a few steps toward the hotel. "Sometimes through their own choice, sometimes through ours. Sometimes people just don't fit in here, you know?"

"We also have another homestead in the High Country called Tuolumne Meadows," Jett said. "People can 'retire' from our experiments and move up there any time they like."

"It's totally separate, and it's a really big honor to go," Cody said. "We have crossover celebrations and everything."

"Why don't people leave after they retire?"

"Leave?" Jett scoffed. "Why would they leave? We're a family here, Autumn. That's one of the biggest reasons we're out here. Besides, look around. Why would you ever want to leave?"

Javi squinted at the hotel's long entryway. "So, how do you get promoted to the hotel?"

"All you gotta do is be awesome," Ryder said. "Participate in my old man's experiments, do your chores, get involved in community events. The Founders will notice."

"The Founders," Cody explained, "are the two ruling leaders of the Community: Ryder's dad Rex and Daniel Lynch, another former meditation master."

"You'll meet them tonight," Jett said, approaching the hotel's large glass and stone doors. "We have a little something special prepared for your arrival."

Jett escorted us through a wide stone lobby. The hotel's original artwork and furnishings had mostly been stripped, but southwestern rugs and leather couches still dotted the foyer.

Candles lined the windowsills in neat rows, and the air smelled warm, like leather and smoke. There wasn't a trace of dust or disrepair anywhere.

"Stay right here," she instructed, following Ryder and Cody toward the back exit. "We'll be back in a flash."

Javi and I stopped as our new companions disappeared from view. Their footsteps echoed through the empty lobby for a moment, and then there was nothing but silence and the crackling of some unseen fireplace.

It felt strange to be alone after so many hours of camaraderie, and our new friends' absence manifested itself as a whooshing blow of sadness and uncertainty so intense, it left me breathless. *Brady would have loved it here.*

Another thought: *I abandoned him to come here.*

I knew the thought was ridiculous. I knew Brady's soul was no more wrapped in that urn than mine had been in the clump of hair my mother cut. And I was here for Brady. I wasn't here for Ryder or my mother or anyone else. I was here because I wanted to prove the Essence theory wrong, and I believed Ryder's father held the key.

Didn't I?

"How are you holding up, Autumn?"

Javi's voice startled me, and I turned, half surprised to see him still standing there. We had been traveling in affable silence for so long that I had almost forgotten we were capable of independent conversation.

He seemed to share my hesitation, and his dark eyes seemed timid as he adjusted the folds of his wrinkled suit. "Do you still think you made the right choice coming here?"

"I do." My answer was automatic. Realizing I didn't need to convince him, I backpedaled slightly. "I mean… it's exciting. And this place is gorgeous. It's just kinda… scary. You know?"

"I know. A bit overwhelming, isn't it?" He steadied himself by placing one wide hand on a leather chair. "And, you know... I believe in this. I really think I believe in this, but I don't want them to force us to become Essence test subjects. We didn't sign up for that."

"I know." His words made me realize how much Ryder had worried me, too.

"OK, we're ready for you in the Meadow now." It was Jett's voice, and she appeared from the back exit with a little leap and a bow. Her grin was wide as she motioned to the door. "Are you guys ready?"

The Meadow was a wide clearing circled by pines and dotted with maples and dogwoods. The lower trees were strung with a flickering assortment of paper lanterns, and these glimmered like stars as the afternoon faded into twilight.

White canvas tents and wooden cabins were scattered in concentric half-circles under the trees to my left, and countless circular dining tables sprawled to my right. Made of raw wood and dotted with wildflower vases, the tables were set with gleaming white plates and silverware.

I made eye contact with Javi as Ryder strode forward. "Welcome to the Meadow, guys. Are you ready to meet your new family?"

He reached sideways and pulled a gilded rope near the back door. This prompted a bell mounted in one of the stone turrets to begin ringing. It was a vibrant sound, clanging and melodic, and it echoed from the building's stone eaves and overhangs.

On cue, the Meadow began to fill.

Lanterns flickered in the trees as teenagers and young adults began appearing from all directions. First arriving in small groups, and then swelling until their numbers blended together, the Community assembled before us in a wash of colors and flowers.

I couldn't believe their sheer numbers. Most of the kids wore street clothes like Ryder, but some were barefoot, and they dressed in long, loose-fitting skirts and tunics. Their hair was long and as wild as mine had been before my mother cut it, and flowers were woven into many of their hairstyles. A few girls had babies propped on their hips, and young children weaved happily through the gathering.

"Ryder." An older man strode forward and clasped Ryder's forearm in greeting. His silver hair was curly, and the dimples in his cheeks left no doubt who he was. Ryder's father.

"Rex Stone," the man said. "We're so thankful you've joined us." He affixed us with a smile so bright, it made me want to blush and look away.

His presence felt as poised and magnetic as Cedar's, and his pale eyes seemed lit with that same inner glow. But where Cedar was distant, Rex seemed warm and so vibrant I could almost feel energy radiating from him.

*The sun,* I caught myself thinking. *Rex reminds me of the sun.*

I stammered a "hello" and leaned into Javi for support as Rex announced our names to the Community. Cheers erupted, and then we were surrounded. Cody, Jett, Ryder and his father acted as a buffer, and they led us to our seats at a very large rectangular head table. It overflowed with wildflowers and clean gray placemats.

"All right, back off, you," Rex said to a group of children as we passed. "You will have plenty of time to meet our new friends after dinner."

Javi and I were soon seated beside Ryder, his father, and a burly red-haired man who squeezed my hand a little too hard when he said, "Daniel Lynch. Good to meet you."

As I turned my attention to my place setting, the most beautiful girl I had ever seen rushed forward and kissed both my cheeks before returning to her table. Her hair was the color of warmed honey, and her skin smelled fresh, like sage and lavender. "I'm Shayla," she said warmly. "Welcome to our home."

Our feast was a blur of roasted vegetables, soups and breads so savory and sweet, they left my mouth watery and my stomach gurgling for more. I had never tasted food so good in my entire life, wasn't even aware food like this existed. I had been conditioned to expect grocery store castoffs, canned goods and potluck dinners at the temple; I had never experienced a meal that emphasized taste this much.

I must have gone into a trance at some point, because Ryder's eyes glinted when he finally placed his hand on mine and said, "Just wait until you taste the bread pudding, Red; it's gonna knock your socks off. Be right back with yours, OK?"

My cheeks burned. I replaced the buttery roll I had been reaching for, and I made awkward eye contact with Shayla as she popped from her chair and followed Ryder to the kitchen. *Smooth, Autumn. Very, very smooth.*

Something strange knotted my stomach at the sight of her with him. Was it jealousy? Shayla hadn't looked Ryder's way once during dinner - hadn't even greeted him when she strode to a nearby table - but now she positively glowed when he opened the door for her. She threw her head back and laughed at something he said, and her fingers were light against his shoulder as she reached to squeeze his upper arm.

"You're just as pretty as she is."

It was Javi's voice. I jumped, and his cheeks reddened. "I'm sorry," he said. "It's... none of my business. I just think you should know."

I couldn't decide which emotion was stronger – my embarrassment at being caught staring or my gratitude at being called pretty. Embarrassment won, and I quickly glanced down at my own plate.

We ate the rest of our meal in silence.

When the last plate had finally been cleared, Rex stood and addressed the crowd. His voice was rich and smooth as velvet. "Our new friends have only just said goodbye to the Centrist Movement. They have lived through many struggles, and they will fear for their Essences in the coming days. It is your responsibility to assuage their fears – just as it was our responsibility when you arrived."

Daniel Lynch stood, too. His voice was deeper, but it lacked the purring quality of Rex's. "Take a moment to remember how you felt when you became part of the Community," he said. "Remember how Cedar and his followers conditioned you to believe your death was just one errant emotion away."

A murmur of agreement filtered through the gathering, and Rex continued. "Cedar is a tyrant and a liar, and his Movement is a fallacy. Our mission here is not only to disprove his theories, but to provide a refuge where former Centrists can receive the treatment and rehabilitation they need – away from the prying eyes of Outsiders or Cedar's spies."

"We are here, united as a family, because we have all survived a terrible ordeal," Daniel said. "We have found a new faith in the rocks and trees and miracles of this land, and we cannot rest until every Centrist is likewise freed." He paused. "Remember our motto. Abundance is the key to longevity."

Rex raised his arms. "Now let us welcome our friends with a proper celebration – one that shows how much transcendence can be achieved through the true amplification of our emotions."

On cue, music exploded through the Meadow. Bonfires burst into flame behind the dining area, and everyone jumped from their tables and began dancing. Jett pulled Javi to his feet, and Cody pulled me to mine.

Music hummed through the gathering – an eruption of drums and guitars and other instruments I'd never heard before. The Community seemed to transform from hundreds of individuals into one living being – a being that pulsed and writhed and danced with so much joy and passion that I couldn't even process it.

I felt Essences burning like wildfires around us, but no one seemed the least bit concerned about it. Instead, they seemed happy, and fulfilled, and completely swelling with life.

I knew I should feel grateful to be here with them, but the thought that I may someday become one of them was way too much to handle. Their energy felt claustrophobic. And reckless. And dangerous.

Cody seemed to read my mind. After a few minutes, he leaned into my ear and whispered, "Ready for bed, Autumn? The dancing'll go on all night, but it's usually too much for new recruits to handle. Sure scared the shit out of me my first night. Wanna get a good night's sleep and then start fresh in the morning?"

I nodded. We squeezed back through the crowd, and we were soon met by Jett and Javi. They were also heading toward the gathering's outskirts, and Jett smiled when she saw us. "Let's get you guys away from this craziness."

"I'm so sorry," Jett said a few minutes later. Her hands were filled with linens, and we were standing before a canvas-wrapped tent cabin. "We would never, ever house two new arrivals of opposite genders in the same tent cabin, but a storm blew through here the other night and knocked out a row of housing. They've been working all day to get the tents repaired, but it hasn't happened yet. We'll get you reassigned as soon as we can, I promise."

Cody flicked on a lantern and pulled open the tent's wooden front door. The light illuminated a small square room with canvas walls, a wooden floor and a wooden frame. A woodstove sat darkened in front of us, and two cots lined the right and left walls.

After showing us how to light the fire, he said, "They'll serve breakfast in the dining hall tomorrow morning. Something light. Probably leftovers from tonight's meal, and then you'll report to Rex for some initial tests and fittings. A tour guide will give you a proper orientation, and then someone will assign you your chores."

"Welcome to the Community," Jett finished, dropping our bedsheets and new clothes before pulling us into tight hugs. "I think you will both love it here."

The awkwardness started the moment Jett and Cody said goodnight. I had already claimed the right cot, and I was sitting, swinging my legs, when Javi turned and said, "I'm sorry I said you were pretty earlier."

He flinched and tossed his bundle of new clothes aside. "I mean, I'm not sorry, because I meant it. But it was a weird thing to say, so I'm sorry if it made you feel uncomfortable."

"That's OK. I..." For some reason, I couldn't look him in the eyes. Instead, I found myself staring at the floor between our feet.

The pulse of drums echoed outside the tent. "I know I'm not off to a great start," he said, "but I really want us to be friends. I know we just met, and I know this whole thing is crazy, but I feel a little less crazy when I remember you're here, too."

"I do, too." I wasn't sure how I felt about Javi, but I knew I liked the crinkle of his eyes and the way he bit his lip when he was nervous.

He seemed nervous right now. Maybe even more nervous than me. And I don't know why, but I realized I liked that as well.

"Good," he said, and his smile was shy when he reached to unfold his clothes. "I'm really glad to hear that."

# CHAPTER NINE

I didn't sleep well. My head was swimming with thoughts of Javi, with thoughts of Brady and with questions about whether or not I had just made the biggest mistake of my life. Music from the gathering echoed from the Meadow until nearly dawn, and my cot creaked like it might collapse at any minute. Javi's repeated tosses and turns told me he probably didn't appreciate my squirming.

Not that his presence lent me to easy sleeping. I was panicked by the idea that I was sharing a bedroom with a boy, and I was so self-conscious that I'd snore or drool or look stupid in my sleep that I kept adjusting my expression to look as pretty as possible in case he happened to glance my way. When that became too tiresome, I turned my back to him, and that's how I stayed for most of the night.

I'm not sure how he kept the woodstove burning. He must have gotten up several times to tend it, but I don't remember any of those moments. That led me to believe I must have slept some, but I sure didn't feel refreshed when our front door began rattling the next morning.

"Morning has broken, you guys! Get up; you're missing it."

Jett was vivacious, filled with laughter and dancing in impatience as we stumbled from our tent. Cody waited beside her, and he greeted us with a much less enthusiastic nod. His hair was skewed in a wild tuft, and it was easy to see he wasn't a morning person, either.

"OK, Javi, you go with Cody. Autumn, you're coming with me."

Jett dragged me from the boys before I had time to protest. My long cotton nightgown dragged behind me as she pulled me through the dappled light of the pine trees.

"I packed a towel and a change of clothes for you; hurry or the Balcony's gonna fill up."

"Balcony?"

She pointed to the cliffs just past the hotel. "There's a ledge up there where the water flows through a couple of natural pools before it feeds down into a creek. The sun warms it up – just slightly – so we use it for bathing."

"You bathe in a creek?"

"No," she laughed. "We bathe at the Balcony. The boys bathe in the creek."

She paused for a moment and then pointed at the hotel. "We don't have electricity at the Ahwahnee, but we do have solar panels in case we need an emergency heat source. The panels also power our refrigerators, and we use them to warm our bath water in the winter.

"We go on occasional supply runs for any outside materials we can't produce here, but we live simply for the most part, and that includes bathing outside during warm weather instead of wasting drinking water. Does that make sense?"

"Yes. But people can't... I mean, you don't bathe out in the open, do you?"

"No." She laughed as we began climbing a steep trail. "Well, actually, I don't know. How do you define 'open'?"

'Open', it turned out, was the perfect description for the scene awaiting us. The Balcony was little more than a ledge – probably only fifteen feet wide from base to edge. Formed by the trickling of a sheet waterfall from a stream high above the canyon, its pools were simple hollows crowded between the ledge and the wall, where water collected briefly before cascading sideways toward a creek.

My cheeks immediately flared when I saw the cluster of half-naked and naked girls crowded around the pools. They brushed their hair and laughed and seemed completely unaffected by the massive, sweeping views of the Valley below them.

That's when I realized we were above the pine trees. I crept toward the edge, cheeks still burning, and I could barely detect the outline of the Ahwahnee through the foliage.

"Hidden in plain sight," Jett explained, coming to stand beside me. "We're too high up here for anyone to see us from the hotel."

Seeing my expression, she glanced back at the girls and added, "This group will be moving on soon. I... I guess I forget how weird this must be for you."

"No, it's OK."

I was lying. As I continued staring out at the Valley, I realized the only naked girls I'd ever seen were my mother and Aunt Marie. And from the moment I could comfortably bathe and dress myself, they'd left me alone to do just that.

I couldn't imagine stripping down out here in the open like this. Although I knew the other girls wouldn't care, I would care, and that's all that mattered.

I was already sharing my bedroom with a boy and listening to people dance until dawn. What was the Community going to ask me to do next?

Strap on a metal wristband that recorded every fluctuation in my heart rate, apparently.

I finally managed to get undressed at the Balcony, but only after everyone left and Jett turned her back to guard the entrance for me. Her face seemed uncharacteristically serious, and she nodded without hesitation at my request. "Of course I'll do that," she said, squeezing my hand. "I used to be terrified of this place."

There was something lingering in her voice, and I thought I detected sadness in the slump of her shoulders as she added, "Don't ever let anyone talk you into changing, OK, Autumn? You can be as modest and shy as you like."

Javi seemed likewise rattled by his experience of showering in the outdoors. "How was your bath?" he asked when we regrouped to head with Cody to Curry Village. Apparently rethinking his question, he turned and walked the rest of the way in silence.

Now, as we sat side by side in Rex's glowing clinic, Javi stared at the complicated metal bracelet shining on his left wrist. Rex was kind – overly explanatory and cautious – as he said, "It's completely painless, and everyone here has one. All it does is record your heart rate."

The laboratory's fluorescent lighting, strange equipment and beeping computer panels jarred me as I studied my own wristband.

"We will download your heart rate readings into our database once a week to track fluctuations and changes," Rex continued. "We will also swab your saliva once a day to check your hormone levels." He swiveled in his chair and motioned to a counter crowded with swabs and test tubes. "By tracking your heart rates and hormone levels through time, we can show the non-alignment of these things to Essence drain and the length of your lifespan."

"Your information is completely confidential," Rex's associate Daniel Lynch said, entering through a side door and pulling on a pair of gloves. His thick muscles were coiled, and his red hair gleamed with an oily sheen. I guessed he hadn't taken it upon himself to bathe this morning.

Rex smiled as Daniel reached for a cotton swab. "Daniel and I are the only people who will ever see your results, and we promise to keep everything between us. Now open up, and let's see what your first swab has to say."

I couldn't get out of that clinic fast enough. I understood why Rex's tests were necessary, but that didn't stop me from viewing my new wristband as a hidden camera or a secret thought recorder. Could it really track everything?

My cheeks burned at the impure thoughts that had been swirling around my head the last few days: the way I'd been so affected by the sight of everyone's mud-covered bodies on the Slip 'n Slide, the way I'd been flattered by Ryder and Javi's attention.

Would the wristband have been able to detect that? And would Rex have known I had been having impure thoughts about his own son?

Without realizing it, I began tracing my fingers over my pendant necklace. *Neutrality is the key to longevity, neutrality is the key to longevity, neutrality is the key to longevity...*

I remembered the Community's counter-mantra – Abundance is the key to longevity – but the words felt wrong in my mouth. *Abundance? What does that even mean?*

I was so preoccupied that I nearly bypassed the girl signaling to me from a nearby Jeep. Cody and Javi nodded and disappeared through the trees, and I approached the rusted vehicle to find a stranger waiting inside for me.

"I'm Kadence," the girl said, extending her hand. "I'm here to take you on your orientation tour."

She was short and curvy, with round eyes and a spray of wispy blonde hair. Her skin was luminous, and her lips were a perfect pale rose. Although I couldn't put my finger on why, I decided I liked her right away.

"What about Javi? Doesn't he need to go on a tour, too?"

"He'll go on his own tour later this afternoon." Kadence turned the ignition switch and patted the faded passenger seat. "Are you coming or not? This thing's ancient; probably can't get it moving again if we don't go now."

As Kadence accelerated through the towering pine trees, I realized my first instinct about her had been right. She was funny. And unpretentious. And as she pointed out the Valley's natural and manmade landmarks, I could tell how much she loved it here. That made me feel a little better, too.

"It's a pretty sweet setup," she explained, pointing out a handful of trails that apparently led to waterfalls, lakes and hidden caves. "The Community really is a family, and we chip in equally to keep this place running.

"Well, not exactly equally," she amended. "Job assignments are based on seniority, but you can petition to get your job reviewed twice a year. So, if you don't like your assigned job, you can always move on to something else."

She took a breath. "Our days are fairly organized. Six days a week, we wake up, eat breakfast, and then most of us have three to four hours of chores. Everyone breaks for lunch, and then we do Essence research for a few hours before nightfall. We meet again for dinner, and then we go about our business. The rest of the night is ours."

"Essence research?" There was that phrase again.

Kadence smiled. "Don't worry; it's not nearly as scary as it sounds. Basically, we just have free time. We can spend it doing whatever we want – but whatever we choose needs to be something that will awaken our senses. Hiking, climbing, dancing... pretty much anything the Centrists would describe as 'emotional', because Rex thinks that's critical to our rehabilitation. He also uses our readings to prove his theories."

I nodded. "Rex takes this whole thing really seriously, doesn't he?"

Kadence chuckled. "That's an understatement. Rex used to be Cedar's number two, so after everything that happened in the temple... I think Rex now realizes what a gifted manipulator Cedar is. He wants to save everyone else from repeating his mistakes."

She pointed to a cluster of wooden buildings on our right. "These are the stables. We aren't permitted to drive – except during orientation tours, recruiting missions and hunting trips. Our cars always break down, and we have to keep replacing them, so everyone gets around by walking, horse-riding or cycling."

Nodding toward a series of pens, she added, "We keep our horses, sheep, goats, chicken and geese over there. Most other livestock are too resource-intensive, so we don't eat too much meat. We usually only harvest our chickens and geese, and we mostly use our sheep and goats for wool and milk."

The stables faded from sight, and then we were looping around Curry Village again. We drove past a series of high-tech-looking dams and a few rows of metal storage tanks. "Merced River, and there's the hydroelectric dams and solar panels," she said. "Rex was an investment genius back in LA. He made enough money outright to get this place started, but we have to live simply to continue being sustainable."

She paused. "Coming up on our right, do you see those little rows of corn? Got those in at the end of March. There's also cucumbers, potatoes, wheat, pumpkins, watermelons, beans… We have a few greenhouses behind Curry Village, so we can grow stuff over winter, too."

We passed the far side of the Ahwahnee Meadow, and then we were twisting through the moss-covered remains of what, at one time, must have been a wooden community. Today, its peeling roofs and planks were collapsed into splinters, and they hung half-framed by their foundations.

"Yosemite Village," she said, and a note of sadness crept into her voice. "This place was the heart of Yosemite forty years ago."

I surveyed the destruction in front of me, the slow decomposition and moldering of what once must have been a thriving community of tourists and adventurers. The ruins felt heavy, like the headstones in a graveyard, and I tried to imagine what the scene must have looked like.

Kadence seemed to read my mind. As she pointed to a massive waterfall churning to our right – Yosemite Falls, apparently – she smiled and said, "We have some vintage photographs in one of the sitting rooms in the Ahwahnee. You really ought to check those out sometime. Totally put this place into perspective."

We passed the falls and pulled through the ruins of another cluster of buildings. "This was Yosemite Lodge," she said, encompassing more broken-down structures with a sweep of her hand. "Another hotel back in the park's heyday. And do you see that high wall behind the remains of the Lodge? That's Camp Four."

The stone wall seemed to encircle a tree-filled encampment of some sort, but it was impossible to tell from this distance. "What's Camp Four?"

"The only place in the entire Valley you aren't allowed to go. Rex keeps emergency food rations, medicines and survival gear there in case we have another earthquake."

She paused. "Keeps kerosene and gasoline there, too. We use new trucks for trips to the city, supply runs, things like that. But we rely on older, gas-dependent vehicles to get around out here. Gas is almost impossible to get in this part of the state, so Rex keeps storage tanks inside, and Daniel drains our vehicles every night." She shrugged. "Makes sense, I guess. He wants to keep order, in case anything weird ever happens out here."

Camp Four's high walls and foreboding entrance troubled me. "Has anyone ever been inside?"

"Not that I know of. A few kids tried to break in a few years ago - wanted to steal some gas and joyride up to Tuolumne Meadows. Rex caught them, and he was so pissed he nearly kicked them out of the Community." She shrugged. "He's a pretty relaxed leader overall, but there are two places in this park that are sacred to him: Camp Four and Tuolumne Meadows. He has a low tolerance for people who don't respect that."

"Tuolumne Meadows." I remembered the name from Jett's explanation. "That's where people retire, right?"

"Right." She motioned to a road that twisted away from the Valley. "There's the route that leads there. It's an incredible honor to be accepted at Tuolumne Meadows - the pinnacle of Community life, really - but it's also a huge decision, because Tuolumne is in the High Country. It's totally separate from the rest of the Community, and no one but retirees and the Founders are allowed to go up there."

"No one else? Not even to visit?"

"No." Kadence's headshake was emphatic. "Rex is very clear about that. Once retirees make the decision to cross over, we need to respect their right to privacy. It's part of the cycle of life out here. Disobedience is grounds for banishment, actually."

"Can retirees ever come back?"

"They can, but I've never heard of one who did. Crossing over is a really big deal, and I guess they just want some peace and quiet."

Our last stop was a narrow trail just before the entrance to the Ahwahnee. Its dirt path led toward a cluster of large white tents and cabins, and these were decorated with multi-colored flags that flapped like rainbows in the breeze.

"Meditation rooms," Kadence said. "A few Community members lead meditation sessions there every morning and afternoon."

"You meditate here?"

"Not that 'smooth out your aura' Centrist stuff, but actual meditation. Meditation as it was meant to be," she explained. "You aren't required to go, but some people think it helps. Awakens your Essence, realigns your chakras, all that stuff."

"You don't sound convinced."

"Oh, no, I love it," she said. "There just seem to be two schools of thought here, so not everyone sees its value. It's really a personal preference."

I studied the meditation rooms. "What are the schools of thought?"

"Well..." For a minute, she seemed to slip from her orientation mode. Drumming her fingers against the steering wheel, she said, "So, Rex and Daniel favor 'active' Essence pursuits – like climbing and celebrating and taking risks – but some of us believe the power of your Essence should be harnessed internally. Like an inner strength, you know?"

I didn't, but I nodded anyway.

"Some people try to do a combination of both – like my friend

Shayla. She's one of the most active people in this entire Valley, but she and I still make time to meditate almost every single day. Depends what you're comfortable with, I guess."

My thoughts flashed back to the beautiful girl I'd met at the dinner table. Before I could stop myself, I asked, "So, what's up with that girl, anyway?"

Kadence's chuckle made my cheeks burn. I stared down at my wristband again, and I wondered if my heart monitor was picking up on the embarrassing way my pulse was now racing.

Before I could worry too long, she answered, "Shayla's great. Amazing, really. Probably the nicest person in this entire Valley."

"Has she ever dated Ryder?"

*Where are these questions coming from?* I grimaced and almost clasped my hand over my mouth to prevent a future outburst, but Kadence seemed to take my question seriously.

"No," she said after a moment. "I don't think so, but nearly every other girl here has." She turned down the Ahwahnee's long driveway. "Autumn, I know you're new here, and I know everything seems really exciting and promising right now. But if I can give you one word of advice…? Stay away from Ryder Stone."

# CHAPTER TEN

"How you liking that wristband so far, Red? Looks good on you."

I fought the flip-flop that skittered in my chest at the sight of Ryder reclined in an overstuffed lobby chair. His boots were dusty, and a book was propped open on his lap.

"What are you reading?" My stride was tense, and my words came out more aggressive than I'd intended.

"Whoa. What's with the attitude?" Ryder flashed a smile and the cover of a well-worn book. "*The Beach*, by Alex Garland. Ever read it?"

"No." I continued walking.

"Hold up a sec." He jumped from his seat and rushed to intercept me. "Why are you in such a rush? Are you pissed at me for something?"

"No." I stared at a spot on the floor. *Watch it, Autumn. That's the face he apparently gives everyone here.*

"Unhappy with your chore assignment?"

I started. "I haven't gotten my chore assignment yet. That's where I'm going right now."

"Oh." He took a step sideways to let me pass. "Well, I just asked, and I'm kinda bummed. I was hoping you'd be assigned to the clinic with me, but it looks like my old man put you at the stables." He shrugged. "It's a good gig – you'll be there with Cody – but I was kinda hoping…" He let the sentence trail off. "I was hoping you and me might get to spend some more time together during the day. You know?"

His words made me woozy, but I forced myself to begin walking away. "Yeah," I managed. "That's too bad."

"Hey, and Red?" Ryder was beside me again. "I'm sorry I didn't see you at the bonfire last night. I looked for you after dinner, but there were just so many people, you know?"

He paused. "I was thinking… There's supposed to be this great meteor shower tonight. Everyone's watching in the Meadow, so… maybe we could share a blanket or something?"

I hoped he wouldn't notice my blush. "No," I stammered. "I… I'm not sure if I'll make it tonight or not. I still have a lot of moving in to do."

It was a lame excuse, but I tried to tell myself it didn't matter. I tried to tell myself I hadn't wanted to spend time with Ryder anyway, but the truth is, I became hyper-aware of him during dinner that night. The meal was a much less ornate affair in the Ahwahnee's interior dining room, and he seemed to be aware of me, too. I kept catching him staring as he stood in the buffet line, leaning like a cowboy against a tall stone pillar.

Javi noticed my preoccupation. When we returned to our tent cabin after dinner, he disappeared and then reemerged with a huge patchwork quilt. Holding it up hopefully, he said, "So I hear there's this meteor shower tonight. I know you've had a long day, but maybe… Wanna watch it with me?"

I didn't – not really – but I said yes anyway. And the smile that split Javi's face almost made me forget about Ryder.

Almost.

The Meadow was packed. It was late, but even the children and babies were still awake, dressed in pastel nightgowns and spread onto quilts and blankets with their young parents.

I couldn't believe I was surrounded by so many wives and husbands and fathers. Hadn't I always secretly longed for the affection and tenderness of Outsider families? Hadn't I always been jealous of their unity, of the way they showed their love for each other without feeling bad about it?

But here, crowded together in the middle of this meadow, I couldn't decide if I felt pleased or terrified by them. Their laughter, their entwined hands and the way the girls rested their heads in the crooks of the boys' arms… It was almost too much to process.

I hesitated for a moment in the grass, but then Kadence waved us over. "Come sit with me," she said. I shook off my discomfort, and I tried to smile and remember her friends' names as Javi spread our blanket on the grass beside them.

As I waited, I couldn't help but look for Ryder in the shifting crowd. When I finally spotted him, half lit on a blanket beside Cody, Jett and two girls I didn't recognize, his face was luminous with candlelight. A curl of smoke twisted from his lips, and one of the girls laughed and reached sideways to run a hand through his hair.

I found myself stewing when Javi reached up to touch my wrist. "Blanket's all ready."

Nestled between Kadence and Javi, with only a few inches of space separating us, I cast one last glance at Ryder and then peered toward the heavens. "Is everyone ready?" a melodic female voice called after a few minutes. "Does anyone need time to find their seats?"

It was Shayla. When no one protested, she clapped her hands and said, "All right, then. On the count of three!"

The Community came alive with chanting: "Three... two... one!" And then we were cast into darkness, hushed by the simultaneous snuffing of every candle and flashlight in the entire Meadow.

Within a few moments, the sky sprang to life. No longer hidden by ambient light – or San Francisco's jarring high-rises – it glistened with violet darkness and so many stars, it seemed impossible to find a swatch of empty sky. Stars upon stars upon stars, washed by a pale wisp of lightness that stretched in a band from one end of the sky to the other.

"That's the Milky Way." It was Javi's voice, and it possessed the same awed humbleness that kept my words lodged in my throat.

I felt stunned. And amazed. Like I'd never even seen the sky before. And then, just when I thought my mind couldn't process any more beauty, the first meteor streaked like an artist's brush across the eastern horizon.

The Meadow erupted with a low exclamation, and then giggles and shushing followed as another meteor followed the first one's path. And then another. And another, racing like spirits across the glowing velvet sky.

"It's beautiful," Javi whispered.

I slowly became aware of the warmth of his body, of the intake of his breath and the pulsing heartbeat that radiated outward from his skin. His heart was hammering, too – I could sense it – and I wondered if he was thinking about the heart monitor on his wrist.

Then I wondered if he was thinking about me – about the warmth of my body, the intake of my breath or the hammering of my heart. We were just a few inches apart, after all, and we were surrounded by so much love and togetherness that it only made sense he would feel it, too.

The idea that he might be paying attention to me became so distracting that I took a quick breath and glanced sideways to check. Our eyes locked, and my question was immediately answered. Javi's dark irises were barely visible in the blackness, but they gleamed with starlight as he lay looking at me across the spread of the quilt.

His expression was intense – unwavering and unapologetic – and the strength of it sent that pulse of energy racing down my abdomen again. A jolt of adrenaline swept through me... or was that desire?

"Hi," I whispered. My voice sounded lame – childish and in no way reflective of the way I was beginning to feel.

"Hi." He echoed my tone, but there was nothing childlike about the expression on his face. Instead, he looked focused – almost as focused as Jett had looked when she curled herself into Cody, breathing heavy and eyes half closed with wanting.

My heart stuttered at the thought. Guilt surged through me, and I immediately looked away. "I'm tired," I whispered. "I think I need to go to bed now."

Before he could stop me, I pulled myself to my feet and rushed back to our tent cabin.

Again, I didn't sleep. This time, it was Javi's twists and turns that kept me awake most of the night.

He wasn't sleeping, either. I could tell that much from the uneven hitch in his breathing, but I wasn't about to roll over to face him. I didn't know what I'd see in his eyes, and I didn't think I could handle another moment like the one we'd shared in the Meadow.

It wasn't even an official "moment", anyway. It was just a blip – a flicker of sustained eye contact, lasting no more than twenty seconds – but Javi's hungry expression said so much. I wasn't ready to deal with the implications of that just yet.

I also wasn't ready to deal with my reaction, or with whatever emotion he may have been able to sense in my expression. Did he think I looked hungry? Could he feel and smell and sense my desire?

I couldn't handle that thought right now. It made me feel embarrassed and self-conscious, and I wanted nothing more than to take that moment back.

But then again, I didn't.

Javi was so big. And strong. And the realization that he could look at me like that... Well, that made me feel beautiful. And powerful. Like all those times I'd caught boys staring at me during temple classes.

But these were terrible thoughts. And their presence in my mind scared me more than anything else. *Watch it, Autumn.*

I gripped Brady's lion a little tighter and repeated the Centrist mantra in my head: Neutrality is the key to longevity, neutrality is the key to longevity...

A pause. *Do I still believe that?*

I heaved a sigh and twisted onto my back – purposefully avoiding the energy that emanated like a furnace from Javi's side of the tent. *Every moment of every interaction I've ever had in my entire life has been based on the Centrist mantra, I thought.*

*And now... just like that... I'm expected to forget it?*

*Now abundance is the key to longevity?*

I felt like everything I'd ever stood for was being ripped out from under me. When I took away the constructs of who I was supposed to be – Autumn Grace, obedient Centrist; Autumn Grace, dutiful daughter – I realized I had no idea who I actually was.

My identity was built around the Centrist Movement – around meditation sessions and shared living with Aunt Marie and my mother. Around chores and neutrality. Around reflection rituals and Cedar.

If my values were suddenly flip-flopped, did that mean I actually was the type of girl who could turn her back on the Movement? Who could be attracted to not one but two boys at the same time?

What about my Essence?

The thought made a lump rise in my throat. I didn't know much, but I knew I didn't want to just forget about everything I'd ever learned. Because even if the Centrists were wrong about some things, they couldn't be wrong about everything. Attachment did lead to suffering, and selfishness and recklessness were very dangerous things.

Weren't they?

A tear spilled unbidden from the corner of my left eye. I hastily wiped it away, and Javi shifted on his cot in response. "Hey, Autumn?" he whispered.

I stiffened and closed my eyes as tight as I possibly could. A few moments passed, and then Javi sighed and sank back into his blankets. Sometime around midnight, his breathing finally settled.

# CHAPTER ELEVEN

I reported to the stables early the next morning – skipping breakfast and sliding out of the tent cabin while Javi was still sleeping. I wasn't hungry, and I didn't want to risk a chance encounter with Ryder – whom I had decided overnight I needed to avoid at all costs.

He was too smooth, too cocky and intrusive, and I didn't like the way he slid into my personal space and sized me up like he owned me. He apparently did that to all the girls here, but I had news for him. He didn't own me, and he would never own me. *I* owned me, and I wasn't giving that up anytime soon. I didn't care how tongue-tied I felt when he was around me.

Javi was a different story. His affection really *did* seem genuine, but it suddenly occurred to me that I didn't even know him. Not really. I didn't know why he was here, and he'd certainly never asked me about Brady. He'd never asked me about *anything*, actually. I didn't blame him – I'd never asked him anything personal, either – but the knowledge certainly made me think twice about the way I'd caught myself feeling last night.

It made me think twice about a lot of things, actually, and it made me remember I wasn't here for Javi or Ryder or Rex or anyone else I'd met here.

I was here for *Brady*, and it was about time I started acting like it.

The stables were cool and long – a wide sweep of wood and light that stretched in the shade beneath a grove of pine trees. A long row of horses stamped and swatted from their spots along a hitching post, and the air was thick with the earthy scents of hay and manure.

It was a strong smell – not quite unpleasant, but not quite pleasant, either – and it stuck with me as I strode inside the barn. Here, the smell mixed with leather, and the air became muted with blocky early-morning shadows.

"You're here early," a girl's muffled voice called from one of the stalls. "Stable crews don't usually get started until closer to eight or nine."

"I wanted to get here as soon as I could," I said, peering toward the source of the noise. "I need to talk to Rex today, so I figured if I came now, maybe I could leave a little early?"

There was the shuffle of something being put away, and then the girl appeared around the corner with a smile. My heart sank. It was Shayla.

"I'm sure we can work something out." She wiped her hands on her thick khaki pants. "It's good to see you, Autumn."

I hated her. I instantly hated her, and I had no idea why.

Maybe it was the curtain of golden hair that swirled like silk as she closed the distance between us. Maybe it was the way she seemed to float rather than walk, willowy and fluid as a dancer. Maybe it was the soft, ivory glow of her cheeks, or the pale eyelashes that batted against eyes the color of a deep mountain pool.

Not that I'd ever actually seen a deep mountain pool. But this is what immediately sprang to mind as I tried to remind myself that I didn't care if she glowed when Ryder spoke to her or not.

"I'm excited you got assigned to work with me," she continued. "Too many boys here, and I can already tell you have good energy. The animals will love you." She paused and checked a clipboard. "We have about three hours' worth of training ahead of us, so we can probably be done by ten if we push it."

We spent the next few hours touring the stables, and Shayla taught me more about the care of livestock than I would have ever thought possible. I learned about alfalfa versus Timothy hay, textured versus sweet feed... I learned how to chop vegetables and muck stables, how to measure supplements and record entries into medical and feed logs. I learned the difference between English and Western saddles, between hackamores and bitless bridles. I learned how to tell billy goats from nanny goats and how to scatter cracked corn so the chickens wouldn't fight over it.

I stayed as far away from the animals as I could, and I cowered a little when the horses looked my way. They were huge, and their rippled muscles and sharp hooves made me uneasy. The way their liquid brown eyes flicked to follow me alarmed me even more.

If Shayla noticed my hesitation, she certainly covered it well. As much as I hated to admit it, she really did seem to be an animal expert. Every creature in her care perked up and stood a little straighter when she approached, and they flicked their ears and stamped their feet whenever she leaned forward to pet or speak to them.

Were they tongue-tied around her, too? Was the whole wide world enamored by pretty blond girls?

I realized at some point that stewing about Shayla certainly wasn't helping me fulfill my promise to maintain a balanced, healthy outlook on life. But I couldn't help it. She was impeccable. The way she slipped so seamlessly from a smile into a laugh, the way she slid her fingers across her horses' flanks... It was like she wasn't even on the same plane of existence as me.

And she was *nice*. Unreasonably so. She took her time explaining my duties – mostly barn cleaning, with a little diet prep thrown in for good measure – and she patiently answered all my questions, no matter how redundant. She was warm and kind and friendly and understanding, and she seemed to light up every room she entered.

She made me incredibly uncomfortable.

I tried to remind myself I didn't care how amazing she was, and I didn't need to prove anything to her. I didn't need to prove anything to anyone.

I slipped out of the barn as quickly as I could, waving goodbye and cutting down the road toward Curry Village. Cool air swirled through the forest canopy, but the asphalt was warm, and the sun shone brightly overhead. By the time I reached Rex's clinic, I had begun to perspire slightly.

I couldn't help the creep of fear that prickled through me as I wiped my temples. Perspiration and endorphins seemed to go hand in hand, and Cedar had always conditioned me to avoid both at all costs.

Now here I was, living in a forest and sweating in the sunshine, and I couldn't quite figure out how that made me feel.

Uneasy, really. Panicked. And certainly ready for a proper explanation.

"OK, you gotta tell me why you think Essence drain is bullshit."

I nearly fainted when the words left my lips. And this time, I *did* clasp my hand over my mouth. What was *wrong* with me lately?

Rex straightened from his clipboard at the sound of my voice. Turning from the wall of cabinets in his waiting room, he smiled. "Morning, Autumn. My son warned me you were a bit of a firecracker."

Firecracker? His words made my stomach flip-flop. What does that even mean?

"Would you like to have a seat?"

I stuffed my hands in my pockets and sank to a seat in a small wooden chair. The lab to my right was darkened, but the door was slightly ajar. A faint green glow emanated from the gloom as Rex strode forward and sank into a seat across from me.

"You're feeling off-balance today, aren't you?" His warmth made me feel like squirming, but his attention also reminded me of Ryder. I couldn't decide if I liked that or not.

"I came here because my brother died," I said. "He was only six."

Rex nodded, and I continued. "I ran into Ryder in the park, and he told me you could prove the Essence theory wrong. It's why I came here; I need to know if Brady died because he ran out of Essence or not."

Rex leaned back in his chair and remained silent. I paused for a second, and then I kept going. "I have been conditioned every single day of my life to believe emotions are bad. Hormones are dangerous, and exercise will kill you. And now I'm here – and it's great you guys don't believe that – but it's only been a few days since I left the city, so I'm going to need more than just your word if you want me to be part of this.

"I just finished cleaning up after *animals,*" I continued, blurting out the words before he had a chance to respond. "Cedar preaches against attachments to animals, but here we are in Yosemite, and there are animals *everywhere.* I can't believe I'm expected to be *OK* with this."

"You aren't expected to be OK with this." Rex's voice was patient. "If you don't like your chore assignment, we can always relocate you somewhere else. Some people just never take to livestock."

"But it isn't about the animals," I said. "It's about trust... and transparency... and the fact that I need to know what's actually going on out here before I decide if I want to stay or not."

Instead of frowning like I expected, Rex simply regarded me with a smile. "I appreciate your tenacity, Autumn," he said. "You are already connecting to your emotions in such a powerful way."

Tenacity? I had only heard that word once, in reference to an Outsider my mother had once seen. He had missed his train and had stood banging his hands against its glass doors until it pulled away from the station.

Rex stood and motioned for me to enter the lab. "Would you like to go on a tour, then? Your friend Javier just finished one himself."

"Javi was here?" I didn't know why the sound of Javi's name left me so flustered. "What was he doing here?"

"Exactly what you're doing." Rex's slow smile told me he'd probably noticed my blush. "Making sure he didn't make a mistake by joining us."

"I founded the Community because I believe manipulators like Cedar should be stopped at all costs."

Rex and I sat beside a wide computer monitor. The room was filled with long tables, refrigerators and rows upon rows of test tubes and neatly organized files. The light bulbs overhead were blinding – a shocking shade of fluorescent white – and one flickered slightly in the corner. This gave the room a weird, buzzing glow.

"My Community exists here as a sanctuary," he said, "but we cannot stop at just existing. As long as monsters like Cedar are in positions of power, the happiness of our children is at stake."

He leaned forward. "Have you heard the whispers, Autumn? The Haight-Ashbury temple is filled to overflowing. Cedar is looking to expand, to build a second temple near Telegraph Hill. Some even think he'll run for office. Try to consolidate his power and turn the entire Bay Area into a Centrist stronghold."

He paused. "I know about what happened to your brother, about the way Cedar's meditation masters let Brady die in the street without lifting so much as a finger to save him. We can't allow a society that promotes such gross negligence to exist."

Before I could manage so much as a nod, he asked, "Who did you leave behind, Autumn? In that terrible, terrible place?"

"My aunt." My voice came out as a squeak. "I left my aunt and my mother behind."

"Let us take a moment, then, to imagine what they are doing right now. Working low-paid, entry-level jobs? Tithing their entire paychecks to the Movement in exchange for paltry weekly allotments that don't even cover their living expenses?"

He frowned. "Or are they surviving on grocery store castoffs and slaving away in the temple? Sewing quilts and souvenirs, when they never see so much as one cent in profit?"

A pause. "Because that's what Cedar does, you know. Conducts. Orchestrates. Sits in his lofty quarters and reaps the benefits of everyone else's sacrifices. Especially the sacrifices of his children."

He clenched his fists. "Don't get me started on his supposed 'neutrality'. Cedar is demented, perverse. Most of his meditation masters are, too." At this, his voice faltered. "Autumn, I have seen so many wicked deeds performed in the name of the Centrist Movement; I have participated in them myself. I did it because I was tricked, seduced into believing I was serving a higher purpose."

He leaned back in his chair. "You've known, haven't you? For years. Some part of you has always doubted his teachings. His methods. Those late-night visits from his meditation masters. Because you're almost seventeen now, aren't you? Your first visit couldn't have been too far from now."

As dread filled the pit of my stomach, he reached forward to squeeze my hand. "Don't worry, Autumn. You're safe now. But you understand why I can't rest until every other Centrist child is likewise freed?"

As I fumbled through an awkward nod, he swiveled to his computer. "Let me show you the data we've been collecting. It isn't enough to simply discuss the fallacy of Cedar's teachings; we intend to dismantle every principle he has ever preached."

He turned to address the darkened computer: "Ryder Stone, please. Patient number zero-zero-three. Inception to present, stabilized with averages."

The computer whirred to life, and the monitor brightened. A neon green line graph appeared against a background of black, and two wiggly lines stretched diagonally upward across its x- and y-axes.

"This is my son's file," he explained. "I have been monitoring his heart rate and hormones since we arrived here. This graph shows the interrelation between the two; it also tracks his highs and lows through time."

He pointed to the horizontal x-axis, which started with the number ten and ended with the number seventeen. "This axis tracks Ryder's age. Right now, there are hash marks every year, but if I had imported a smaller amount of data, I could see months, weeks, days, even minutes or seconds."

He pointed to the vertical y-axis. "This tracks the highs and lows of Ryder's heart rate and hormones. So, if we consult the data" – here, he motioned to the two squiggly lines, one a brighter shade of green than the other – "we can see that his hormone fluctuations tend to follow the patterns of his heart rate. So, if he's keyed up at the top of a mountain, for instance, his heart rate and hormones will reflect this."

The sight of Ryder's heart and hormone lines squiggling across the screen left me strangely unsettled. I felt like a voyeur – like I was reading his mind or scoping out his secrets.

"Let me show you Ryder's first kiss," Rex continued. "I don't usually know the catalysts for each patients' fluctuations – and it's certainly none of my business to find out – but I'm specially privy to Ryder's information, as he reports his milestones to me whenever possible. We use the timing system to backtrack events and assign profiles to each one."

He turned and addressed the computer again. "Ryder Stone, patient number zero-zero-three. April 30, 2033, 2.30pm-6.30pm."

I felt a tightening in the pit of my stomach when I saw the two green lines appear again. This time, they started relatively low on the graph, and they arched slowly upward, weaving up and down until they spiked and peaked somewhere around 4 o'clock. The peak held for quite some time before the lines began their slow descent an hour or so later.

Rex pointed to the moment the lines began to dip. "He was twelve when it happened. And this is when she was called back to the stables."

"The stables?" My heart sank. Surely Shayla wasn't Ryder's first kiss. Was she?

My cheeks burned, and I looked away from the monitor. "OK, so how do you use this to research Essence drain?"

"Excellent question." Rex turned to address the computer again. "Elsa Holly, please. Patient number zero-seven-eight. Inception to death, stabilized with averages."

Death? A lump rose in my throat as another set of green lines appeared on the screen. This time, the x-axis began at nineteen and ended at twenty-three. The up-and-down fluctuations weren't nearly as exaggerated as Ryder's.

"Elsa joined us five years ago," Rex explained. "Passed away just this last summer."

I studied the abrupt ending of the graph. Its last reading peaked at the very edge of its upper limits. Elsa was terrified when she died.

"Bear attack," he said, noticing my hesitation. "A terrible day for the entire Community. I'm sorry to show you this – it's hard to relive it – but what's interesting about Elsa's chart is the fact that she lived a relatively quiet life until the moment of her death." He motioned to the fairly even flow of Elsa's emotions through time. "Mostly kept to herself. Didn't exercise or explore or put herself out there at all."

His expression became somber. "She eventually decided to leave the Community, but she startled a bear on the outskirts of our camp. We found her heart rate monitor a few days later."

He shook his head as I gasped. "If I were Cedar, I would tell you Elsa lived a very cautious life. She was extremely careful with her Essence, yet fate snuffed her out far too soon, wouldn't you agree?"

"Yeah, but maybe Elsa was just born with a very low supply of Essence? You never know how much your body stores to begin with."

"That's exactly what your friend Javier suggested, and I would be compelled to agree if this were a singular occurrence. But the data we have collected suggests a very powerful non-alignment of hormones, heart rates and life spans across the board. Regardless of the variables."

He paused. "Let me show you some files from Community members who have retired and crossed over to our second encampment in Tuolumne Meadows." He addressed the computer: "James Elliott, please. Patient number zero-two-five. Inception to retirement, stabilized with averages."

James's file flashed on the screen. It started at sixteen, ended at twenty-one and was filled with ups and downs that surpassed even Ryder's.

"Here are a few more," he continued, ordering up a handful of other retirees' files. Each graph peaked and dipped crazily, and the last reading on each file maxed out at the upper end of the spectrum.

"Our retirees, for the most part, are exemplary members of the Community," he said. "They have given us everything they can possibly give us. When they make the decision to retire to Tuolumne Meadows, we remain eternally grateful for their sacrifices."

He ordered the screen to darken again. "We compare these graphs to those unfortunate enough to be taken by Mother Nature, and what we've found so far is absolutely no correlation between heart rates, hormones and life spans." He paused. "Our data is irrefutable, even if everyone *is* born with a different supply of Essence."

"So, why are you still collecting data? Why haven't you already confronted Cedar?"

Rex took a breath. "I would like nothing more than to destroy the Movement tomorrow, especially now that it has been weakened by the controversy surrounding your brother's passing. But we must first collect as much data as possible to ensure a solid scientific result. By the first of August – the seven-year anniversary of our little Community – we will have a high enough relative chi-squared to exceed a ninety-nine percent confidence level–"

He chuckled when he realized I wasn't following. "Which is a fancy way of saying we will have enough data for an unimpeachable result. Cedar may be able to fight back against anecdotes and anomalies, but he can't fight back against a plethora of scientific evidence. He also can't fight the brewing opposition that has risen in response to the way he has handled your brother's passing – especially when the world finds out Brady's own sister left his Movement to join our cause."

Rex smiled and patted my arm. "The first of August is only the tip of the iceberg, of course. Our data won't be complete until the end of our lives. But with these results, no one will be able to claim our long lives here are just statistical flukes. We will have real scientific credibility, which we will need to categorically destroy the Movement."

He swiveled away from the desk. "We will continue collecting data after August, but we will also begin to shift our focus. We will begin compiling our findings into pamphlets for distribution, and we will start converting as many Centrists as we can. We will also attempt to turn public opinion against the Movement. Once Outsiders realize how dangerous Cedar actually is, they will stop viewing his Movement as a harmless hippie anomaly.

"We will accuse him of gross negligence, of child abuse, of sexual assault, of violating child labor laws... We will expose Brady's death as the senseless tragedy it was, and we will dismantle the entire Movement brick by brick. We won't stop until Cedar and his meditation masters are locked away forever."

He took a breath. "What we're looking for over the course of the next few months is an amazing final push. We have already tested our methods, and we know what we're doing out here is safe. So now we want our study's final numbers to be off the charts.

"My son picked you," he finished, "because he tells me he sees a spark in you. He knows how hard you've taken your brother's death, and he thinks you have the drive and passion necessary to become an important part of our team."

He paused. "Can you imagine how different Brady's life would have been if he had been allowed to embrace inner spirit? If he had been able to run and play and experience life the way it's supposed to be experienced? Without *fear*?"

He stood and began leading me toward the exit. "You do want to help us free other children like Brady, don't you, Autumn?"

"I do." I didn't seem to have any control of my words, much like I hadn't been able to control my words around Ryder. But as Rex escorted me out the front door, I felt determination solidify inside me, and I realized how much I really wanted to do this.

I wanted to help bring Cedar down.

# CHAPTER TWELVE

I ran into Javi outside the entrance to the clinic. He must have seen me enter, because he was sitting waiting on a split rail fence. His long legs were stretched in loose-fitting pants, and his hair was windblown.

"Got to you, too, didn't he?"

I nodded. "He did. And I want to do this, Javi. I really want to do this now."

"I do, too." Javi looked taller this morning, and straighter, with a fierce expression and eyes that glinted almost black as charcoal. He stood.

"They've got me cleaning rooms at the Ahwahnee," he said. "An unlucky chore assignment, but I finished early today, and I think we should go on a hike." He motioned toward a dirt trail. "Rex tells me there's a set of waterfalls up this way, and I'd like to see them."

He paused. "And I want to hear why you're here, Autumn," he said. "If we're going to try to do this together, it seems this should be our first step."

We cut away from Curry Village and starting up a winding, sun-dotted trail. The air smelled crisp, like moss and sediment, and the air felt warm as it settled on our shoulders.

The trail was wide and steep as it curved alongside the granite canyon walls. A clear creek gurgled to our right, and rocks rose sharply to our left. Their towering height made me feel a bit claustrophobic – like I was stuck between buildings in San Francisco's financial district – but this place didn't remind me of the financial district *at all*.

It was wild here. And green. Instead of hearing cars, trains and chattering businessmen and women, all we heard were chirping birds, trickling water and the crunch of gravel as it ground beneath our feet.

We hiked in silence for a few minutes, and then I felt my breath shortening. The pain I'd felt in Golden Gate Park was back, but instead of panicking, I simply took a deep breath and reached sideways to stretch.

*A stitch. This is called a stitch, and everybody gets them.*

Javi frowned, but I shook my head. "I'm fine," I said, and I hoped my voice didn't betray my lingering fear. "It's apparently no big deal. You're just supposed to stretch, and it will go away."

"What are you supposed to do when you can't breathe?" Javi's words were labored, and it relieved me to see I wasn't the only one having trouble with this.

"It's the altitude," I said. "It's harder to breathe when you're high in the air, and this place is a lot higher than San Francisco." I straightened as the pain in my side began subsiding. "We'll get used to it. I think it only takes a few weeks for your body to adjust."

Javi motioned to the trail twisting before us. "This is scary, isn't it?"

"What?"

"This. Everything. The idea that we're out here hiking, and we might not die, after all."

"Yeah." I wiped the sweat from my brow and glanced back toward the trailhead.

"I wonder if we'll ever get used to this," he said. "And I wonder which fear is worse: the fear of feeling nothing, or the fear of feeling everything?"

"What do you mean?"

"It just seems like you shouldn't feel everything all the time, just like you shouldn't feel nothing all the time. You know?"

"I guess. But Rex said you should do whatever you want. So if you want to be neutral, I guess you could be neutral. Right?"

He didn't look convinced. "I guess so."

We made our way higher and higher, past rockslides, cottonwood groves and drop-offs that grew increasingly steeper the farther we traveled. We didn't say much – couldn't say much, really, with our huffing and puffing.

When we finally reached the wooden footbridge, it was Javi who spoke first: "Wow. Would you look at that?"

I followed his line of sight. There, raging a mile or so upstream, I found myself staring at a waterfall so violent and massive, I felt myself shrinking back slightly. It was still far away, but its vertical drop-off was so daunting it made me dizzy. Wedged in the narrow span between two cliffs, it towered at least three hundred feet above the valley floor. The water that catapulted from its crest exploded in a heaving spray so thick, it completely shrouded its base in mist.

Javi consulted a wooden sign. "Vernal Fall, it says, and there's apparently two ways we can get to the top."

I reached his side and studied the sign. "It's only about half a mile to the top if we take this Mist Trail," I said and pointed to the path on our left. "The trail we're on right now is much longer."

"Mist Trail it is." Javi surveyed the longer trail with a smirk. "Why in the world would anyone go the long way?"

Nearly six hundred stone stairs later, Javi and I both understood why someone might choose the long way. The Mist Trail – aptly named, I realized, when I became soaked – was nearly vertical. Its winding stone steps cut straight into the side of the cliff, and they crumbled and wiggled under our feet as we struggled to the top.

I was terrified. I climbed more than I hiked, and I slipped on the wet moss and crawled on my hands and knees in some places. I would have turned back several times if not for Javi's quiet support. He walked a few paces behind me, and he caught me whenever I began to slip.

He looked scared, too, but he also looked exhilarated. His dark hair was plastered to his forehead by the time we reached the summit, and his cotton pants clung to him, dripping and nearly transparent from the water. He was wearing dark undergarments, I noticed, and I would have blushed, had I not been so exhausted.

The trail petered out on the right side of the waterfall, and a wide, relatively flat stretch of granite and meadow opened behind it. The cliff's drop-off loomed dangerously to our left, but a wide stretch of corroded chain link fencing blocked it for the most part.

My fear of heights kicked into overdrive, and I made sure to give the cliff a wide berth as I walked to inspect the point where the gushing creek cascaded into the waterfall below. I had never seen anything like it before. The water, relatively calm on top, dropped over the side in a raging explosion of roaring power. Water droplets burst and scattered apart in midair, and they collided and recombined dizzily as they streamed downward.

The view from up here was even more unfathomable than the one from the bottom, and I felt my head spinning when I stared for too long. *Vertigo*, I thought, clinging to another word I remembered from my temple lessons. I staggered backward and sank to a seat on a rock.

Javi followed, and we sat together in silence. After a few moments, he tilted his head and grinned. "We made it."

I surveyed the jumbled cliff before us and felt victory and relief coat my insides. We *had* made it. We had scaled the side of a cliff together, and nothing bad had happened to us. Our Essences hadn't faltered once.

The grin that swept across my face must have told Javi everything he needed to know, because he beamed when he motioned to what looked like a widened swimming area behind us. "Wanna take a walk?"

I nodded. We approached the water, blocked artificially from the waterfall by a series of stone boulders. The roar of the falls lessened, and it was easy to imagine there was no waterfall raging behind us.

"So, what made you leave the city, anyway?"

The question was unexpected, but Javi's tone was so sincere that I only hesitated a moment before answering, "My little brother, Brady, died a few months ago."

"Brady was your brother?" The color drained from his face. "Autumn, I'm so sorry; I had no idea."

"No, it's OK. But... Brady was a good kid, you know? He didn't ever do anything he wasn't supposed to, so when he..." I cleared my throat. "Well, that's why I'm here, I guess. I don't want his... *life*... to have been for nothing. If Essences really are bullshit, Centrists need to know that."

Javi nodded and leaned sideways until our shoulders were touching. It was a good feeling – warm – and it didn't make me uncomfortable like I expected. Instead, I felt reassured. Like I wasn't alone anymore.

"Why are *you* here?"

"My girlfriend killed herself two years ago."

Javi's words were so unfathomable that I nearly tumbled to the ground. Instead, I jerked sideways and whirled to face him.

"I know, I know." His smile was slow and sad. "There are so many things wrong with that sentence that you don't even know where to begin."

"I don't." My cheeks reddened. "Javi... I'm so sorry. I've never heard of anything like that before. What *happened*?"

"Well, the first rule we broke was the one that says you aren't allowed to date."

"Right."

"But we did. Obviously. We grew up living next door to each other, and the feelings we had for each other just wouldn't go away." He bit his lower lip. "We started seeing each other when we were fifteen – sneaking out at night, cutting classes at the temple, all that. It was stupid, and we knew it was stupid. But we felt invincible, you know – after a while – because nothing *happened* to us. Our Essences seemed fine, and no one ever suspected anything."

His eyebrows knotted. "We didn't *do* anything too dangerous, anyway. We just kissed, and we held each other and talked about our future. We justified it because we figured I'd be a meditation master someday. Maybe I'd be assigned to her, anyway."

He picked up a fragment of rock and began rolling it between his thumb and forefinger. "One night, her mother caught us kissing in the alley. Gabriella was terrified she would tell Cedar, so I suggested we desert – make a dash for San Jose, or Monterey, or anywhere, really, where we could be away from the Movement."

The rock fell from his hands. "Gabriella said she couldn't leave. Said it would bring too much shame to her family. So that night... I don't know exactly what happened. Maybe her mother *did* tell Cedar; maybe Cedar decided to send her away somewhere. Or maybe she just couldn't live with her guilt." At this, his voice cracked. "Whatever the reason, she hung herself that night. I didn't find out until the policemen arrived the next morning."

I didn't know what to say. My fingers quickly found his, and my shoulder pressed into his side until his breathing evened out slightly.

We stayed silent for a moment, and then his tone changed. "Here's the thing that's never made sense to me. Gabriella's list of transgressions didn't mention me – or suicide – once. Cedar covered the whole thing up, said her cause of Essence drain was too much laughter and the secret stash of romance novels she'd hidden in her bedroom."

His voice became heated. "How can it be that we carried on a secret relationship for more than two years, but Cedar blamed her death on *romance novels*?"

He looked so struck by the inconsistency that I felt my knot of determination solidify. Gabriella's list of transgressions was exactly like Brady's.

"How many more?" I said. "How many more transgression lists have been lies?"

Our metal wristbands clinked together as I grabbed both his hands. "I can't tell you how sorry I am about Gabriella, Javi, but more than that, I'm pissed. I can't believe we've allowed ourselves to be controlled by Cedar for so long. I can't believe the things he's made us do."

"How about the things he's made us *not* do?" The fervor in Javi's voice mirrored my own. "My whole life, I've been terrified to feel *anything*, but look where that got Gabriella. Look where that got Brady."

I nodded. "I *hate* him, Javi. I'm sick and tired of his lies, and I want to do this. I want to help Rex destroy the Movement."

I glanced toward the swimming area, to the gurgle of clear water and the reflection of the sun off its ripples. The weight of my wristband felt heavy, and I instantly knew where we could start. "Javi, have you ever gone swimming before?"

# CHAPTER THIRTEEN

Javi's shirt was off before I could even finish my question. Ripping it over his head, he kicked off his new hiking boots and fumbled with his pants' drawstrings.

Then he was standing there with his hand extended – bare chest gleaming in the sun and long legs tense beneath dark undergarments. His expression was resolute, and he waited for me without a trace of uncertainty in his eyes. "Let's do this, Autumn."

I couldn't help my hesitation, and I couldn't help the blush that crept through my cheeks at the sight of him. But I could make the decision to do something about it.

So I did.

I loosened the ribbon that kept my flimsy blouse tied, and I dropped it to the ground. I kicked off my shoes and stepped out of my pants, and then I was standing there, nearly naked, too. My Community-appointed undergarments were much more flattering than my bulky Centrist ones – soft blue panties and a matching cotton bra – but the thought that I was actually standing here letting a boy look at me was still so foreign and uncomfortable that I only paused for a second before I darted toward the swimming area.

"Do you know how to swim?" I called over my shoulder as I ran.

"No! Do you?"

"No!"

"Can't be that hard, right?"

He ran a few paces behind me – I could hear the slap of his feet against the granite – but I tried not to think about what my butt might look like from that angle as I approached the creek and splashed into the water.

"Wait, wait, wait!" I shouted, stopping a few paces in when the creek's icy chill stunned me. It was glacial – absolutely freezing even in May – and I began to rethink our decision to swim until Javi crashed into me and sent us both catapulting forward into deeper water.

Javi's cry was strangled. Surfacing in a flurry beside me, he struggled and kicked, backpedaling toward the shallows and dragging me with him.

We clambered up the bank, shivering and sputtering and finally collapsing on a sun-warmed rock. "Wow," he said, fighting his coughs as I wiped the hair from my eyes. We made eye contact and instantly erupted into laughter. Javi looked like a drowned rat, and I'm sure I looked no better. My hair was an absolute mess, and my pale skin had begun taking on blue undertones. My teeth were chattering, and I'm sure my lips were turning blue as well. Even Javi's skin was starting to look sickly. Goose bumps and sand particles covered his chest and stomach as he lay on his back and laughed until he cried.

Tears were streaming from my eyes, too, by the time we were finished. The sun had warmed my frigid skin by then, so I may have looked a little less ridiculous when he propped himself on his elbow and said, "Wanna go in again?"

It suddenly occurred to me that I actually *was* lying here in my underwear next to him. I stole a glance downward, and although I was relieved to see that my clothing still wasn't see-through, my nipples were certainly making quite a show through the thin fabric of my bra.

I quickly covered my chest with my arms.

I was too late, I think, because the playful expression in Javi's eyes changed when he saw me survey myself. This led him, I'd imagine, to glance downward as well, because he shuddered slightly and inhaled in one shaky breath.

Energy hovered between us, and I felt my body become electrified. Before I realized it, I was up on my elbow, and my desire to taste his lips finally became overpowering. I had never kissed a boy before, but suddenly I wanted to feel what it felt like to press my body against his.

Our lips were only a few inches apart when I heard the leaves crunch behind us. And then, a loud voice boomed, "Red! Javi! You found the swimming hole!"

I jerked backward and locked eyes with Ryder. He stood a short distance away, shirtless and flanked by two boys I didn't recognize.

There was a defiant set to his jaw, and his eyes drilled into Javi's as he asked, "Having fun, guys?"

Javi straightened, and an edge crept into his voice. "Water's colder than it looks."

"It is at that." Ryder tossed his backpack to the ground. His signature confidence returned, and he grinned broadly as he strode toward us. "Boys and I blew off chores to scope out Taft Point for our summer highlining route. Should be set to go soon, if either of you wanna join us."

He motioned to the group behind him. "Trey and Adrian. Guys, this is Javier and Autumn. New recruits." He winked and reached for the buttons of his pants. "Think we could use a swim, too. Room for a few more?"

I was astonished when Ryder dropped not only his pants, but his undergarments, too. His back was to me, but every curve and muscle of his butt was clearly visible when he took off running and crashed into the deep water.

Trey and Adrian quickly followed. Although I never saw their fronts, I clearly saw both of their backs as they cast off their clothes and catapulted naked into the swimming hole after him.

I realized my mouth was hanging open when Javi snarled and straightened from the ground. "Assholes," he said and extended his hand for me. "I'm so sorry, Autumn. Let's get out of here, OK?"

Stunned – both by his anger and by the nakedness that had just flashed before my eyes – I let him pull me from the rock and lead me back to our clothes.

He turned to block me as I struggled into my pants. "He knows you just got here," he fumed, rage barely concealed. "How could he possibly think it's OK to strip down naked in front of you?"

I didn't answer. Still shocked, I pulled my blouse over my head and gathered my hair into a sloppy ponytail.

"I'm so sorry." He turned to pull on his own pants. "That was unbelievably disrespectful. Let me take you home, OK?"

I tried to tell myself I was horrified – and I kinda was, I guess – but mostly, I was just surprised. And later that night, when I replayed the sight of Ryder running naked toward the creek, I felt a little amused, too.

The sight of his white butt, so out of sync with his tanned back and legs, was pretty funny. I wondered what his front looked like – giggled a little when I tried to picture it – and then I remembered the highlight of my afternoon was supposed to be my almost-kiss with Javi, not my almost-sighting of Ryder's package.

Javi and I had been thankfully reassigned to separate tent cabins, so I didn't need to worry about his presence in the cot beside me. This relieved me, but it still struck me as odd that – as incredible as the feeling of almost-kissing him had been – it was Ryder's interruption that kept running through my mind.

That smoldering moment when he sized us up across the clearing… His eyes had been filled with… what? Outrage? Envy?

I felt a little giddy at the idea that he may have been jealous to see me with Javi, but I stopped myself before I could go any further. After all, Ryder apparently dated everyone around here. So even if I could have him, I didn't want him, anyway. Right?

*Get yourself together, Autumn.*

"Get a good look?"

I jumped at the sound of Ryder's voice. The rake in my hands clattered against the stall wall in front of me, and I whirled to see him waiting in the stable aisle. His arms were crossed, and dimples creased the smoothness of his cheeks.

"What are you doing here?" I reached for my fallen rake and picked a stray piece of hay from my hair. "Blowing off chores again?"

"Nope." He took a step forward. "Clinic's a piece of cake; I just organize samples for my old man until he gets bored and tells me to beat it." He narrowed his eyes playfully. "But you didn't answer my question. Get a good look?"

"At what?"

"At *it*." He tilted his head and motioned to his pants. "The business. You know."

"No." My blush was becoming painful. "No, Ryder, I did *not* see your business yesterday. Thank you very much."

He beamed and turned around. Glancing at me over his shoulder, he said, "How 'bout the ass, then? Get a good look at that sweet thing?"

"That sweet thing?" I couldn't help but laugh. "If by 'that sweet thing' you mean 'the whitest butt in the world,' then yes, I did see that."

"Ah, Red, you're killing me over here." He slumped against the stall door. "I go out of my way to impress you, and here you are, breaking my heart all over again."

"As if your heart is capable of being broken," I said with a smirk. "I've heard all about you, Ryder, and I think heartbreak is probably last on your list of concerns."

"Shows how much you don't know about me." He sighed and hung his head. "Next, you're going to tell me it *didn't* destroy me to see you kiss that dude yesterday."

"I didn't kiss that dude yesterday!" I don't know why my protest came out so fast. "Javi, I mean. I didn't kiss *Javi* yesterday. I *almost* kissed him, but you managed to kill that moment pretty quickly."

"Good." His grin was radiant. "Then I'll make it my mission to continue killing those moments whenever I can." He paused and leaned a little closer. "Seriously, Red, you don't want to waste your kisses on that guy. He can't make you happy like I can."

"Like you can? Did you actually just say that?"

"I did." His eyes lingered as he turned to go. "You know I've been crazy about you ever since I met you. My heart is yours, whenever you're ready to collect it."

I tried to think of something snappy to say – some way to make the situation funny again – but by the time I'd gathered my words, Ryder was already gone.

# CHAPTER FOURTEEN

The next few days stretched, softening slightly and blending into a wash of sunshine, cool breezes and lightning-fast baths at the Balcony. Javi and I didn't try to kiss again, but we did settle into an easy camaraderie. By the end of the week, we began meeting after chores for hikes and stopping by the meditation tents to spend time with Kadence.

She was fantastic. Although she giggled at our futile attempts to allow ourselves to experience the world through our opened chakras, she still seemed pleased by our meditation efforts. She was also assigned to be our official orientation leader, so we began meeting for lunch and listening to her Community lessons beside the Merced River.

Our "lessons" were essentially a crash course on life outside the Centrist Movement. We learned about literature, politics, biology and the prevalence of hormones that were apparently running on overdrive through every teenager's veins. We learned that love and passion and sex weren't considered dangerous out here – were even encouraged somewhat – and Kadence giggled every now and then as she talked, saying things like, "And here you were, probably thinking there was something wrong with you!"

We learned words for emotional subtleties we'd never experienced, and we talked about the differences between the ones we already knew: anxiety versus insecurity, jealousy versus envy, confusion versus bewilderment, sympathy versus empathy.

The knowledge was enlightening – new, but not new, somehow. Temple classes touched on sociology and biology and current affairs, but they also emphasized Essence drain as the root cause of nearly all of the world's evils. The knowledge that I was now encouraged, even expected, to act in opposition to my upbringing was dizzying.

Kadence made us practice. We took turns yelling, laughing, singing... It was terrifying at first, but we gradually grew to look forward to it – sprawling on the riverbank and screaming until our lungs hurt.

Those first few days were magical. Once we'd completed our introductory lessons, we shifted our attention to what Kadence called our "inner journey". It was during these classes that we learned to appreciate the openness of our senses.

"So there's this guy who used to live here," she said late one afternoon. The three of us were sitting cross-legged, and a few wispy clouds dotted an otherwise flawless sky. "Name was John Muir. Came here in the 1860s or '70s, I think; you can find some pictures of him in the Ahwahnee."

She smiled. "He's the one who fought for this place to become a national park. And do you know what he said? 'Climb the mountains and get their good tidings. Nature's peace will flow into you as sunshine flows into trees. The winds will blow their own freshness into you, and the storms their energy, while cares will drop off like autumn leaves.'"

She waited for us to react, but I didn't know what to say. I had never heard words strung together like that, but I knew they resonated somewhere deep inside my gut. I could tell by the light in her eyes that they resonated in hers, too.

She smiled. "Don't try to digest that just yet. But tuck it away and hold it somewhere. And when you're out here, think about it. Feel it. See if you can come up with any words of your own. This is what living in the Community is really all about."

Not all our classes were quite so serious, and Kadence felt free to tease us as we struggled through the course she called "Responsible Relationships".

"The Community encourages relationships, but they aren't a hundred percent necessary," she said. "It's really up to you, and it's all about your comfort level. But if you do decide to date, it's important to be honest and communicate with your partner. And if you choose to become physical, you need to take certain precautions to make sure you both stay safe. How familiar are you guys with birth control?"

The idea that sexual relationships were actually encouraged here was mind-boggling, and Kadence's rules for dating were equally overwhelming. "It's an isolated population," she explained. "It wouldn't be so important if we lived somewhere else, but if one person gets a disease here, it can spread like wildfire through the whole Community. So you have to register all your new partners with Rex and Daniel. They keep a database."

Although I lingered for a moment on the idea that I was finally allowed to experience a boy's tenderness, the thought of having to have *that* conversation was enough to keep my clothes on for the rest of my life.

Ryder was strangely absent for most of the rest of the week, but he showed up in a flurry Friday afternoon – tromping through the stables and appearing by my side as I weighed supplements in the kitchen.

"Moonbows," he said by way of a hello, jumping to a seat on the counter beside me.

"Nice to see you, too." I reached for a towel. "Where have you been all week?"

He waved that away with a grin. "Busy. I'm terribly busy and important, you know, but I've come to let you know you have plans tonight."

"I do?"

"You do." He followed my movements as I began loading feed buckets in the corner. "You're coming to the Falls with me, Jett, Cody... the whole damn Community, really, or at least the fun ones."

"The Falls? Which falls?"

"*The Falls*, Red. Yosemite Falls. You obviously still have a lot to learn here."

"Oh–kay?" I let the word draw into a question. I knew he was baiting me, toying with me somehow, but I couldn't help the flutter of – what? curiosity? flattery? – that sifted through me at his attention.

"So, the Falls *rage* this time of year; it's all that melted snow from the High Country." He bounced from the counter. "If you catch a full moon just right – and this only works in late spring – you can actually see rainbows reflected in the waterfall's spray." He paused and gestured dramatically. "Moonbows."

"Moonbows," I repeated.

I tried to picture what a night rainbow might look like, and I must have smiled, because Ryder grinned and leaned against the counter. "Thought you might like that."

"What do you do during moonbows?"

"Party your ass off. We bring sleeping bags and drinks and snacks; some of the boys and I set up a slackline across the creek, and we basically dance around and make like *Where the Wild Things Are* till the sun comes up."

He must have read my confusion, because he sighed. "*Where the Wild Things Are,* that's a book. Damn, Red, we gotta get you a proper education."

"OK, so you watch moonbows until the sun comes up. What about your chores?"

"Red, you gotta stop placing so much emphasis on your chores." Ryder scanned the kitchen. "Shayla doesn't care what time you come in, long as you get your shit done. This place even has a fridge; why don't you get tomorrow's diets ready now so you don't have to worry about it later?"

"Can I do that?"

"Sure thing." He reached for a knife. "Hell, I've even been known to chop a carrot or two in my day. Pass me some veggies, Red. We'll bust this out."

I did what Ryder said, weighing and measuring and packing away all the veggies we chopped before he dashed back to the clinic and I took off for lunch. I still didn't completely understand the appeal of moonbows, but the invitation definitely sounded intriguing – especially since it led to a few flustered minutes of side-by-side work with him. Moonbows also sounded like a great way to spike some of my heart readings – which I was definitely inclined to do, since my first weekly reading with Rex was the next morning.

When I mentioned the plans to Kadence and Javi over lunch, Kadence said, "Yeah, you and Javi should totally go. It's a

Yosemite must-see, and it doesn't happen that often. Shayla will understand if you're a little late to chores tomorrow morning."

"You don't want to come with us?"

"Nah." She wrinkled her nose. "Don't get me wrong; it's totally amazing, but once you've been there and done that, it loses its luster a little, you know? Plus, it's always super crazy out there, and I'm feeling kinda tired, so… You guys just go and enjoy it without me."

Before Javi and I could protest, she smiled. "I'm serious. I will be so mad at you if you don't go." She tried to look threatening. "No more free meditation sessions, either. You can figure out how to open your chakras without me."

After much prodding, Javi and I finally agreed, and we showed up at the crumbling Yosemite Falls trailhead sometime after ten o'clock. "You don't want to get there too early," Kadence had explained, suiting us up in warm coats after dinner. "Better to make a dramatic entrance."

Dramatic entrance? I still wasn't exactly sure what she meant by that when Javi and I started walking toward the thundering falls. She had also insisted we couldn't bring a lantern or a flashlight, and I cursed this logic as we stumbled through the night. We kept getting snarled up in bushes, and we made countless wrong turns before we finally settled in a few paces behind a group of kids neither of us recognized.

As we neared the base of the Falls, the din of laughter and conversation spilled through the waterfall's roar. A huge mob of bodies became visible through the pines, and I felt an inexplicable jolt of nerves at the sight of so many people gathered together at once.

*We barely know anyone here.*

I don't know why this made me feel so self-conscious. It was nearly pitch-black, so it wasn't like anyone could see me, anyway. But I was suddenly so overwhelmed by the idea that Javi and I might look stupid in front of everyone that I nearly fainted in relief when I felt a tight grip on my bicep. "Autumn!"

It was Jett – thank goodness it was Jett – and her blinding white smile was visible even in the darkness. She was wearing a brightly colored sweatshirt, and her hood's fake fur tickled my nose as she pulled me into a hug.

"Oh my gosh, I've barely seen you this week! I'm so sorry; the stupid greenhouse guys have been working me like a dog. It's all about the planting season, you know, so I've had zero time to do anything fun at all. Hold on a sec, Cody's around here somewhere... Hi, Javi! Looking good in that jacket!"

She ushered us past mobs of people and circles of guitar and drum players. A space opened up near the waterfall's base, and she shoved us toward the platform railing. "Check this out, guys."

Yosemite Falls made Vernal Fall look like a bathtub. The water heaved and exploded before us, roaring downward from a summit so high it stretched out of my sight. The spray was so dense it obscured most of the base from view, but there – right there in front of me, in the middle of everything – a vivid rainbow stretched from one side of the creek to the other. It shimmered in the moonlight, disappearing and reappearing from view.

The sight of its fragile beauty was so overwhelming and unexpected that I didn't realize I had grabbed Javi's hand until he squeezed mine back and whispered, "I know, right?"

Jett appraised our entwined hands and quirked one corner of her lips. "Tell you what," she said. "I'm gonna rustle up Cody, grab some drinks, and I'll be back in a bit, OK? Stay here a few minutes by yourselves?"

There was so little room on the platform that Javi and I were nearly smashed together. We made eye contact, and a flutter of desire sprang alive in my chest. It was the first time I'd felt it since our hike to Vernal Fall – the first time my feelings for Javi hadn't been clouded by my feelings for Ryder.

Which were stupid, I had reminded myself all week, angry a flirt like Ryder could affect my feelings for a guy as deep and genuine as Javi.

It wasn't something I was proud of, but the thought had been present ever since Ryder showed up in the stables and told me his heart was mine. That was a dumb line – he probably said it to every girl – but I hadn't been able to shake the feeling that maybe he really *did* fall for me a little that night we played together on the Slip 'n Slide.

I realized my thoughts were slipping again. And instead of allowing myself to be swept away in the moment with Javi, I was actually thinking about Ryder again. And I was kinda wondering where he was right now.

*Dammit, Autumn.*

Jett's return with Cody was soon a welcome relief.

"OK, so the trick is, you gotta drink it fast." Jett pinched her nose and waved Cody's flask to demonstrate. The four of us were sitting on a log near the only fire permitted to burn at the gathering. "It's called moonshine, and it tastes like gasoline, but it does the trick. You just gotta slam it."

"Why?" Javi frowned. "What's the point of drinking it if it doesn't taste good?"

"Because it gets you wasted, bro." It was Ryder. He appeared with a wink from the darkness behind us. "Cedar's cronies taught you guys about alcohol, right? A huge cause of Essence drain in the twentieth century – nearly solely responsible for the beginning of World War Two?"

"What does it do to you, really?"

"It's not nearly as scary as it sounds," Jett assured me from Cody's lap. "It just relaxes you a little. Takes your inhibitions away. Makes you laugh a little harder and become a little braver."

"It basically makes you into 'You, Plus' or 'You, Enhanced'," Cody said. "It doesn't change who you are, just makes you a little more amplified."

"Unless you drink too much," Ryder said, fishing a cigarette from his pocket. "Then it turns you into a raging idiot. Next thing you know, you wake up in bed next to a complete stranger."

He grinned and turned to placate me. "Just kidding, Red. Javi. But seriously, don't drink too much, or you'll regret it tomorrow."

I eyed the bottle in Cody's hands suspiciously. I'll regret it? He's kidding, right? I don't want to act like an idiot if I drink this, and I *definitely* don't want to wake up in bed next to a stranger.

"Relax, Red," Ryder said, lighting his cigarette in the fire. "I don't even have to turn around to know you have that horrified look on your face."

"I don't have a horrified look on my face."

"You do, Autumn," Jett said with a giggle. "You really, really do."

I glanced at Javi, and he squeezed my knee supportively. "I'm not sure we're into this tonight, guys," he said. "Just got here, you know. Although you're selling it really well, Ryder..." He let the sentence trail off, and I was surprised by his acrid tone.

I can't explain why this irritated me, but it did. Before I knew it, I found myself blurting, "No, wait. You said this stuff makes you braver? Does it affect your heart rate? Make you feel things more?"

"It can," Cody answered. "It'll slow you down if you sit around and do nothing, but if you get up and start having fun with it…"

"All right." I nodded. "Let's do it, then. I'm in."

# CHAPTER FIFTEEN

The first thing that happened when I tasted the burning liquid – which was not nearly as delicious as it smelled – was that the world became a little fuzzy. Not weirdly fuzzy, or alarmingly fuzzy... just softened slightly, blurred a bit at the edges of my vision.

I kinda liked it, actually; it made me feel less self-conscious as I followed our group back through the crowd. I was gliding – striding through there like I belonged – and I *did* belong, you know? I was with Jett, who was the most fun girl I'd ever met, and I was with Ryder, and his father basically owned this place.

Javi decided not to drink, and his shifty, worried expression made me feel a little uncomfortable at first. But soon his concern blended into the background of the evening, and the foreground became filled with colors, laughter and introductions with a whirlwind of people whose names and faces became indistinct after a while.

We returned to the creek, and I noticed that Ryder and his friends had pulled a wide, flat piece of rope from one side of the water to the other. They had secured it between two big trees, and it stretched, waist-high, across the clearing – just far enough downstream to be spared the waterfall's spray.

"Slackline," Jett explained, rolling her eyes as Ryder and Cody crowded toward it. Javi followed them warily.

"What's a slackline?"

"See that girl?" She motioned to a willowy blonde girl with her back to us. The girl tested the rope with her hands and stood back to watch it vibrate. "That's Shayla; you may have seen her around."

My chest tightened. Was there ever a time Shayla *wasn't* the center of attention?

"Shayla's kind of a legend around here. What she's gonna do in just a sec is pull herself up to stand on the rope. Once she catches her balance – way harder than it looks, because the rope jumps around and vibrates – she's gonna walk across the creek and get to the other side."

"But..." I felt my eyes widening as I surveyed the jagged rocks and water beneath her. "What happens if she falls?"

"That's the stupid part," Jett said. "If she falls, she hurts herself. Probably badly."

"But..." I struggled to process this. "Why would she do that?"

"For the adrenaline rush she'll feel when she makes it across. Like I said, Shayla's kind of a legend around here. Has some of the most impressive readings in the entire Valley."

"Does Cody slackline, too? Does Ryder?"

"Almost all the boys in the Community do it." She rolled her eyes again. "Most of the girls don't – Shayla's really the only one – but it's kind of a rite of passage around here. I tried it a few times, and I nearly broke my ankle."

Shayla balanced herself on the quavering rope, and then she pulled herself to a standing position in one fluid motion. She remained motionless until the rope's vibrations subsided, and then she began walking forward slowly – one bare foot in front of the other.

Her intensity and grace were mesmerizing. The air seemed to go out of the entire gathering as everyone stopped to watch her, but she didn't even seem to notice. She was solely focused on the rope below her, and her arms were held outward, spread for balance.

I frowned. "Ryder mentioned something about looking for a highlining route at Taft Point the other day. Is highlining the same thing as slacklining?"

"Highlining is slacklining between two cliffs. Ryder was talking about having three thousand feet of air between him and the ground."

I couldn't even picture this. "No way," I said. "Why in the world... What would happen if he fell?"

Jett shrugged. "Some highliners attach safety ropes to their lines, so they just bounce around for a while until they can pull themselves to the other side. Others wear parachutes, but some..." She shook her head. "Some *idiots* – like Ryder and his boys – they think it's fun to just take their chances. Addicted to the rush, I guess. Morons."

"Ryder doesn't wear a safety line?" I couldn't explain why, but I felt a flutter of desire at the thought. I pictured Ryder's bare back – muscles tensed as he walked through the empty space between cliffs – and I shuddered. "Isn't that–?"

"Ryder's an idiot." Jett's voice was sharp, and she turned from the slackline just as Shayla reached the far side of the creek. Shayla jumped from the rope and turned with a little bow as the crowd erupted in cheers. "They're all idiots."

Catching herself as we strode back into the crowd, she paused and attempted a smile. "Sorry," she said. "I just... get tired of worrying, you know? I know they're doing it for their Essences, and I know Rex encourages them to push themselves. It's just… It all just seems a little reckless, you know? It's… frustrating."

She retrieved the flask from her sweatshirt pocket. "Let's forget about it, OK? The night is young… Wanna dance or something?"

The current in the air was electric, and campfire smoke enveloped my skin as Jett and I strode from group to group, passing the flask back and forth and listening to the music spilling from the guitars and drums.

I had never heard music like this before. It was *fun*, not dreary or monotonic, and its beat infused the night, humming through the pine canopy and pulsing like a heartbeat in the auras of all my new friends. I melted into their rhythm after a while, and I swayed a little and giggled when Jett prodded me and said, "Look at you, Autumn! Girl's got rhythm!"

I should have been terrified. I should have excused myself, taken a deep breath and repeated the Centrist mantra a few times for good measure. But I didn't. And here's the thing: it didn't even occur to me that I should.

Instead, I found myself smiling. And laughing. And enjoying everyone's company without fearing for my Essence once.

Maybe it was my heart rate monitor. Maybe it was the moonshine. Maybe it was the way I kept catching the Community boys staring at me when they thought I couldn't see them.

After a while, the fuzziness at the edges of my vision increased. Jett assured me it was normal – laughed when I attempted to explain it to her – and then I was laughing, too. We were sitting somewhere near the edge of the campfire, and I just felt so *good* all of a sudden that I couldn't help my burst of giggles. The air was swimming with light, and we were surrounded by so many smiling, happy faces that contentment just poured out of me, thick and rich as honey.

"Autumn," Jett said after a minute, rousing herself to sit up straight. "Autumn, I think it's working. I think you're getting drunk."

"Drunk?" I struggled to my feet and staggered a little when the world spun. "No way, Jett. *You're* getting drunk."

"I *am*. I totally, totally am. And you are, too."

I'm not quite sure what happened next. I know I laughed – I think we both did – but then we were out in the crowd again. We were jostling and talking and stopping to watch the group of fire dancers throwing flaming sticks into the air and catching them.

I know we looked at the moonbows again for a while, and I know the waterfall spray felt cold and dark and beautiful against my face. I remember sneaking off to pee in the woods at some point, and I snickered as my legs wobbled. Jett stood guard and promised she'd protect me from "wandering eyes".

I met another girl named Autumn – and this was hilarious to both of us for some reason – and I picked up someone's guitar and puzzled over the tight line of strings that buzzed and sounded terrible under my fingertips. And then Javi was beside me, and I was irritated by his concern as I swayed back through the crowd.

"I'm fine," I remember saying, waving him away and weaving toward the slackline. "I'm fine, fine, fine. Just 'Me, Plus'. 'Me, Enhanced.'"

The ground felt soggy beneath my feet, but I really *was* fine. I was great, actually: excellent and confident and wonderful. I wondered how I had ever lived without feeling this feeling, and then I decided I wanted to slackline, too.

I wanted to highline over a cliff someday, and I was so giddy and excited by this that I decided I absolutely, positively needed to tell Ryder right now. So, I staggered along the banks looking for him. I smiled to myself, and I imagined how excited he would be to see me.

But then I saw him. And I was no longer fine at all.

He was standing with his back to me, but it was very clear who the girl in front of him was. Shayla. Although they weren't kissing, they definitely seemed drawn to each other. She was laughing, and her golden hair was fluttering around her shoulders as she squeezed his bicep and leaned to whisper something in his ear.

Bile rose in my throat, and then I turned around and stormed off as they started at the sound of my intrusion. I was trudging along the creek, tripping on rocks and fighting the inexplicable tears I felt welling in my eyes, when I ran into Javi. And then I knew exactly what I wanted to do next.

I vaulted toward him, wrapped my arms around his shoulders and pulled him into a hard kiss. I didn't know exactly what I was doing, but I knew I liked his shudder when he wavered against me.

"Autumn," he sputtered, pulling away. "What are you doing? Are you OK?"

"I'm fine." I pushed him against a nearby tree. "I'm fine, and I'm wonderful, and I really want to kiss you right now."

"Autumn." He dodged my lips and held me at arm's length. "You're... You've been drinking, and I don't want to..."

"I'm fine," I insisted. "I'm just 'Me, Enhanced'. And 'Me, Enhanced' has been wanting to kiss you for a really long time."

His face became serious. "Autumn, I don't want you to do anything you're going to regret tomorrow..."

"I'm not going to regret this. I want to kiss you, and I want to kiss you right now. Do you want me to or not?"

"I do. I have since the first time I saw you at the temple, but I don't want..."

"Then just let me already."

My hands threaded through his hair as I stood on my tiptoes, and I leaned against his chest and pressed my lips against his. His eyes went cloudy, and his arms tightened around my waist like clamps.

I felt strong and beautiful and completely intoxicated by the power of it. I was actually making Javi tremble.

He didn't seem to know what to do with me for a moment, and then another shudder coursed through him and he groaned and parted my lips with his tongue. His hands gripped my hips so hard I thought they might leave bruises.

I didn't care, because I suddenly couldn't be close enough to him. I raked my hands through his hair, and he wrapped his arms around my lower back and pulled me to the damp forest floor below him.

My heart nearly exploded. We were kissing on a bed of moss, and I was leading his hands to my chest. I was fumbling with my jacket and the ties on my blouse, and his hands were cupping my bra through my shirt's open fabric. The ache that raced through me was so overpowering that I think I must have lost control for a moment, because I don't remember anything at all except the flood of desire that was suddenly so strong that I pushed him to the ground and rolled to sit on top of him.

Something rustled in the bushes behind us. I sprang to look backward, and I came face to face with Ryder. Again.

His eyes widened, and then he retreated. And then I was readjusting my blouse, jumping from Javi's lap and taking off after him.

Why? I still wonder how I managed to leave Javi's side, what I said over my shoulder as I turned to run after Ryder. Did I simply say I had to go, or did I say something more, like I'd seen Ryder with Shayla, and that's why I'd raced into his arms, looking for comfort?

I don't know the answer. That part of the night has become a blur. I'm not even sure when Javi left the Falls, but I do know I caught up to Ryder somewhere near the slackline. His eyes were cold, and his frown was more like a scowl when I rushed up to him and said, "What's your problem? Why do you care, anyway?"

"Because I *like* you, Red," he snapped. "I *like* you, and I'm sick and tired of watching you make out with Javi. OK?"

"You don't like me." I crossed my arms. "You like Shayla, and besides, you apparently date everyone here, so it's not like I'm-"

"Shayla's my *friend*, Red. Where are you getting this?"

"Kadence." I didn't mean to tell him, but the word just poured out.

The look in Ryder's eyes told me I'd hit a sore spot. "Kadence? You're gonna listen to *anything* that girl has to say about me?" He shook his head. "You know what? Never mind. You've clearly made your choice. Go back to Javi; he's probably pissed enough at you for leaving."

I wavered, and I think my lower lip may have even trembled when I said, "But... But I don't want to be with Javi..."

"Then why were you making out with him, Red? Why were you sitting on his lap with your shirt half off? You have a pretty weird way of showing him you don't want to be with him."

"I..." I felt a tear slide down my cheek. The euphoric feeling of the night – the energetic swell of happiness and confidence I'd been buzzing with all evening – seemed to be crumbling around me now.

I wanted to collapse, to go home and be neutral and forget about everything that had happened, but instead I found myself stammering, "I... I was looking for you. And then I saw you with Shayla, so I..."

I stopped, too ashamed to continue, but Ryder didn't make me elaborate. Instead, a funny thing happened. His expression softened, and he took a step toward me. "What are you saying, Red?" he asked, and his voice became surprisingly tender.

Humiliated, I glanced at the ground and realized a few of the ties on my blouse were still off-kilter. I struggled to fix them, and I didn't notice Ryder was reaching for me until he cupped my chin between his thumb and forefinger.

"Red," he whispered. "It's OK. I'm not mad at you. Are you telling me you kissed Javi because you thought I liked Shayla?"

Making eye contact with him somehow made it feel too real. Besides, the world had begun tilting a little, and its jerky spins were beginning to make me nauseous.

Ryder must have realized something was wrong, because his tenderness faded. "Red," he said, reaching to steady me. "Are you OK? You look a little pale all of a sudden. Want me to take you home?"

I tried to nod, but the motion sent the world into overdrive. The stars spun, the waterfall stopped churning, and the last thing I remember is the whirl of the pine canopy as the night came crashing down around me.

# CHAPTER SIXTEEN

I thought I was going to die when I woke up the next morning.

It was just after sunrise; I could tell that by the weak light filtering through the room's filmy curtains. A white plaster ceiling stretched above my head, but the rest of the room was a bit of a mystery. I seemed to have a nine hundred pound weight gluing me to my pillow, and this made anything beyond slight movements impossible.

My head was pounding like the drums at the Falls, and my insides felt like I'd somehow swallowed one of those flaming fire sticks. A burning, acidic taste sat in my mouth, and I don't think I'd ever been so thirsty in my entire life.

It occurred to me that I had no idea where I was, but even this paled in comparison to my sudden and burning need to vomit – which I did, off the side of the bed, into a metal garbage can apparently prepared for the task.

I noticed a hand towel, a glass of water, and two white pills arranged neatly on the nightstand to my right. Wiping my mouth, I reached for the water and began slurping.

As I sank back into the bed, I tried to fight the hazy film currently coating my brain. A nebulous feeling of guilt swirled somewhere just out of my reach, and it irked me that I couldn't quite place it.

We were watching moonbows. And then there was moonshine... and Jett... and the slackline... I remembered the music, the fire dancers... *Did I really go to the bathroom in the woods?* And then there was the creek, Ryder and Shayla... And then...

*Oh, no. No, no, no, no.*

I rolled onto my back and covered my face with both my hands.

I kissed Javi. I kissed Javi *hard*, and his hands were under my shirt, and... No, no, no.

Guilt and mortification surged through me. Javi hadn't been drinking, so I was sure his memory wasn't spotty like mine. What did he think when I pressed him up against that tree? When I bolted away and left him lying there?

I frowned, unsettled. Why *did* I leave him lying there?

"Welcome to my bedroom, Red. Told you you'd forget everything and wake up next to a complete stranger." The voice was Ryder's. As he entered from the hallway to my left, his words brought me reeling back to the present.

Oh, no, that's why.

I felt an electric jolt shoot through me. "What happened?"

Ryder's grin was wide. "Told you to watch out for that moonshine."

"But what...?" I didn't even know what I was trying to ask. "Ryder, I'm so... I made a fool out of myself, didn't I?"

His voice became surprisingly reassuring. "It's fine, Red. I promise. It's moonbows; everyone gets stupid at moonbows."

"But I..." The more I remembered, the more I wanted to vomit again. "I was so out of control... I can't believe I..."

Ryder reached across the bed and smoothed the hair from my forehead – an unexpected act of gentleness that made me start. "Red, it's really fine. Really. No one's gonna judge you for what you did or didn't do at moonbows."

"But I did a lot." I struggled to sit up. "I kissed Javi on the ground, and my shirt was almost off, and I came running after you to..."

I paused. Why *did* I go running after him?

"To tell me you were in love with me?" Ryder's grin spread, and that boyish swagger returned. "Remember that, Red? When you said you were in love with me?"

"I didn't say that!" I thought I'd die of embarrassment. "I didn't say that... Did I?"

"I don't know." His eyes became playful. "What do you think? Think you're in love with me?"

"No! I'm not... I'm just..."

"Kinda in love with me?"

I was so humiliated I couldn't even meet his eyes when he glanced at my trash can and added, "Are you feeling any better?"

"I'm so sorry." I sank a little farther into the bed. "I kinda want to die right now."

"Red, seriously, it's fine." He pushed the trash can aside and reached for my hand. "It's really not a big deal; happens to all of us. And you wanna know the best part?"

"There's a best part?"

"Yeah. Of course there is." He cocked his head. "We can stop playing games now, if... well, if you meant what you said last night about... you know... wanting to spend more time with me, too?"

I could have been imagining things, but I swear he actually looked a little nervous when he added, "You know, about what Kadence said about me? It's not true, but it's not a hundred percent untrue, either. I used to be a lot different than I am now, but I *am* different now, Red. And I want to show you I'm worthy of being the guy that's *your* guy. Would that be all right with you?"

Before I could answer, he bounded from the bed. "Wait. Don't answer that. Let me do this right. Romance you, sweep you off your feet… All that old-fashioned, chivalrous-type stuff. It'll be awesome."

The jostling of the bed reminded me why I was incapacitated here in the first place. I winced and sank back into the pillow. "Can we wait until I'm strong enough to stand again? I *will* be strong enough to stand again, won't I?"

"Absolutely." Ryder headed toward the door. "It's called a hangover; you should be right as rain by tomorrow. In the meantime, why don't you stay in bed and rest for a while?"

I shook my head and immediately regretted it. "Can't. I have chores…"

"You and the chores, Red. Don't worry; I'll take care of them." He twisted the doorknob. "I'm gonna pop downstairs and grab us some breakfast. Why don't I wake you back up in a bit?"

When I awoke – a couple hours later, judging by the window's changing light – a thick loaf of bread smeared with butter had replaced the hand towel on my nightstand. The garbage can was gone, and a shining glass of water sat next to a sprig of pale wildflowers.

I smiled and reached for them. They were papery, rose-like blooms – white in the center and faded to pink on the edges. I had heard of people bringing flowers as gifts before, but Cedar denounced the practice as wasteful. No one I'd ever known had actually given or received a flower.

The emotions I felt welling inside me while I held the tiny, perfect buds are difficult to describe. My body still felt weak, but my heart swelled until I felt like it might burst from my chest. Suddenly, the rest of the world didn't matter so much anymore.

Yes, I'd done stupid things last night. I was sure Javi was mad at me, and who knows what he'd told Kadence. I didn't know what had happened to Jett, and I had no idea how many people had seen Ryder take me to his bedroom.

But you know what? I was pushing my heart rate readings, and I was helping Rex disprove the Essence theory. I was sitting here holding flowers from a boy, and that boy seemed to actually like me.

I thought back to Kadence's warning about Ryder, and then to Ryder's rebuttal: *You're gonna listen to* anything *that girl has to say about me?*

Maybe she was wrong about him. Didn't he at least deserve a chance to prove himself?

Sometime later, after I'd finished my bread, chugged my water and taken the two white pills, I managed to finally stagger out of bed and get my first clear look at Ryder's bedroom. It was a sparse space – with a thick white comforter, filmy curtains and dark wood furniture – but it was scattered with books and small tokens and souvenirs. Tidy stacks of river stones, clusters of dried sage, petals, driftwood and tiny white seashells... All these items were lovingly arranged on counters and shelves and bookcases, and I smiled at their sentimentality.

There were two old-fashioned photographs in the room – an unexpected touch of personalization that took me by surprise. One was a small, framed image of a white-blond child and a handsome young man grinning from a cliff's steep overlook. Half Dome gleamed in the background, and the words on the left corner read, "Glacier Point, October 13, 2031".

The man was immediately recognizable: a younger version of Rex Stone. Which means the little boy must be Ryder, I thought. I picked up the frame and studied the little boy carefully, and my feelings for Ryder surged at the knowledge that he had once been young and hopeful and bowlegged, just like everybody else.

I walked toward the second photograph: a large black-and-white image framed on the wall nearest the window. In it, a wiry, shirtless man stood balancing on a highline. A cliff loomed in the background behind him, and the highline stretched in front of him – disappearing into the foreground on the lower right side of the scene. A spectator, ant-sized and indistinct, watched him from the far cliff.

The man stood suspended over a vast stretch of nothingness. His right leg was firmly planted on the highline, but his other foot hovered nearly horizontal to his left. His arms were twisted for balance, and his muscles were tense. His face was homed like a laser on the rope before him, and his black hair gleamed in the sunlight.

It was no wonder Ryder did crazy things for fun, with this man giving him inspiration all the time. I peered closer and tried to make out the words in the lower left corner: "Dean Potter, Taft Point, 2009".

My mother was five years old then.

The bedroom door creaked open. I turned, expecting to see Ryder again, but Javi's steely gaze met me instead.

He held a broom in one hand and a bucket of cleaning rags in the other. His jaw was tense, and his eyes were narrowed into slits. "Morning, Autumn," he said, voice icy. "Get a good night's sleep?"

"Javi, what are you doing here?"

"Cleaning the Master's bedroom." He strode forward and kicked a rug back into place. "This is what I do now, apparently. What are *you* doing here?"

Before I could answer, he glanced at the rumpled bed and the flowers resting on the nightstand. "Should I change these sheets now or what?"

"What? Javi, no... This isn't what it... Nothing happened between Ryder and me last night. I just started feeling sick, so he brought me back and let me stay here. We didn't..." I cleared my throat. "We didn't *do* anything, Javi. We didn't even kiss."

"Well, that was generous of you. Limit of one guy per night, then?"

"Javi." I felt tears welling in my eyes. "I didn't mean to... I'm sorry I left you last night. I don't know what I was doing... I barely even remember leaving..."

"That's because you drank about a gallon of moonshine, Autumn. You practically attacked me, and then you left." He scowled. "You were acting ridiculous. And I know it wasn't you – I know it was the moonshine – but I didn't like it. I didn't like seeing you act like them."

"Like *them*?" His words rankled me. "Like *who*, Javi? Like Jett and Ryder and Cody? Like the people who told us about this place and brought us here in the first place? Like *those people*?"

He met my challenge. "Yeah," he said. "Like those people. You know, not everyone in the Community acts like Ryder or Jett or Cody. There are people like Kadence, too. People who understand you don't need to act like an idiot and tear your clothes off to get your heart rate elevated."

"Tear my clothes off?" I thrust my finger into his chest. "You may act all judgmental on me now, but you didn't seem too offended by my decisions last night. As a matter of fact, I think it was *your* hands inside my shirt, and it was *you* who pulled us to the ground. I may have been drinking, but I remember some things. And you wanted me just as much as I wanted you."

"Yeah, but I didn't get up and leave you! I didn't go running off after some other girl, and I certainly didn't spend the night in that other girl's bed."

He had me there. I felt my argument weakening, but I couldn't give in, so I scowled and thrust my finger harder into his chest. "You're just jealous," I said. "You're jealous because *you* wanted to spend the night with me, and I chose Ryder instead."

The instant the words left my lips, I knew they were the wrong ones.

Instead of fighting me, Javi just scowled. "You're right," he said, and he stalked to collect his cleaning supplies. "You're right, Autumn. I thought what you and I had was special. I thought it had the potential to grow into something big – maybe even something huge – but it looks like I was wrong. Apparently, you like assholes."

With one swipe, he knocked a pile of river stones off Ryder's dresser. The pebbles jangled crazily to the floor, and they ricocheted and scattered like grains of sand.

"Just so you know," he said, "he *will* hurt you. Maybe not today; maybe not tomorrow. But soon. I guarantee that. And you know what? I never, *ever* would have." He clenched the door handle and spat before leaving, "Tell the Master he can clean his own goddamned bedroom."

# CHAPTER SEVENTEEN

I tried running after Javi, but I didn't have any explanation for what happened, and he knew that as well as I did. The only thing I could manage was a weak "I'm sorry," but that didn't help things much.

It didn't help things at all, actually, because he countered with, "What are you sorry for, Autumn? For choosing him over me? Because you did. You realize that, don't you? You chose *Ryder Stone*, the biggest asshole in this entire Valley."

"Javi..." My lower lip trembled, and I felt the ripping away of what had quickly become one of the only constants in my life. One of the only things that made me feel like I was home here.

"What?" Javi's lower lip seemed to be trembling, too. "What do you want to say, Autumn? Because I know you don't want to say you've made a mistake. I know you don't want to say you'd rather be with me than him. Tell me I'm wrong."

I couldn't, and he knew that as well as I did. But as I watched him turn and storm down the gleaming stone steps, the pain in his expression was so overwhelming that I wished more than anything I could.

It was nearly noon when I finally made it to Curry Village, and my skin felt clammy as Rex removed my wristband and downloaded my heart rate and hormone readings into his database.

"Got your new file all set up," he said, smiling proudly as he addressed his computer: "Autumn Grace, please. Patient number two-four-seven. Inception to present, stabilized with averages."

My name appeared on the screen, and my very own wiggly green lines stretched from the dates May 22, 2038 to May 29, 2038.

"Impressive first reading, Autumn," he said, leaning back in his chair. "Looks like you had some really strong spikes this week. I'm proud of you."

I sat a little straighter as he pointed to the graph. "Shall we go through your readings a bit?"

I nodded. Soon he was zooming in, localizing data and explaining the graph's ups and downs to me. "Looks like you took my words to heart when you left my office on Sunday. What are these huge spikes around two o'clock?"

"Vernal Fall." I felt myself blushing. "Javi and I hiked, and then we went swimming. We saw Ryder and his friends up there, and… it was a fun day."

He smiled – was it knowingly? – and then we moved on to the next few days. He laughed at my complete disdain of horses and applauded Kadence for taking us out of our comfort zones, and then we looked at last night's readings: the bizarre peaks and squiggles that spiked like crazy during moonbows.

"Last night was a good night for you," he said. "Were you at Yosemite Falls with my son and his friends?"

"Yes, sir." I don't know why his question flustered me so much, but it did. I abruptly dipped my head. "The boys set up a slackline over the creek, and Jett and I had some moonshine. It was... um, fun. But I sorta drank too much, and I..."

"You did exactly what you should have done for our cause."

I felt my blush deepen. "Thanks," I said, stealing a glance at him. His ice-blue eyes caught mine, and my stomach fluttered as he smiled and patted my shoulder.

"Autumn, these readings are very powerful, especially for a new recruit. I can't tell you how proud I am that you're already putting yourself out there like this." He rolled his chair away from the desk and popped to his feet. "Let me get you some medicine. You probably feel fairly nauseated today, don't you?"

Contentment purred upward inside me, and I nodded, overwhelmed by the detached way he wasn't judging me for my actions. I'm not sure why I had expected him to react like Javi, but I had. Maybe it was the way Cedar and his meditation masters had always been the ones to discipline me back home; maybe it was the way my mother and the other women in my life always seemed to judge me from afar.

Adults were always the ones imposing their beliefs on me, always telling me I wasn't living up to their expectations. Was it possible Rex really *didn't* care if I drank too much moonshine or lost control every now and then? Was it possible that, for once, I was actually doing everything exactly the way I was supposed to?

Rex returned with a glass of water and two dark pills. "Charcoal," he said. "It will soak the excess alcohol from your system. Make sure to drink plenty of water, and get lots of rest this afternoon. You should be good as new tomorrow."

He glanced at the computer screen. "Just finished my son's readings, actually. He had a pretty solid spike just before two himself. You didn't have anything to do with that, did you, Autumn?"

"No." My cheeks were definitely burning now. "No... I didn't... I..."

"Very well." He smiled. "It's none of my business, anyway. But if you do decide to engage in physical relationships here, just remember to register your partners, OK?"

I would have forgotten about morning meditation completely if Kadence hadn't caught up with me outside the clinic. Her cheeks were flushed from running, and a crease marred the perfect smoothness of her forehead.

"Autumn, are you OK?" She held me at arm's length. "I was so worried when you didn't show up this morning. Is everything all right?"

Her proximity startled me, and I found myself freezing so she wouldn't smell the alcohol on my breath. "I'm fine," I stammered. "I just... I wasn't feeling so good. I'm sorry I missed..."

Before I could finish, someone began running across the parking lot toward us. It was a blond man in fatigues, and he carried a large white bundle in his arms. It was Brian, the guard I'd met at the park's entrance, and his eyes were glassy as he reached the clinic door.

In his arms, he held a person. A light-haired person wrapped in sheets, and the sheets were quickly becoming stained with rivers of dark crimson blood.

"Shayla!" Kadence sprinted toward him. "Brian, where did you find her? Is she all right?"

Brian pushed past her. "Rex, you gotta get out here! I found Shayla!"

The color in Kadence's face drained at the sight of her friend. Shayla was unconscious, and her head lolled to one side as Brian shifted her weight in his arms. Her temple was caked in dried blood, and her normally silky hair was matted to her blouse. A dark stain seeped from a spot near her temple.

The world seriously began to spin, and I felt vomit rise in my throat as Kadence stammered, "Brian, what happened?"

"Not sure." His voice was unsteady, and I wondered if he might vomit, too. "I found her near the base of the Falls this morning. She must have slipped off the slackline at moonbows last night."

Slipped off the slackline?

Rex and Daniel surrounded us. Daniel held Kadence as she screamed and cried and went limp in his arms, and Rex took Shayla from Brian and yelled to his assistants: "Clear off the operating table! There may still be time to save her!"

Within a few seconds, I was alone again. The world was spinning, and I was thinking about slacklines and bloody sheets and head wounds. And then I was crouched on the gravel, and my buttery, perfect loaf of bread was being heaved into the bushes at my feet.

It was more than an hour before Rex reemerged from surgery. Kadence, Brian and I were sitting like statues on the split rail fence when he opened the clinic door and announced, "She lost a lot of blood, but we managed to get her stitched and stabilized before it was too late."

Relief flooded through Kadence, and she jumped to her feet. "Rex, that's amazing! Where is she? When can I see her?"

Rex touched her forearm. "Shayla has decided to cross over, my dear. This accident has shaken her up quite a bit, and she thinks it's time for her to shift her attentions elsewhere. Daniel is preparing to take her to Tuolumne Meadows as we speak; she may not be returning for a while."

"What?" Kadence's face paled. "Rex, no way. Shayla isn't ready to cross over yet; she's only eighteen. And even if she *were* ready, she'd say goodbye to me first; I know she would."

"Kadence." Rex's voice became paternal. "You know as well as I do that the urge to cross over sometimes strikes us suddenly. Shayla has been through a lot; I need you to support her in this decision."

"But Rex, no! Shayla would never cross over without telling me first. You have to change her mind; you have to let me see her."

Rex and I exchanged a look as he gathered Kadence in his arms. "Please understand where Shayla is coming from, Kadence. She believes crossing over is critical to her recovery, so we must respect her wishes – no matter how much we hurt for her. She loves you, my dear; I'm certain she will be back as soon as she regains her inner balance."

"But she *won't*." Kadence's tears were wet against Rex's shirt. "They never come back, Rex; you know that as well as I do."

"Kadence." His voice was tender. "Tuolumne Meadows exists as a refuge for those who have already given themselves to our cause. Retirees are free to go back and forth as they please, but if they choose not to... Kadence, if Shayla chooses to stay in the High Country, you must be willing to let her go. We must think of what's best for her, not for us."

He met my eyes. "Autumn, will you please help me? I must begin preparations for Shayla's crossing-over celebration. Will you help Kadence back to the Ahwahnee?"

I felt the swell of purpose filling me. "Yes, Rex," I said. "I'll take her home."

Shayla's crossing-over celebration was held the very next night. She didn't attend – retirees never did, apparently – but the Ahwahnee Meadow was decorated in a wash of candles and lights and flowers so beautiful they painted the scene like a canvas. Everyone wore white, and Rex looked resplendent as he cast his eyes toward the heavens and thanked the universe for allowing us the opportunity to see Shayla from one stage of her life to the next.

"Once it wells inside us, the decision to cross over is a signal of transformation as intrinsic to our existence as the moment a caterpillar decides to shift from chrysalis to butterfly. It is the pinnacle of Community life and a milestone that cannot be rushed. Let us spend the evening celebrating Shayla's decision to embrace it."

I was stunned by the open displays of joy, by the tears and remembrances and the singing of transformation songs. I had never heard the stringing-together of such beautiful words before, and the synergy of the Community's melody reached inside me, infusing my insides as much as the night around us.

I thought of Shayla, of the beautiful girl I'd barely known, and I wondered why she had decided to leave and maybe never return. Tuolumne Meadows sounded like paradise, but Shayla had the rest of her life to enjoy it. Why had she decided she needed to leave *right now?*

Guilt surged through me as I thought of all the horrible things I'd thought about her. I hadn't hated her at all, really; I'd simply been jealous. Now she was gone and I might never have the chance to make up for it.

Before I knew it, I felt myself moved to tears. I hadn't been able to find Ryder, Jett or Cody, and I was too nervous to look for Javi or Kadence. So there I stood, teary-eyed and alone, until the gathering began to break up.

Within a few minutes, I felt a hand on my shoulder. Javi's stance was guarded, but his eyes were earnest when he said, "You all right?"

Relief welled inside me. I sniffed and wiped my bleary eyes before answering, but then Ryder was there, too.

"I got her, OK?" Ryder's voice was severe, and his arm looped around my waist before I could react. "I'll take care of her."

Javi's expression skewed, and he took a step forward. "You don't own her, man."

"I know. And you don't, either."

Javi looked injured for a second, and then his face hardened. He cast his eyes from Ryder to me and then back again, and then he turned and spat on the ground. "You know what? You're right. I'm outta here; you guys are perfect for each other."

I wanted to chase after him again, but Ryder stopped me before I could. "You OK, Red?"

I pulled away from him. "What the hell was that?"

"What?" He looked surprised. "I'm… sorry. I didn't mean to overstep; I just didn't want him to make you uncomfortable."

"He wasn't making me uncomfortable; *you* were. You acted like a jerk, Ryder."

"I'm… I'm sorry. I obviously overreacted."

"You think?" I felt like shaking him. "Ryder, remember I've never been in this position before. So, all of this tension between you and Javi… It's just too much. I can't handle it."

I sniffled, and my eyes filled with tears again. "I don't know what I'm doing right now, OK? I have no idea how I'm supposed to act, and I'm not sure what's considered acceptable here. So, the last thing I need is you guys getting into a stupid fight over me. It's ridiculous."

Ryder stopped me. "Red, I'm sorry. I sometimes forget what this must be like for you." He said nothing for a moment, and then he began leading me away from the gathering. "I wasn't being exactly truthful when I told you I'd attended my own Free Soul Ceremony. It's part of the spiel; it's just what I'm supposed to say. But I was *two years-old* when my dad left San Francisco, so all I know about the Centrist Movement is what I've seen from the outside."

I stiffened. "You lied to me?"

"Everything I just said, and that's the one thing you cling to?" He started to smile, but his expression fell when I didn't answer. "I lied about that one little detail, Red, but everything else I said was a hundred percent true. Besides, who are you going to trust more? Someone who knows where you're coming from, or someone who doesn't?"

"But if you lied to win my trust..."

"It wasn't a big lie, Red. It was just a little one. Why are you so stuck on my Free Soul Ceremony?"

I stopped walking. "It wasn't a little lie, Ryder; it was a *huge* one. Your Free Soul Ceremony is the most important Centrist ceremony you ever experience. How could you possibly know what I was going through if you'd never-"

"What's the big deal?" He tried to smile again. "It was just a stupid ritual."

"It wasn't a stupid ritual; it was the moment we realized we were responsible for our own Essences. It was the scariest thing we ever had to go through." I felt my voice rise. "You couldn't have possibly understood what leaving meant to us if you had never felt the weight of that responsibility in your chest."

"Red." He reached for my shoulders. "I'm sorry; I really am. I didn't mean to trivialize what you went through. I know your Free Soul Ceremony was your most important ceremony..."

"But how could you know that? How could you know anything about me?"

"Red, I'm sorry. I just wanted to save you, OK? I saw how unhappy you were in Golden Gate Park, and I knew you needed to get away from there. I didn't mean to mislead you; I just wanted to free you." He took a breath. "I just wanted to bring you here. To a place where you could laugh. And be safe. With me."

The words seemed to hover in the air around us, and the rest of the world faded slightly as he met my gaze. The defeated slump of his shoulders was nearly imperceptible, but the open, insecure look in his eyes was not.

"I'm sorry, Red," he finally whispered. "Truly. Please forgive me."

Butterflies fluttered in my chest, and I softened. "Ryder, if we're going to try to do this, you can't lie to me. About anything. Ever. I don't think I can handle it." A pause. "Do you promise?"

"I promise." His relief was barely contained. "I won't. Why would I? I have nothing to hide." He met my gaze again. "I'm sorry about what I said to Javi, and I'm sorry I lied to you about my Free Soul Ceremony. Will you please let me make it up to you?"

When I didn't immediately respond, he said, "Will you please let me take you for a walk? I know this great spot by the river where you can ask me anything you want, and I promise I'll tell you the truth. What do you say?"

# CHAPTER EIGHTEEN

The last place I wanted to go was the woods, at night, but Ryder assured me wild animals only prowled the outskirts of the Valley. "This part of the river's our territory, and they know that. But if it'll make you feel better, I'll grab a gun before we go."

It didn't, but he grabbed one from the Ahwahnee anyway – tucking it in his belt and assuring me the safety was on before he led me across the remnants of a wooden bridge near Curry Village. He found a span where the boards weren't collapsed, and then he sank to a seat and dangled his feet over the edge. The water churned steadily below, but he didn't seem concerned as he motioned for me to join him.

"Remains of the Housekeeping Camp bridge," he explained, extending his hand to help. "This bit – this uncollapsed spot right here in the middle – I come here sometimes when I need to think."

I gripped the railing and dangled my feet beside his. The chill of the river rose through the darkness, and I felt a shiver whisper up my shins.

"Come here." He wrapped his free arm around me. "Feels a little cold until you get used to it."

I nodded and leaned gratefully into the crook of his arm. His smell was different from Javi's – smokier, with undertones of musk and sweat – but it seemed more masculine, too. It reminded me of adrenaline.

After a few minutes, he sighed. "Been a crazy day, huh? Can't believe Shayla left us."

"You've known her for a long time, huh?"

"Yeah." He smiled. "She was one of our first recruits; joined us when she was twelve. I can't believe she won't be around anymore."

That niggling sense of insecurity resurfaced. "Shayla was your first kiss, wasn't she?"

"Yeah." He laughed, and his eyes seemed nostalgic. "She was. She was a year older than me, and I thought she was the most perfect girl I had ever seen. But then we grew up. I became a recruiter, she became disgusted with me, and that's pretty much the end of that story."

"Why did she become disgusted with you?"

He shrugged. "My new role didn't really fit with what she wanted. And I got so busy recruiting that I didn't have much time for her."

"So… how many people would you say you've recruited now, grand total?"

He stretched his legs. "Maybe eighty? I've only been at it for a few years, so that's a pretty good pace."

I nodded. I wanted to say, "And how many of those recruits have been girls? And how many of them have sat here right on this very spot with you?"

But I didn't. Instead, I said, "So, when you say you've recruited these kids... What does that mean, exactly? How much of what you tell them is planned in advance?"

He chuckled softly. "If you're asking me if I faked what I said to you that night in Golden Gate, I didn't."

"That's not what I'm asking." I was glad the darkness hid my blush. "I'm just saying... Why did you pick me? Why did you pick any of us?"

He leaned back and surveyed the sky for a moment. "You really wanna know?"

"Yes. I really do."

He sighed. "We look for Centrists who are broken in some way."

"What? What do you mean, you–"

"No, wait. Let me finish. We don't look for broken *people*; we just look for Centrists with cracks. Followers who've already started questioning Cedar's teachings. These people usually turn out to be the best advocates for our cause, because they already have something invested in what we're doing." He reached to touch my hand. "We knew you were broken the minute you came running into that park, Red."

My tears were back, and they clouded my vision as he reached to gently wipe them away. "I'm sorry about Brady," he whispered. "And I hate that I had to be such a dick about it when we were in the city. It's just... That's kinda my role, you know? Cody's the kind one, Jett's the charismatic one, and I'm the charming, clever asshole. It's kind of a team thing."

Broken. He'd thought I was broken. I wasn't sure why this knowledge bothered me so much, but it did. It *hurt*; it made me feel weak – and exposed – like he'd picked me out of pity. Like he'd simply felt sorry for me.

"Why did you pick Javi?"

"Dude was pacing like a lunatic outside the meditation masters' building. He's almost eighteen, you know? Time to start training to become one of them, or time to get out. He couldn't seem to make a decision, so he was just walking, walking, walking. Looking back and forth, chewing his nails, raking his hands through his hair." He shook his head. "Recruiting outside the meditation masters' building is kinda like shooting fish in a barrel."

"What about Amneet?" When he looked puzzled, I added, "The girl with the black hair?"

"Ah, Amneet. I'm sorry, we just go on so many trips…" He thought for a second. "We met Amneet outside the temple, and it was clear she wasn't looking forward to her lot in life." He looked at the sky again. "Amneet was more of a wild card. Didn't seem broken, just seemed pissed off. Sometimes our spiel works with those types; sometimes it doesn't."

I bit my lower lip. "So, it's a spiel. It's all scripted."

"No. It's just…" He paused. "Red, you gotta understand. This isn't a game to us. We aren't just out grabbing random kids off the streets. Every time we bring home a new recruit, we invite them to join our family."

I couldn't help my snort. He must have interpreted it correctly, because he chuckled and said, "I know what you're thinking: Javi. You don't think I'm treating him like family right now, do you?"

"Well… I mean, *you're* the one who brought him here in the first place…"

"Yeah? Well, that was before I knew he was gonna go after my woman!" He grinned and reached sideways to tickle me. "Just kidding, Red. You're your own independent woman, and I pity the man who tries to tame you."

Try as I might, I couldn't hold back my giggle. Wriggling away from him, I said, "All right, let's talk about you, then. What's your deal?"

"I have a deal?"

"Apparently. You said Kadence wasn't right about you, but she wasn't wrong about you, either. What does that mean?"

"Ah, Kadence." His self-assurance faded a little. "That whole thing."

"Yeah. That whole thing. She said you date everybody here. Was she lying?"

"I'm not the person Kadence thinks I am…"

"But?"

He cleared his throat. "But… I may have been that person at one time."

Anxiety knotted my stomach. He must have sensed it, because he quickly continued. "Look, you have to realize. I started recruiting when I was *fourteen*. Do you know what kind of an idiot a fourteen year-old boy is?"

"I have an idea."

"Yeah, but *do you*? I was expected to be the flirtatious one; I was told to charm every single suitable girl into coming away with us." He stared at the dark water. "It was an act back then; it really was. But I was just a kid, you know? When those girls actually started falling for me…" He shook his head. "They had never been given the chance to experience any of those emotions before, so when we got back to Yosemite… Do you have any idea how intoxicating it is to feel like you have that kind of power over every single girl you meet?"

I thought back to the way Javi had trembled under my fingertips, and I realized with a start that I knew *exactly* where he was coming from.

"It… isn't healthy, you know?" he said. "It's a façade. Empty. Seduction for seduction's sake; it doesn't mean anything."

"So… how many girls have you been with?"

He winced and met my eyes. "Define 'been with'."

"That many, huh?"

"Red… I'm sorry. It's just… You need to understand where I'm coming from. Our upbringings were completely different." He reached for my hand. "Imagine if you grew up here, if your job was to be the charming one. Would you have acted any differently?"

I shrugged. "So, what changed? Why did you decide you didn't want to be that guy anymore?"

"Grew out of it, I guess. Realized there's more to life than that power." At this, he leaned a little closer. "Besides, I've moved on to more fulfilling pursuits. You see, I got a preoccupation with this little redhead lately."

"Is that right?"

Heat rose in my cheeks, and the river below my feet no longer chilled my toes. Instead, my insides caught fire, and they burned from a place near the center of my chest when Ryder licked his lips and cupped my cheeks between his hands.

He leaned toward me, and my breathing became shallow when he closed his eyes and pulled me to his chest. The current that had been building between us ignited the instant our lips met, and it spread from my heart down through my abdomen until my vision felt cloudy and my entire body ached.

When I'd kissed Javi, I'd felt powerful and beautiful and strong. When I kissed Ryder, I felt like I'd turned into jelly – like I was going to liquefy and scatter into a million pieces on the bridge span.

I forgot about the river; I forgot about the night. I forgot about every single thing except the feeling of Ryder's lips against mine, the tangle of his hands in my hair and the heat of his breath against my neck.

I felt like I would pass out, like I would collapse in Ryder's arms and never, ever get up again. And that feeling... that hungry, powerless feeling of my heart racing against his chest...

The moment I kissed Ryder, I felt like I was waking up.

# CHAPTER NINETEEN

Ryder woke me the next morning by banging impatiently on the door to my tent cabin. "Hidden waterfalls won't discover themselves," he announced, holding up a pair of fluffy towels for me to see.

My eyes still were bleary from sleep, and my insides were jumbled from the kiss we'd shared. I hadn't slept much; instead, I'd just twisted and turned and replayed those delicious feelings over and over all night long.

I ran a hand through the tangled bird's nest that had once been my hair, and I hoped Ryder wasn't as shocked by my early-morning appearance as I was by his. But my shock was the good kind of shock, and I'm pretty sure his wouldn't have been. His shock would have been the shock you undoubtedly feel when you accidently rouse a forest creature from its night bedding.

I hoped he wasn't comparing me to a raccoon or a bear right now, but his expression was all smiles when I closed the door and then reemerged in my Community-appointed pants and blouse a few minutes later. I tried to contain my hair in a ponytail, but its curlycues and flyaways were way too much for me.

His voice was warm and slightly formal as he extended his hand to help me down my steps. "How did you sleep last night?"

"Good." It was a lie, of course, but I had no intention of telling him that thoughts of *him* had kept me awake all night.

He didn't seem to share my hesitation, because he laughed and said, "Must not have shaken you up the way you shook me up, then. You kept me awake all damn night, you know that, Red?"

I tried to act nonchalant, but I must not have done a very good job, because he grabbed my hand and said, "Come on, you must have thought about me a little bit, right? For half a second?"

"I don't know. Maybe half a second."

"I see how it is." He grinned. "Just enjoying the fact you got me wrapped around your little finger, is that right?"

"I have no idea what you're talking about. And where are you taking me, anyway? I've got chores…"

"Already taken care of." He held a tree limb out of my way as we started up the trail near the Balcony. "We're doing something even better today."

"Oh, yeah?"

"We're swimming. There's this place called Secret Falls, and it's filled with natural slides and waterfalls and all kinds of good stuff. Even a few still pools where the water stays warmer. You looked a little chilled at Vernal Falls the other day." He turned and grinned at me. "Really, I'm just looking for an excuse to see you with your clothes off again."

"You will *not* be seeing me with my clothes off," I announced a short time later.

We stood near Secret Falls – which wasn't a falls so much as a bunch of small slides that cascaded and filled a jumble of clear pools. Some were big, some were small and some were secluded in the narrow spaces between boulders and high trees.

The light was white gold, and the air felt warm as we shimmied up boulders until we got to the edge of one of the pools. We were the only people in sight, and Ryder took the opportunity to pull off his shirt and jokingly invite me to remove mine. "And your pants. And those annoying undergarments, too."

I couldn't help but laugh as I stuck a tentative foot in the pool. "No way. And it's freezing. Not warm at all. You lied to me."

"Are you kidding? I promised I would never lie to you." Ryder crouched beside me and wiggled his own foot in the water. "That's bathtub warm, Red. Try again."

"Nope, still cold. Freezing, actually, and I learned my lesson at Vernal Falls. I think I will sit this one out, thank you very much."

"No way." He grabbed my hand and pulled me toward the water. "Red, you gotta learn to do stuff that scares you sometimes."

"I do plenty of stuff that scares me."

"What have you ever done that scares you?"

"I came here, didn't I? I got on your muddy Slip 'n Slide, and I left the Movement, and I kissed you on the Housekeeping Camp bridge last night..."

"That scared you?"

"Yeah." I hadn't meant to sound vulnerable, but I guess I did.

Ryder stopped pulling my arm, and his swagger disappeared. "Yeah," he whispered, holding my gaze. "Scared me too, Red. *Autumn.*"

My real name stuck on his tongue, and he looked a little sheepish when he added, "I guess I never really asked. Which do you prefer?"

"What do you mean?"

"Red? Or Autumn? Suppose I just took it upon myself to rename you."

"I like Red." I smiled. "I've never had a nickname before. Kinda makes me feel like I belong here."

"Belonging. That's a weird concept, isn't it?"

"Yeah. Sure is."

Something swirled in the air between us – quiet and expectant and deeper than either of us had intended. We stayed silent – each one looking at the other, each one waiting for the other to speak first – and then finally Ryder said, "You know what? Let's blow off swimming for now. I can take you to my favorite spot, and we can get to know each other better." To lighten the weight of the air around us, he winked and added, "You can even keep your clothes on if you like."

A short time later, Ryder and I sat stretched in the limbs of large, flowering tree. "Pacific dogwood," he had explained as we climbed, plucking a pale white blossom and tucking it behind my ear.

He helped me to a spot where two limbs bowed outward, and they formed a perfect pair of benches as they stretched and bloomed above a deep, crystal pool. The canopy was dense, and the flowers and pale green leaves gave the clearing a dreamy, vibrant glow.

An emotion stirred in my chest, and I reflected on the Community's counter-mantra: *Abundance is the key to longevity.*

*Abundance,* I repeated in my head as I glanced at my fingers across the tree's smooth bark. *I feel rich right now.*

Ryder must have sensed my awe, because he smiled and said, "Beautiful, isn't it? I come here sometimes when I want to remember what life's all about."

I reached for another blossom. "And what *is* life all about?"

"This. Everything. My old man's not just out here to disprove the Essence theory, you know. He's out here to ensure that everyone, everywhere, gets the chance to experience beauty like this. You can feel it, can't you?"

I tilted my head. "Feel it?"

"There." He reached for my heart, and the warmth of his fingers against my collarbone made my breath catch. "There," he repeated. "Right there in your chest. That glowing feeling, like your heart's gonna burst through your skin? You can feel it, right?"

I nodded – although I wasn't quite sure if the skittering in my heart was caused by the beauty of the dogwood or the whisper of his fingers against my skin.

"That's your Essence, you know." His expression became serious. "Not the bullshit Essence Centrists tell you about, but your real Essence. Your spirit. That intrinsic quality that makes you who you are." He smiled. "Do you know who you are, Red?"

"What do you mean?"

"I mean, you obviously know who you are, but do you *know* who you are? When you pull away all the constructs?"

I must have looked confused, because he touched another blossom and continued. "I'll give you an example. Some people probably think I'm just some dumb, cocky recruiter, but you know what I want to do, Red? I want to become a doctor, just like my old man, and I want to help people. I want to make the Community as strong as I possibly can. You know what I'm saying?"

I nodded. I had never really thought about what I wanted to be before. Hadn't really considered I'd be given an option. Cedar and his meditation masters assigned everyone jobs in the temple or used their connections to find entry-level positions for us out in the Community. They purposefully picked jobs that kept our minds blank, didn't want us filling our heads with dangerous Outsider notions.

"I'd like to be a teacher, maybe," I said after a moment. "Not in a temple, but in a school. A real one. I want to show kids like Brady how to lead good lives."

Ryder smiled. "That's beautiful, Red. Perfect. Really perfect. And you wanna know the secret to that?"

"There's a secret?"

"Of course. In order to get from here to there, we can't suppress our Essences. We have to *amplify* them." He leaned closer. "You know how you amplify your Essence, Red?"

"No." Again with the automatic responses. I realized I wasn't thinking about much as long as Ryder's face was this close to mine.

That glowing warmth inside my chest was overtaking me. And the feeling of being here, of being present in this dogwood tree, surrounded by blossoms and sunshine and a boy who really seemed to like me... That feeling became so all-consuming, I forgot he'd even asked a question.

It wasn't until he hesitated with his lips just inches from mine that I realized he was waiting to tell me something. But what? What had we been talking about, anyway?

I think he must have read my mind, because he repeated, "The way to amplify your Essence, Red, is to push yourself further than you've ever thought possible. The harder you push yourself, the more alive you feel. And you know what I think would make you feel alive right now?"

"What?" My insides were suddenly foggy. I felt limp, and I didn't protest when he clenched his hands around my shoulders and leaned even closer.

"Red, do you trust me?"

"Hmm?"

"Do you trust me? You know I'll always catch you, right?"

What was he talking about? I managed a weak nod before I closed my eyes and swayed into his arms. His fingers were warm, and his breath felt hot against my lips when he tensed and leaned in to kiss me.

But he *didn't* kiss me. He yanked me sideways off the limb instead, and we both crashed into the crystal pool below.

The icy water slammed the air from my lungs. I felt my insides seize up, and I became so overcome by panic that I must have blacked out as I struggled blindly in the pool. I didn't know where the surface was, and I didn't know where the bottom was – but just as quickly as I was submerged, I was pulled to the surface by two strong hands. And then Ryder was holding me in his arms and laughing.

"What the hell was that about?" I sputtered. I tried to tread water, but he was already holding me to his chest and kicking us to shore.

"Awesome, right?"

I couldn't break free of his grasp. My hair was plastered to my face, and my clothes were glued to my skin, but Ryder didn't seem at all bothered by my fury. Instead, he actually looked *entertained*, and the realization that he'd put my life in danger just so he could laugh at me... I was so furious, I didn't know what to do.

We approached the bank. Before I could pull away, he rolled on top of me and pinned me to his chest. "I'm sorry, Red; I didn't mean to scare you. But I promised I'd catch you, and I did. And look at you. You just jumped ten feet from a tree into a pool. And you *swam*, Red. Did you ever in a million years think you'd be *swimming*?"

"I..." I paused. He was right; we'd jumped into something deep and dark and scary and unknown. And we were fine.

"You know I'm right, don't you?"

I tried to frown, but I was suddenly filled with a giddy sense of accomplishment – like I'd beaten something I didn't even realize I needed to beat. But I had. And I did. And Ryder had helped me do it.

His grin told me my reaction was written all over my face. "I'll always be here to catch you, Red," he repeated. "I want you to know that. And you know what else I'll always be here to do?"

"What?" The heat of his embrace was quickly trumping the chill of the water.

His eyes became playful. "I'll always be here to tickle you, too."

"What? No!" I tried to squirm, but it was too late. He pinned my arms to the rock and began tracing circles in the narrows of my waist.

I couldn't help but laugh, and I couldn't help but struggle, but then his lips were on mine, and I wasn't thinking about anything anymore. Anything except the glowing of my heart as it raced to burst through my skin.

# CHAPTER TWENTY

"We must honor Shayla's dedication by continuing our quest for truth."

Rex addressed the entire Community from the back porch of the Ahwahnee. Shayla's last heart rate readings, downloaded into his database this morning, inspired him so much he felt compelled to assemble everyone together at once.

Shayla's heart rate was apparently elevated right until the moment she had her monitor removed. "She was a model Community member," Rex said. "According to her readings – both from this week and the last several months – it is certain Shayla believes in our mission here. She believes in it with every ounce of her soul, and her decision to cross over will reverberate through this Community from this day forward." He raised his voice. "Let this be a lesson to all of us. We must never forget the reason we are here, and we must honor Shayla's devotion with our every action."

Daniel came to stand beside him. "Understanding that the initial phase of our research will be drawing to a close in August,

Rex and I urge each of you to come up with a personal goal between now and then. In the spirit of Shayla, we would also like you to spend some reflective time remembering why our research matters to you."

"What did you give up to come here?" Rex asked. "Who did you leave behind? Why? Remember that decision, how it sank into your gut and became part of your soul when you arrived here." He cleared his throat. "Shayla gave up her family, her life as a Centrist and her little sister Tabitha to join us. Let us never forget her commitment."

Daniel's movements were crisp. "Some of you have just become part of our Community, while others have been here for years. No matter how long you have been part of our endeavors, I urge you not to let your determination wane. Don't become complacent with your heart rate readings, because we will never have this opportunity again."

"The only way to dismantle the Centrist Movement is to take advantage of every single second we spend here," Rex finished. "In the spirit of Shayla's commitment, please remember this as we move forward."

I was standing in the back of the gathering – still dressed in my work clothes – when the crowd began to disperse. I hadn't seen Ryder since he'd dropped me at my tent cabin yesterday afternoon, and the lingering kiss he'd given me on my front doorstep had been enough to keep me off-balance all morning.

But my thoughts were far from Secret Falls as I watched the Community members filter back across the Meadow. I felt stirred and inspired by Rex's words, and I decided right then and there I needed to come up with a goal for myself.

I found a seat on a nearby pine log and closed my eyes. If I really wanted to help dismantle the Movement, I needed to do something big. Something huge. Something way more impressive than sitting here in the Meadow with the sun's rays shining on my face.

Like Ryder said, I needed to do something that scared me. Something that amplified my Essence. Something Rex and Ryder would be proud of.

The answer came to me almost instantly: I needed to do something Shayla would have done.

*I'm going to walk the highline at Taft Point. And I'm going to do it without a safety line.*

I was so excited about my plan that I almost didn't notice Kadence and Javi walking through the pine canopy. But Kadence was livid, and her words carried with the weight of ice water: "Bullshit. It's complete and total bullshit. There's no reason why we should celebrate Shayla's injuries with a speech like that."

"I know," Javi answered. "It doesn't make sense. Seems really irresponsible."

"She's lucky she didn't die, you know? Why push everyone else into making similar mistakes?"

We made eye contact across the clearing, and Kadence rushed toward me. "Autumn, thank you so much for helping me to my room yesterday. I don't think I could have made it without you."

I wanted to ask her why Rex's speech had upset her so much, but Javi cleared his throat to get her attention. She paused for a second, and sadness briefly flitted through her features.

"Autumn, I heard you and Ryder might be…" She wrung her hands together. "Listen, I just want you to know that I'm happy for you. If Ryder is the guy you've decided you want to be with… I just don't want things to be weird between us."

Her expression pinched, and she exchanged another look with Javi. "Just… remember to be careful, OK?"

I stared blankly at her for a moment, and then I did the only thing I could think of; I thanked her for her concern and then faked a stomach ache so I could get out of there quick.

It was a dumb move, but it worked. Its only drawback was the look on Ryder's face when I came staggering into the Ahwahnee, hand clenched over my belly.

"What are you up to, Red?" His voice was deliberately slow, and his eyes glinted as he tilted his head to study me.

He was standing near one of the fireplaces, surrounded by mounds of rope and gear I didn't recognize. Two boys were busy laying out equipment behind him, and they stopped what they were doing and turned when I entered.

"Oh, shut up," I said playfully. "Like you've never faked nausea to get out of a conversation before. Even Centrists know that trick."

"Seems I have underestimated you." He chuckled and turned back to his gear. "What are you up to right now? Wanna come climbing with us?"

"Climbing?"

"Yeah. Rock climbing." He motioned to the boys behind him. "Trey and Adrian. You guys remember Autumn from Vernal Fall, right? Three of us were about to spend a few hours at Church Bowl. Don't suppose you wanna join us?"

I nodded, even though I wasn't sure exactly what he was talking about. "Yeah, I definitely would."

I wanted to tell him about highlining, about my brand-new goal at Taft Point, but I wanted to be alone with him first. I wanted to see that spark in his eyes when he heard my decision, and I wanted him to pull me into his arms and tell me he was proud of me.

I decided I would wait.

Church Bowl was a vertical cliff face a short walk from the entrance to the Ahwahnee. I set out with Ryder and the boys, and it felt good to tramp down the pavement in the middle of the group.

Trey was unmistakable – tall, dark-skinned and dreadlocked. He spoke in a slow, deep voice, and he spent most of the walk discussing climbing routes with Adrian.

Shorter and stouter, Adrian had thick hands, toffee-colored hair and blocky, tan shoulders. He didn't have much to say to me, either, but his voice filled with enthusiasm when we reached Church Bowl. Then he and Trey were gone, rushing to the cliff and carefully laying out their gear again.

"Aren't big talkers at first," Ryder explained, hanging back with me. "You'll grow on 'em after a while." He bumped me lightly on the hip. "That is, if you keep me around long enough."

Keep you around long enough? His touch sent a jolt through me. "Depends on how nice you are to me, I guess."

"That so?" He enveloped my shoulders with one swoop of his arm and motioned to the rock wall. The boys were busy pulling on strappy harnesses and inspecting a bizarre assortment of clamps, ropes, wires and metal objects I didn't recognize. "Wanna give climbing a shot, or would you rather sit back and watch today? We're starting easy, so this would be a pretty good day to give it a whirl if you're into it."

"I want to try." I paused. "Oh, and Ryder? I was thinking about what Rex said, and I've already come up with my goal for the next few months."

"That right?"

"Yeah." I swallowed. "I've decided I want to learn how to slackline."

He grinned. "That's a great goal, Red; I'll teach you myself."

"No, wait, I'm not finished. I want to highline over Taft Point, just like Shayla would have. And I want to do it like you. Without a safety line."

"Red." If I was expecting him to cheer or jump for joy, he certainly didn't. "I don't know about that. Highlining is crazy dangerous, and you just got here, you know? Shayla's been highlining for years. Why don't you set your sights a little lower, on something like a creek slackline?"

"I don't want to do a creek slackline." My voice came out whiny, but I didn't care. "I want to do a highline. I thought you'd be proud of me."

"I am." He held me at arm's length. "No, Red, don't misunderstand. I *am* proud, and that goal is totally badass. I just... don't want to set you up for failure, you know? Shayla worked a really long time to get as good as she got, and even she fell, you know?"

"I'm not going to fall." I frowned. "I'm going to do it. Amplify my Essence, just like you said. Will you help me?"

His expression softened, and the slow smile that crept over his face was definitely worth the wait. "Yeah, I will. Sure you're into it?"

"I am."

"All right. Let's do this, then." He pulled me in for a quick peck on the forehead, and then he turned to address the boys. "Hey, assholes! Guess who's decided she's highlining Taft Point with us?"

"What?" Trey's voice was incredulous. Straightening up from the clamps he was inspecting, he shot me a smile almost as wide as Ryder's. "Hell yeah, sister. Let's get your ass up on that line."

# CHAPTER TWENTY-ONE

Apparently you can't just highline Taft Point. You have to train and train and train for months or even years sometimes, so Ryder insisted we get started that very instant. That meant blowing off climbing and instead setting up our very own slackline at Church Bowl's base.

Only it wasn't quite that easy. Ryder had to dash back to the Ahwahnee to grab some "webbing", so I had to wait and listen while Trey told me all about this Chinese guy named Ken he'd once seen "go splat" when he panicked halfway between Taft Point and the other side.

"It was heinous. Dude was trapped out there in the middle, as far from the beginning as he was from the end. I'll never forget the look on his face." He shook his head and worked the climbing line secured to the harness on his waist.

Adrian hung from the other end of the line. Suspended high on the rocks and attached by what appeared to be a safety pulley, he yelled down after a while, "Less blabbing, more belaying, please. Thank you very much."

After a few minutes, Ryder returned with a thick, flat rope slung over his shoulder. He must have seen the horrified look on my face, because he shook his head and said, "Trey, really? You already told her about the Chinese guy?"

"Sorry, man." Trey shook his head. "Heinous, though. It really was."

Ryder met my eyes. "It was. It was absolutely horrible, but Ken's the only one who's ever died on the highline, and that's because he didn't take his training seriously. Which means if you really want to do this, we need to get started right away."

He paused. "You can change your mind any time you want, you know. And for the sake of argument, let's assume you'll have a safety line, OK? Better for my heart that way."

"OK." I didn't want to admit it, but the cliff-sized weight in my chest lifted at his words. "A safety line sounds good. For now. And I can always change my mind about that, right?"

Ryder took a few moments to show me our gear – a much less complicated assortment than what Trey and Adrian used to rock-climb.

"OK, let's get terminology straight first. This," he said, motioning to the coiled rope at his feet, "is called webbing. It's made of nylon, and it's weaved to be flat, almost like a seatbelt. Even when it's pulled tight, it's still pretty springy; that's why it always jumps around when you walk. Different from the old tightropes of circus days."

He picked up three D-shaped metal clasps. "These are called carabiners; we'll use them to secure the webbing between trees." Chuckling at my nod, he said, "There are tons of ways to string a slackline, but the easiest is what we're gonna do today. See two trees you like?"

"What?"

"For starters, you wanna look for two trees about twenty feet apart. Strong ones. In a nice, flat place where the ground isn't too rocky. See any trees like that?"

I pointed to two pines, and he nodded. "Perfect." He picked up the webbing and a few large sticks. "Wanna help me wrap 'em? We're gonna want the line to be low, maybe even with your mid-thigh?"

Ryder instructed me to hold the sticks vertically against one of the tree's trunks while he wrapped the webbing around it. "To cushion the tree, you know," he said. "Don't want it to get rope burn."

Once the webbing was secured by a carabiner, we stretched the remaining length across the clearing and secured the other end to the second tree. I cushioned its loop with a few more sticks while Ryder wrapped it, and then we took turns pulling it tight with the second and third carabiners.

When the slackline was officially ready, Ryder instructed me to take off my shoes. "You gotta feel the webbing, Red," he said, kicking his own pair into the dirt. "Every tiny vibration, every little inconsistency and flicker. You gotta know that webbing better than you've ever known anything in your entire life. Can't fake it, or you'll fall."

I smiled at the intense way he scrutinized me while I took off my own shoes. "Got cute feet, Red," he said, planting a quick kiss on my cheek.

"You wanna take your time standing up," he continued, coming to stand beside the webbing. He placed his right foot on it – like Shayla had during moonbows – and then he stood still for a moment, eyes focused forward.

"See how I'm not just popping up to stand? Taking a moment to feel the webbing and gather my thoughts before I start. Gotta clear all that shit out before you get up. Just... whoosh. You know?"

He closed his eyes. Tension seemed to drain from his face, and then... Whoosh. One quick exhale, and he was standing.

He was... beautiful. Of all the words in the world, it was the one that jumped to my mind first. In an instant, I knew it was the right one.

Gone was the Ryder I thought I knew – the Ryder that smoked cigarettes and swaggered and laughed and flirted with me. Gone was the guy I'd met in Golden Gate Park, the guy who'd skinny-dipped on top of Vernal Falls and kissed me on the Housekeeping Camp bridge.

In his place was this *man* – this laser-focused, intense and centered man. His expression was calm, and his eyes never left the slackline as he took one step, then two steps, then three steps forward. His arms, held outward from his sides, swayed slightly as he corrected his balance, and his movements were fluid and graceful as a cat's.

Desire swept through me at the memory of those arms wrapped around me, and I felt pride swell inside me as well. *Ryder thinks I'm capable of doing this, too.*

In several short steps, he made it to the other side. As he turned to face me, his face melted into a grin. "Ta-da!" he said. "And that's all there is to it. Ready to give it a try?"

I'll admit it; I was smug. Ryder made it look so easy that I was certain I'd be up and strutting around on that thing in no time.

As he jumped down and motioned for me to begin, I approached the slackline and mimicked his opening stance: right foot elevated and parallel to the webbing, left foot solid on the ground. The position was a little harder than I expected, but I blamed that on how much longer Ryder's legs were than mine.

I stood very still for a moment, and then I attempted to straighten my right leg, just as he had. That's when things started to fall apart.

It's apparently really hard to lift your entire body with only the strength of your thigh to support you. And apparently my thigh wasn't up to snuff, because my body barely budged. I popped up about three inches, and then I felt my leg collapse beneath me. My knee buckled, and then I was back on the ground.

My face burned, but when I looked in shock at Ryder, he did his best to control his smile. "No worries, Red. It's crazy hard at first. Your muscles'll build in time, but standing up is one of the hardest parts. Why don't you try again, and I'll give you a boost if you need it?"

I returned my attention to the webbing, but my leg collapsed the second time as well.

"It's OK," he said. "Let's see what a little help does for you." Coming to stand at my side, he instructed, "Put your left arm on my shoulder. And then push up when you're ready to straighten your leg."

I nodded, but the nearness of his body flustered me. When I straightened my leg and tried to stand, the webbing vibrated, and I tumbled sideways into his arms.

"Can't you just hold my hand and lead me?" I asked, frustration edging into my voice.

"Can't do it, Red." He gently deposited me back to the ground. "And you shouldn't hold onto my shoulder when you get on your feet, either. It's a crutch, and it'll hold you back. Gotta find your own balance, you know?"

I must have frowned, because he chuckled and flicked my nose. "You're cute when you're pissed off. You know that?" Turning to pat the slackline, he continued. "The thing about this is it's not a party trick. It's a tool; it makes you find your center.

Makes you push everything out of your head and focus on only one thing. If you get unfocused, you start to wobble. And if you start to wobble, you start to fall. End of story."

He slouched against the nearest tree. "Remember your Centrist meditation exercises? All that aura-smoothing shit? Well, that's crap meditation; not the real thing at all. But in order to get those auras smoothed, you have to quiet your mind. Slacklining's like that, but now you gotta concentrate on your physical self as well as your mental self. What's your body doing? Where's your gaze? How does that webbing feel beneath your toes?"

He smiled. "Don't rush into walking this time. Just push up and balance on one foot. See how long it takes to find your center. When you find it, start walking."

I nodded. Turning back to the slackline, I propped my right foot on the webbing and grabbed Ryder's shoulder for balance.

I concentrated on the feeling of my breath as it left my lungs, on the slow relaxing of my face as I breathed in again. From somewhere to our right, I could hear Trey and Adrian laughing, but soon their voices faded a little. The sun felt hot against the top of my head, but the rest of my body felt cool. Sharp. Focused.

Instead of bolting to a standing position like before, I straightened my right leg slowly. The webbing jerked again, and I could feel the muscles in my thigh quivering, but I didn't give up this time. Instead, I extended my arms like he had, and I took a moment to catch my balance.

*Whoosh.* My breath felt like it weighed a thousand pounds as it left my lungs. And then, *whoosh,* another breath back in.

My eyes drilled into the slackline so hard they began to burn, but I didn't look away. I'm not even sure if I blinked, and the jerking of my arms slowly subsided as my body began to find its center.

The feeling was hard to process. A slow melting and reformulating of my insides that startled me so much I jerked sideways to see if Ryder was watching. The movement sent vibrations humming through the line again. The next thing I knew, I was falling.

I managed to land on my feet this time. When I straightened, I didn't feel frustrated or antsy like I had before. Instead, I felt energized. And determined. And a tiny bit fixated. Someday, I would be able to do this.

"I want to try again."

# CHAPTER TWENTY-TWO

After a few hours of training, I managed to take a few steps before slipping. The falling wasn't even that bad, either, because I quickly learned to leap to the ground the second I felt my balance faltering.

Not that I'd be given that luxury at Taft Point, but Ryder told me I shouldn't spend so much time focusing on the end goal. "In order to slackline successfully, you need to be in the here and now, you know?" he'd said, lighting a cigarette and leaning against a nearby boulder.

I did my best, and the sense of accomplishment I felt at the end of the day was enough to swell my body with a bubbly feeling of effervescence. Ryder must have sensed it, because he swooped in for a kiss when I bent to put back on my shoes. "Looked good up there, Red. I'm proud of you."

I tried to hide the pleased feeling I felt welling inside me. I also tried to hide the way these funny, spontaneous kisses were flustering me so much. "Ryder, I only walked four steps today. Hardly Taft Point–worthy."

"Yeah, but it's your first day. Some people never even get that far."

We left the slackline and began walking toward Trey and Adrian. They were busy repacking their gear, but Trey called, "Nice job, Red! Best new girl I've seen in a long time."

I felt myself blushing again, both at his compliment and at the fact he'd called me by Ryder's nickname.

Adrian seemed equally impressed. "You got good form," he said. Mimicking my arm movements, he added, "Gotta let the tension move through you a little more, though. Let your arms go completely loose, like tentacles."

"I will. Thank you."

He picked up the rope coiled at his feet. "Got a good one, Ryder. Gotta hang on to her."

"I think I will." Ryder smiled and wrapped his arm around my waist. "So, you assholes better stay away from her, OK?"

Since my orientation lessons with Kadence were officially concluded – and I didn't really know what to say to her or Javi anyway – I purposefully avoided our meditation sessions and spent almost the entire next two weeks practicing my slacklining at Church Bowl instead.

Ryder came with me sometimes, and Trey or Adrian usually joined in, too. They popped up on the slackline and demonstrated turns and twists and even funny crouching moves where they bent on one knee and offered a prayer to whatever higher power may or may not have been looking out for us.

Jett and Cody even became regular fixtures after the first few days. Jett disapproved of the whole idea, but she mostly just hugged me and told me she'd remember this when I finally came around and decided slackliners were idiots, too. Cody took a much more pragmatic approach, and he often brought snacks and offered to give me boosts whenever Ryder wasn't around.

By Friday, I didn't need boosts at all. I was also consistently walking from one tree to the other, and I could almost make it halfway back without falling. By Thursday of the next week, I was making it to the tree and back more times than I wasn't.

I also settled into a comfortable routine with the entire group, and it wasn't unusual for Trey or even Adrian to seek me out in the dinner line and crash to a seat next to me. They were all calling me Red now, and they'd started taking bets on how soon I would be overtaking them on the slackline.

Kadence and Javi didn't seem as impressed. I had barely talked to them since Shayla's crossing-over celebration, but they often locked eyes with me in the dining hall. Even when I was in the midst of laughing and joking with my new friends, I still felt coldness ache in my chest at the sight of them.

They seemed to be busy, too. Ryder told me one afternoon that Kadence had begun spreading the word that she didn't appreciate the way Rex had handled Shayla's accident. She said it was reckless, and she encouraged everyone to ignore Rex's call for increased risks.

This sent tiny ripples coursing through the Community. It also rankled many people – none more than Rex, Daniel and Ryder.

"So what," Ryder said late one evening, "she thinks we should just forget why we're here in the first place? Maybe start smoothing our auras and trying to stay neutral?"

It was my one-month Yosemite anniversary, and Ryder, Jett, Cody, Trey, Adrian and I had decided to celebrate by camping, drinking moonshine and relaxing around a fire near a place called Squaw Caves.

It was my first time drinking since my moonbows incident, and my enthusiasm was mellowed slightly by my memories of the horrible hangover I'd felt the next day. I decided to drink much slower this time, and the liquid's burning taste was nearly intolerable as I chased it with my water bottle.

"Kadence is just trying to slander us," he continued. "Has had it out for us, ever since she got here."

"Kadence doesn't have it out for you," Jett insisted, flicking a piece of bark into the fire. "She's just different than you. She misses her friend."

"She's a stiff," Adrian sneered. "She just wants to cause trouble."

"A stiff?" It was my voice, and the sound of it surprised me.

"It's the word we use for people who don't believe in pushing their heart rates to the limit," Trey explained. "They always seem to undermine Rex's research."

"But they've never outright questioned it before, so this is big, even for them," Ryder said. "Stiffs like Kadence have always said they think my old man's research is inflammatory. Think he should just let the Essence theory go and forget about Cedar entirely. But my old man isn't like that, you know? Cedar *wronged* him, and he wronged him in a major way. He won't be able to rest until he frees every single Centrist. We shouldn't, either."

I picked at a stray thread on my blanket. "But Kadence wears a heart rate monitor. Everyone does. So she can't disapprove of what he's doing too much, right?"

"Well, yeah, she knows who gave her a home," Trey said. "But she doesn't push herself like the rest of us. None of the stiffs do."

Ryder seemed to suddenly come to. "You know what?" he said. "This is bullshit. Sitting here bitching about Kadence won't help anything, and I'm sure this whole thing with Shayla will blow over soon, anyway." He made eye contact with me and smiled. "I think we should all just concentrate on making Red's one-month anniversary a special one. That's the reason we're all out here, right?"

As everyone murmured their agreement, he pulled a clear plastic bag from his backpack. "By the way, I have a surprise for you guys."

"Shut up," Jett said, reaching for the small white pills. "Where'd you get MDMA?"

"Fresno. Last supply run. My old man got some to help me keep my readings high. Sure he wouldn't mind if I shared the love with you."

He began passing pills to everyone, and I took mine without question. Rolling it in my hands, I said, "MDMA?"

Jett grinned and held the pill between her teeth. "Used to be used in this stuff called ecstasy. Crazy popular before the Great Quake, but - surprise! - Centrists think it's dangerous."

"What does it do to you?"

"Acts kinda like moonshine, but way better." Jett chewed her pill and swallowed. "It releases all these great hormones in your brain, and it just makes you... happy."

I frowned. "I'm not going to act stupid if I take this, am I? I'm not going to forget everything again?"

"No." Ryder laughed. "No memory loss, and no puking, either. Trust me, Red, you're gonna love it."

I popped the pill, and the group followed with an enthusiastic round of applause. Their laughter made that cozy sense of belonging swell inside me again.

"Thanks, guys," I said, wiping my mouth. "What are we supposed to do next?"

Trey grinned and popped to a standing position. "May take a while for the pill to kick in. In the meantime, hide-and-seek, count of fifty? Campfire's home base, and I'm it. Let's get moving."

I didn't know what he was talking about, so I sat there stupefied until he began counting down from fifty. Instantly, everyone scattered.

I would have remained sitting there dumbfounded if Jett hadn't grabbed my hand and squealed, "Come with me, Autumn. I'll show you how to play."

We made it through a few rounds of hide-and-seek before everyone started to feel the MDMA's effects. When they did, the game petered out, and Trey began playing his guitar while the rest of us lounged around the campfire.

I didn't feel like laughing or dancing with everyone quite yet, and my head drummed as I stared at the ground between my feet. I felt like puking again, and I probably would have if Ryder hadn't appeared by my side.

His pupils were dilated so wide, his irises seemed almost black, and his hand was warm as he massaged the space between my shoulder blades. "Don't worry," he said. "You feel nauseous sometimes at first, but the feeling will pass. Just relax, OK? Concentrate on my hand on your back, and you'll feel better soon."

I nodded. When I closed my eyes, the nausea lessened. In its place I felt an antsy creep of anticipation. A tingling sensation started at the top of my head and began filtering its way down through my limbs.

My skin began to feel magnetic, and the warmth of Ryder's hand began spreading in warm waves down my back. It was startling – that feeling of melting that spread like butter through my spine. When I opened my eyes, I felt my entire world swelling.

Ryder smiled beside me, and I could tell by the look in his eyes that he knew exactly how I felt. "Better, right?"

I couldn't even answer. My heart was churning, and my insides were suddenly so charged that I couldn't put my thoughts into words. My heart had oozed into liquid, and the purring feeling of contentment that was humming inside me made anything but smiling impossible.

"Knew you'd like it."

I nodded. We sat in silence for a few minutes, and then the planes of Ryder's face became so beautiful that I had trouble concentrating on anything else. I wanted to touch his skin – to feel those sloping cheekbones and full, wide lips – so I extended my hands and cupped his face between them. He closed his eyes, and the meeting of our skin was so intense that I felt the warmth of his cheeks and the coolness of my palms blurring together into one.

The strains of Trey's guitar and the echoes of laughter began infusing my insides, and the sound melted through my entire body until I felt myself buzzing with happiness. I was here. In the middle of the woods. In the middle of this beautiful night, and I was connected to so many amazing people that it was suddenly hard to tell where they ended and where I began.

Adrian picked up a drum, and the harmony of the two instruments began singing through me. From far away, the sound reminded me of a heartbeat.

Or *was* it a heartbeat? My heartbeat? Ryder's heartbeat? The heartbeat of our mothers while we were in their wombs, or the heartbeat of this place – this moss-covered place called Squaw Caves that called us together and sheltered us beside a campfire?

Jett and Cody became entwined as Trey hung his head over his guitar and Adrian played the drums at his side. Jett grabbed my hand, and then we were dancing.

We were drawn into the beat, and suddenly I realized how equal we all were. Here in this forest, with all of our Essences and auras swelling, with the music slamming into us and passing through us. I realized with certainty that neutrality wasn't the thing that kept us centered; it was this. It was the music that filled us and the friendships that sustained us. It was the joining of our hands and the singing of our souls – because we were here together, in this bubble, and we were alive.

I suddenly felt so energized that I wanted to run, so I said, "Hide-and-seek again. Please?"

The music faded, and then we were all smiling as Adrian held up his hands and said, "OK, my turn. Count of fifty."

Ryder and I tore off into the trees together, but I couldn't keep quiet long enough for us to find a hiding place. All I wanted to do was learn every single thing about him, so we slipped away from the game and climbed to the very top of the boulders – to a flat stretch of rock that opened to the sky and to a moon so beautiful, I could almost feel it shimmering on my skin.

Then we were facing each other, cross-legged on the granite, and Ryder's hands were dancing like waves against my shoulders. I was glowing, and I was lost in the depths of his eyes – in the shifting black vastness of his pupils. I could see into his soul, and I swore his soul was pulling me into him. Like we were one soul in two bodies.

His face was changing now, shifting a little at the edges, but I realized it didn't matter what we looked like, anyway. All that mattered was what we looked like on the inside. And his insides were beautiful. Just like his outsides.

I wanted to touch him again. This time, my hands found their way to his chest, and he pulled me toward him. The feeling was explosive, like two fireworks colliding in midair.

I realized there was no place I'd rather be. I was kissing Ryder on top of a boulder, and my heart was churning like a train inside my chest. His hands were cupping my shoulders, and then they were inside my shirt. He was crouched on top of me, and his pants were unbuttoned and mine were unbuttoned, too.

I'm not sure exactly how things happened next, but I know the stars were glimmering like diamonds in the velvet sky behind Ryder's head. I know the Milky Way danced through the heavens, and I know every single thing about that moment just felt right.

# CHAPTER TWENTY-THREE

I woke with a start sometime around dawn. The granite felt rough against the contours of my back, and Ryder slept soundly beside me. Even though he'd slipped down to the fire circle and gathered blankets for us at some point, the padding didn't do much for the rock's unforgiving surface.

My head hurt – not in the foggy, bleary way it had after the moonshine, but in a hollow way. Like everything inside my brain had been glassed over.

My entire body ached, and my legs shook a little as I rolled to my side and tried to re-bunch my blankets into a pillow. *Did last night really happen? Ryder and me… Did we really…?*

Panic welled inside me. I thought of Kadence's lessons, of the registry in Rex's office, and I realized that any shred of neutrality I had once been able to claim was officially gone now. I felt… different today. And I wasn't sure I liked it.

Ryder stirred and made eye contact with me. His pupils were back to the right size again, and his whites were bloodshot. He looked like his insides had been glassed over, too.

"Morning, Red." His voice was little more than a croak. "How'd you sleep?" He felt around beneath his blankets and added, "You have my pants over there, by any chance?"

My cheeks burned. Even though I was completely covered by the clothes I'd fumbled back into last night, I felt more exposed than ever.

I wanted to curl up inside myself, but I didn't have the hazy, regretful feelings I'd had after moonbows. These feelings were different. I felt vulnerable, like all my insides had been ripped completely out of my body. My heart and lungs and bones were laid out in front of Ryder, and he could do anything he wanted with them. I was powerless to stop him.

"Ryder…" I didn't even know what I was trying to say, but the lump rising in my throat meant panic was on the way. "About last night. You know… what happened between us? I just want to make sure…"

I wrung my hands together. I felt like something profound had shifted between us, and I wanted him to know that. "I don't know exactly what the rules are for this kind of stuff, but I feel like what happened between us was a really big deal. Wasn't it?"

Ryder smiled. "Course it was, Red. This was a huge deal for you, and I get that. Was a huge deal for me, too. You don't regret it, do you?"

"No." I didn't know why I was being so weird all of a sudden, but I felt like everything that had ever existed between us hung on this conversation. "I just…"

Before I could answer, his expression changed. "Shit," he said. "What time is it? I was supposed to meet my old man first thing this morning." He looked around. "I'm so sorry, Red, but I really gotta run. He'll have my ass if I don't show up on time. You seen my pants?"

My panic came flooding back. In an instant, my heart and lungs and bones were outside my body again, and I was clutching my blanket lamely as he found his pants and began struggling back into his shirt.

I wanted to cry. I felt like I had just given my entire soul to him, and now he was leaving me.

Before he turned to climb down the boulder, he planted a quick kiss on my forehead. "I'm so sorry, Red. I have a recruiting trip this week; gotta hit the road first thing tomorrow. My old man and I still have to organize details so... I'll find you later, OK?"

I didn't know what to say, so I just nodded. And then he was gone, and I was lying by myself on a boulder with rocks jabbing into my back.

I returned to the campfire circle a short time later. Trey and Adrian were still sleeping, but Cody was busy tending the fire while Jett sliced a loaf of bread. Her pale roots and spiky black flyaways poked in all directions.

"Autumn!" she said. "I know you're probably not super hungry, but you really ought to eat something. Also, drink water. Tons of water. How are you feeling?"

"Groggy. Weird."

I wanted to tell her that I felt like my insides had turned to dust, but she stopped me before I could. "We call it the comedown," she explained. "Not nearly as bad as a hangover, but... It's like you've already felt all the emotions you were allowed to feel for the day, so there's nothing left. You know?"

I did know – kinda – but I also knew I'd feel a lot less scattered if Ryder hadn't just left me. "Ryder said he has to go on a recruiting trip," I said abruptly, taking the bread she offered. "Aren't you and Cody going with him?"

"Yeah. Don't need to start getting ready until later, though." She must have read my face, because she quickly added, "But hey, Ryder has a lot more work to do than we do. He has to set up all the logistics with Rex, and…" She paused, and her expression became serious. "Hey, Autumn? Don't worry about Ryder, OK? Rex can be kinda demanding. It's not… you… or anything."

I nodded. "I need to go, too, actually. Chores. I'll see you around, OK? Thanks again for everything."

"You sure?" She tilted her head. "Can't you blow 'em off or go in late like us? Comedown Day's kind of fun, actually. We all just crash out and curse and feel weird together."

"No, that's OK. Thanks, anyway."

She held my gaze for a minute, and the sadness that crossed her features reminded me of the wistful way she'd stood watch for me at the Balcony that first day. I thought she might protest, but she finally just nodded and glanced at Cody. "Hon, do you mind walking Autumn back to the trailhead?"

Cody and I set off through a dappled morning – fresh and cool but quickly warming as the sun burned through the remaining dew. Cody's hair was skewed into an unruly cowlick, and he led the way down the trail without grace.

"Feel like a drunken bear this morning," he explained as we walked. "I'm tripping all over the place."

I tried to smile. Cody and I hadn't spent much time together by ourselves, but his stoic support had always comforted me. I felt like I could certainly use it this morning.

"Feeling all right?" he asked after a minute. "MDMA didn't agree with me the first time I tried it, but then again, I wasn't dating anyone back then. Always more fun when you have someone to share it with."

I nodded. "Yeah, it was… nice."

"She's right, you know." He pushed aside some branches and held them back for me. "What she said about Rex? Dude demands so much from Ryder that it's not even funny. Keep that in mind, OK?"

"OK."

"You know, and…" He glanced at me again. "Well, Jett dated a lot of people before she dated me. So when we started spending time together…" He shrugged. "Well, it was kinda hard to see through the bullshit, you know? To see past all the things everyone told me about her? But look at us now. It's been ten months, and I've never been happier. I really think she's the One."

He absently brushed his hand against a pine trunk. "I guess what I'm saying is, I think everyone deserves a second chance – including guys like Ryder that maybe haven't had the greatest beginnings." He attempted a smile. "Even if they do ditch you on Comedown Day. You know what I'm saying?"

We said goodbye at the trailhead, and I made it the rest of the way to the stables without incident. The only thing alarming about the walk was the nebulous feeling of insecurity that still swirled like a tide inside me.

I wasn't even exactly sure why I felt so insecure. It wasn't as if Ryder had said or done anything wildly out of the ordinary this morning. He had been funny and affectionate and flirtatious, and he'd apologized multiple times for leaving me.

That meant his feelings for me hadn't changed, right? And why would they have changed, anyway? It's not like I'd given him anything he could break…

I shook my head. I had. I had given him something beautiful and fragile and nonreturnable, and it was the helplessness of that giving that left me so unbalanced.

I couldn't protect myself from him anymore.

I was chopping animal diets in the kitchen when I heard the footsteps. When I turned, I couldn't help the fluttery feeling of expectancy that followed. Maybe it was Ryder. Maybe he had flowers. Maybe he had decided to blow off the recruiting trip and spend time with me instead.

But it wasn't Ryder. It was Kadence, and she must have seen the disappointed look that flashed in my eyes, because she frowned and said, "Geez. Sorry to disappoint. Have you seen Javi around here today?"

"Sorry." I took a breath. "I didn't mean…"

"It's fine." She leaned against the doorframe. "We've missed you at morning meditation sessions, you know. You could come back."

When I didn't say anything, she sighed. "Well, have you seen him? Ahwahnee groundskeepers said he might be here picking up eggs."

I shook my head. "He may be out back."

"Will you tell him to find me if you see him?" She narrowed her eyes, and then her expression changed. "Holy shit, Autumn. You did MDMA, didn't you?"

She didn't look mad anymore, just worried. And as she rushed toward me, her worry changed to fear. "Autumn, you did. I know you did."

"So what? Why do you care?"

"Because it's dangerous." She reached for my shoulders. "How much did you take? When did you take it?"

"Last night. It was just one pill; what's the big deal?" I freed myself and turned back to my cutting board.

"Autumn." She reached for me again. "Listen to me. MDMA's illegal – not just for Centrists, but for everyone. It screws up your brain. Can even kill you if you aren't careful. Who gave it to you?"

"Rex." I frowned and thrust my chin at her.

"*Rex* gave you MDMA?"

"He gave it to Ryder, and Ryder gave it to me. He bought it to keep Ryder's heart rate up, so it can't be all that dangerous, can it?"

"It can." The color drained from her face. "You're sure Rex gave it to Ryder?"

I narrowed my eyes. "What are you trying to do, Kadence? Get Rex in trouble? Find out what he's doing so you can report it back to your *stiffs*?"

I sneered the last word, and the look on Kadence's face told me I'd hit home. "Stiffs? Is that how you see me now?"

I shrugged. "I don't know. Maybe."

"Autumn." She sighed. "Look, I know you believe everything Rex and Ryder have to say. But I don't, and I don't want you to get hurt." She narrowed her eyes again. "Wait. What's that bruise on your neck? Autumn, is that a hickey?"

"What?" My hands flew to protect my neck. "What are you talking about?"

"There. Right there on your neck. That big purple spot. You and Ryder didn't sleep together, did you?"

The shuffling of more footsteps signaled Ryder's entrance. And then: "Seems kinda private, doesn't it, Kadence?"

His voice was calm, but his smile wasn't reflected in his eyes. As he strode forward to stand by my side, I could see his jaw was clenched.

Kadence's eyes narrowed. "You know you shouldn't have given her MDMA, Ryder. And Autumn, if you slept with him last night, you need to get checked out at the clinic right now. You actually can't wait."

"Why didn't you tell me MDMA was dangerous?"

I blurted this the moment after Kadence wheeled on her heel and crossed the threshold. "And why do I need to get checked out at the clinic?"

Ryder remained motionless, but his expression changed, too. "Red, don't listen to Kadence. She has no idea what she's talking about. MDMA isn't dangerous; she just doesn't understand it."

"OK. But what about the clinic?"

His frustration faded. "Well, that's why I'm here," he said. "Listen, I'm sorry I bolted on you earlier. I shouldn't have left you like that, but my old man..."

"Why do I need to get checked out at the clinic?"

"It's... It's standard procedure. A precaution, really. No big deal. I'll go with you."

I shook my head. I didn't know much, but I knew I didn't want to have to explain myself to Rex.

Ryder seemed to read my mind. "My old man isn't in the clinic on Fridays, so it'll just be Daniel. Come on, Red, I'll even treat you to dessert afterward."

# CHAPTER TWENTY-FOUR

The strawberries were gooey, and they coated my fingertips with the sugary dusting that Ryder made a big display of perfecting. We were seated on twin lawn chairs on the Ahwahnee's back porch, and the sun felt warm as we plucked them from a large ceramic bowl.

Ryder had been right about the clinic. Although Daniel seemed surprised to see Ryder by my side, he confirmed that MDMA definitely wasn't dangerous if taken in moderation. After applauding my decision to take pregnancy prevention seriously, he simply marked Ryder's name in my file, handed me a pack of birth control pills and gave me a small white capsule to wash down with water.

"Levonorgestrel," he had explained, shaking it out of a large glass bottle. "May make you feel a little nauseated, but it will block your ovaries from releasing an egg. No egg, no fetus. End of story."

I wasn't sure how I felt about interfering with my body's purpose, but Daniel assured me the capsule wouldn't terminate a pregnancy. It would simply prevent one from occurring in the first place, and "in a place as small as Yosemite Valley, we need to limit conception to couples who have made the decision to wed."

*Wed.* The word sounded almost as strange as the concept, so I was relieved when he changed the subject. Glancing at Ryder, he said, "You're hitting the road soon, aren't you, son?"

"Yes, sir."

He made a note in Ryder's file and turned toward the exit. "Very well. You should probably expect a visit from your father before you leave."

I would have been more concerned about Daniel's comment if Ryder hadn't blown it off by saying, "Probably just wants to congratulate me on picking such a babe."

As we sat eating strawberries behind the Ahwahnee, I was so relieved to have Ryder by my side that I didn't even care if Daniel mentioned me to Rex or not. Ryder had said he was sorry for leaving, and he'd stuck by me at the clinic. He had said he would never leave me like that again.

Without meaning to, I found my thoughts returning to the stables. "Do you think we should apologize to Kadence?"

"What? Why?"

"For this morning? For being short with her? She was just trying to look out for me…"

"No. Definitely not." Ryder rolled a strawberry between his fingers. "My old man knows what he's doing, you know? And even if she can't understand that… Well, she *should* understand that. None of us would even be here if it weren't for him."

I nodded. My next question came out of nowhere, but I couldn't stop myself: "Ryder, have you and Kadence ever dated? Because there seems to always be this weird tension between you."

He chuckled and popped the strawberry in his mouth. "You're a perceptive one, Red. But, no. We never dated. I kissed her once, but I guess I was a dick to her the next day, and she hasn't been my biggest fan ever since."

"I see." This news did kind of bother me. So did his answer to my next question: "Have you ever dated anyone else I know?"

"Yeah." He stared at his hands. "Jett and I dated for a while."

"Jett?" I couldn't help my jaw drop. "You dated *Jett*? Why didn't you tell me?"

He shrugged. "I'm sorry, Red, but it was a long time ago. It was right when she got here, and I was still in my scheming stage, so…"

I jumped to my feet. "I can't believe you didn't tell me you dated *Jett*." I don't know why, but his omission felt like a betrayal. Like I was the only person in the entire world who hadn't known.

"It wasn't a big deal, Red. It's ancient history, and everything's good between us now. She's dated a bunch of guys since, and she's really happy with Cody, so…"

I thought of Cody's words, of the way he'd had trouble seeing through the bullshit. Suddenly, I understood why. The bullshit was actually a long line of guys, and the first guy in that line was Ryder.

"How are you and Jett possibly still friends? And how are you and Cody friends at all?"

"Because Cody's an awesome guy." Ryder stood now, too. "He loves her, and she loves him, and we all agree that I was just a great big mistake, so…"

His composure crumbled. "Red, don't walk away. Don't… judge me for something I did two years ago. Please?"

He reached for me, and I may have been seeing things, but I swear he looked choked up when he added, "Please, Red. I've never been honest with anyone in my entire life, but I want to be honest with you. I don't want to screw things up between us."

I couldn't help it; I softened. He reached for me, and his voice was quiet when he said, "Red, I'm sorry. About Jett, about Kadence. I'm sorry about this morning, and... I just wanna be a good guy, you know? This is new for me."

I started to answer, but I was interrupted by a polite throat-clearing. And then: "Sorry to interrupt, but may I speak to you for a minute, son?"

Rex stood a few feet behind us, and his expression was gracious when he added, "Good morning, Autumn," before ushering Ryder away.

They stopped about fifty feet from me – far enough that I couldn't overhear their conversation, but close enough that I could study the similarities and differences between them. Ryder was taller, but he was lankier, too. His shoulders hunched forward as they talked, and it was clear that – regardless of Ryder's confidence – it was Rex who ran the show around here.

The conversation continued, and Ryder suddenly frowned. He threw an arm in the air, and then he shook his head and stalked away. Stopping a few feet from his father, he stood with his eyes to the sky.

A pit formed in my stomach. I couldn't tell exactly what was going on, but it seemed bad. And something in my gut told me it was about me.

Ryder finally nodded and turned to finish the conversation. Rex clapped him on the shoulder and left, and then Ryder stood there staring at me across the back porch.

I didn't know what to do, so I waved and waited for him to tell me what had just happened. But he didn't. He simply held my gaze for a few moments, and the look of defeated remorse that flashed in his eyes was so intense and heartbreaking it made my stomach drop to the floor.

Without a word, he turned and walked inside the Ahwahnee. And he didn't come back.


At first, I thought I must be mistaken. Surely he wouldn't just walk away and never return, right? But the minutes stretched, and the pit in my stomach solidified into a weight. I felt glued to the chair – vulnerable again and bewildered.

*What just happened?* I wanted to chase Ryder and find out, but I also wanted to catch up to Rex and figure out what could have possibly been so devastating.

I chose Ryder. Rushing up the stairs to his bedroom, I took the steps two at a time, and my inner monologue became a racing swell of questions: What did Rex say? Why did you leave? You promised you would never leave me again.

I finally made it to the fifth floor. Javi was there – pushing an old-fashioned maid's cart down the hallway. We made eye contact as I cleared the landing, but his expression darkened, and he quickly looked away.

Javi's presence startled me. We hadn't run into each other lately – probably by his choice – but our moment of unguarded eye contact was enough to throw me off. He had said Ryder would hurt me; could he have possibly been right?

I didn't allow myself to think about that. Instead, I simply huffed and marched past him. Ryder's bedroom was the second-to-last one on this level, and its door sat ajar. I stormed inside and found Ryder calmly folding clothes by his bed.

"What was that about?"

He flinched at my entrance, and I could tell he didn't know what to say. "My old man thinks..." He cleared his throat and dropped a shirt on the bed. "He thinks it's best if I concentrate on my research right now."

"Your research?" I didn't understand, and then it hit me. My wall of fury crumbled, and insecurity stung so hard at my insides that my voice became a whisper. "Your research... instead of me."

"Right." He clenched his jaw. "Thinks my readings will go soft if I spend time with you."

"But Ryder, I'm walking Taft Point with you! I'm helping you, and we're proving the Essence theory wrong together."

"I know. That's what I said."

"And your readings... Well, look at what happened last night. How can he possibly say this isn't good for you?"

"I know. I told him that, too, but..." He tapped the clothes in his hand. "He says our readings will peak at first, but once you and I have... settled, our readings will plateau. And right now, at the end of our first phase of research, he doesn't think it's the best time for me to..."

"But there are couples all over the Valley! Hundreds of them, and *families*... And how can he possibly justify-?"

"Because I'm the show pony." Ryder's expression collapsed. He tossed his clothes aside. "I need to hold myself to a higher standard than everyone else here. I'm patient *number zero-zero-three*; my readings are more valuable than anyone else's."

"But Ryder..." Tears sprang to my eyes. "What are you saying? You're not actually listening to him about this, are you?"

"I can't say no to him. I can't possibly say no to him; look at everything he's done for me."

"Ryder, listen to me. You just finished telling me you didn't want to screw things up between us. You said you wanted to be honest with me. Were you lying then, or are you lying now?"

"I wasn't lying then." He stared at his bed.

"OK. So you were telling the truth then. And the truth is that you want to be with me?"

He nodded.

I reached for his hand. "Ryder, we're going prove the Essence theory wrong. We don't have to be apart to do that."

He nodded again, and his hand tightened around mine. A light seemed to form behind his eyes, and his voice became determined when he whispered, "We just won't let ourselves plateau."

"Right." Relief swelled inside me. "We just won't plateau. We'll show Rex this is the right decision, and our readings will be even stronger than they would have been otherwise."

"He won't even have to know. Until after, when we've done what we need to do."

Hesitation seized me, but I fought it and nodded. Ryder was right; Rex didn't need to know until we'd proved him wrong.

"We'll kick Taft Point's ass, and we'll do it together," he finished, pulling me to sit on the bed beside him. "Will you practice while I'm gone?"

"Every day." I fought the swell of discomfort that rose inside me at the thought of having to date him in secret, and I tried to muster a smile. "And I'll get Trey and Adrian to help me move the slackline to two trees that are farther apart."

"Great." He began rushing around the room and tossing things in his suitcase. "Taft Point is almost exactly one hundred feet from one side to the other. I think you're ready to stretch the line to fifty or sixty now at least."

His smile widened when he rushed back toward me. "Red, you're brilliant," he said, kissing my forehead. "We'll show my old man we know what we're doing, and we'll stay elevated in the process. It's the perfect plan, and you're the perfect girl for it. You with me?"

"I'm with you."

He wrapped his arms around me and kissed me with an intensity I hadn't felt from him before. He kissed me like he needed me, too.

# CHAPTER TWENTY-FIVE

I stayed true to my word. With Trey and Adrian's help, I practiced slacklining every single day that next week. By Friday – the day of Ryder, Jett and Cody's return from the city – I felt comfortable walking seventy-five feet from one tree to another.

I was so excited about my progress that I stayed at Church Bowl long after Trey and Adrian had gone back to the Ahwahnee to prepare for the new recruits' welcome feast. When Ryder, Cody and Jett sped past the Ahwahnee's entrance gate – this time in a sleek, black all-terrain vehicle – I jumped from the line and decided to chase after them.

The path to the Ahwahnee was shady, and it couldn't have been a more beautiful afternoon. The sun hung low in the western sky, and the air was warm and languid. The Ahwahnee kitchen smelled thickly of cooking bread, and lanterns already twinkled from the Meadow.

As I approached the truck, Cody waved from the driver's seat. Jett popped out from the back, and then Ryder extended his hand to steady the new recruit.

Who just happened to be a girl.

Who just happened to be gorgeous.

"So, this is the Ahwahnee," Ryder said. "Pretty sweet, huh?"

The girl had her back to me, but I could see she was tall and lean, with thick black hair and skin as tan as Javi's. Her profile revealed a button nose, high cheekbones and a beaming smile.

"Absolutely gorgeous," she said. Her accent was lilting – South American, maybe? – and her drab wool dress didn't hang on her body the way mine had. Its boxy shape only seemed to accentuate her curves.

"Thought you'd like it." Ryder made eye contact with me across the parking lot and winked, and then he swooped his arm around the girl's lower back and began leading her forward. "So, more than two thirds of the Community lives in the Ahwahnee; the rest live in Tuolumne Meadows. If you want a room in the hotel, all you gotta do is be awesome. The Founders will notice."

Jett began walking on the girl's other side. "The Founders are the Community's two leaders – Ryder's father, Rex, and another former Centrist, Daniel Lynch…"

Jett's words dissipated as the group approached the Ahwahnee's entrance, but I found myself glued in place. Everything – from Ryder's casual flirtation to Jett's enthusiasm – was a mirror image of my first day in Yosemite.

I don't know why this unsettled me so much. It only made sense they would give similar orientations to new recruits. It just bothered me to realize that even the moments I'd thought were spontaneous may have been scripted after all.

How far did the script extend? Did Jett usher me to the Balcony that first morning because she liked me, or did she simply do it because it was her job?

What about meals? Was it the recruiting team's job to sit with new kids until they felt comfortable enough to find friends?

Would Jett have been so excited to see me that night at moonbows if I hadn't just arrived in the Valley?

What about Ryder? I swallowed and tried to push the question aside. Ryder and I were fine; we were more than fine, actually. He'd said he was tired of being the flirtatious one; he'd said he wanted to be honest for once in his life. But... What if he said that to everyone?

I swallowed. It wasn't possible. Ryder had acted out of character; he'd even gotten in trouble for it. There's no way you can make that up, right?

The clanging of the Ahwahnee Meadow bell signaled the start of the welcome feast. It also jolted me from my inner turmoil.

*I guess there's only one way to find out.*

The new recruit's name was Maria, and her mother had apparently moved from Costa Rica to join the Movement when she was eight. She was almost eighteen now, and she was completely opposed to the prospect of staying neutral forever – especially since her favorite memories of home involved festivals and dancing and colors.

She giggled more than anyone I'd ever met. As I sat watching her during dinner, I wondered how in the world she'd lasted in the Movement as long as she had.

"Easiest snag ever," Jett whispered, cutting squash from her place beside me. "We found her strolling along Kezar Drive singing to herself, and she was even doing a little dance as she walked. She's lucky we saw her before a meditation master did."

I felt strange around Jett today – disillusioned, I think, both by her recruitment script and by her history with Ryder. Why hadn't she told me?

Ryder sat beside Maria at the head table, and he seemed to be in fine form tonight, touching Maria's wrist as she buttered her bread and glancing sideways to laugh or point whenever she asked a question.

He was mesmerizing up there – confident, relaxed and charming – and I could certainly see why Maria's cheeks looked so flushed. She was captivated by him, just like me and every other girl in the Valley.

The pit in my stomach made anything other than picking at my food impossible. Although Ryder looked my way and smiled a few times, he certainly didn't make an effort to come over and talk to me. Even when dinner concluded and the music and festivities began, he simply slipped into the crowd with his hand on the small of Maria's back.

Kadence and Javi noticed. I caught them staring at me a few minutes into the celebration, and I felt a pang in my chest at the sight of them. Did they actually *pity* me?

I didn't need their pity, just like I didn't need to stand there and wait for Ryder to come find me. It was late, and I was tired, and I didn't need to stay there, anyway.

I turned and tramped back to my tent cabin.

When someone began knocking on my door a couple hours later, I assumed it must be Kadence or Javi. I unfurled myself from my blankets and stomped toward the door – intent on telling them I didn't need their pity, now or ever – but it wasn't Kadence or Javi. It was Ryder, and he rushed forward and buried me in his arms with a ferocity that was nearly crushing. "I missed you so much, babe," he whispered. "How've you been? How's training?" His light eyes were intense, and his presence nearly filled the tent cabin. "Been thinking about you all week. Have you made it to fifty feet yet?"

It was as if he had never left, and the transformation was so startling, it took a minute for me to process it. When I finally did, I pulled myself from his grip. "That's it?"

His face fell. "What do you mean, 'that's it'?"

"You ignore me the entire night and spend all your time flirting with the new girl, and all you have to say is, 'Have you made it to fifty feet yet?'"

"Red." Ryder's eyebrows furrowed. "You know all that was bullshit, right? Just part of the act?"

"I don't know." I crossed my arms. "I'm not sure what's an act and what's not anymore."

"What are you talking about?" He reached for my hands. "Everything was fine between us when I left; what changed while I was gone?"

"Nothing changed, Ryder. It's just… it's really hard to see you flirt with another girl. You must understand that."

"I do. It's hard for me, too. I don't give a shit about Maria; I just have to act like I do until she gets comfortable here."

"But where does it end? Do you have to spend all your time with her? Hold hands with her? Kiss her on the Housekeeping Camp bridge?"

"Red, no." He squeezed my hands. "I don't have to do any of those things with her. I just have to orient her to the Valley, and then I'm free of her. My old man will be satisfied as long as *someone* sweeps her up; maybe Trey or Adrian would like to…"

"Wait, wait, wait." I pulled my arms free. "It's part of your job description to play matchmaker, too? Was that your responsibility with me?"

"No, of course not. And it isn't my responsibility with Maria, either. I just think an easy way to get rid of her would be to introduce her to my friends." He met my eyes. "Red, I want to be with *you*. I don't want to be with Maria or anyone else, OK? How many different ways do I have to say this?"

My anger loosened slightly. "You're sure that was bullshit?"

"Yes." His answer was firm. "It was most definitely bullshit. And it will continue to be bullshit. You're the one I want, Red. You're the one I'm going to conquer Taft Point with. As soon as we've proved ourselves, we can let the whole world know. How does that sound?"

"It sounds good." My heart swelled as he tightened his arms around me. He kissed my forehead again, and then he tilted my chin upward until our lips met. I felt my insides catch on fire, and then my arms wrapped around him, too.

The woodsmoke from the stove, the salty scent of his skin, and the tinge of wind and sweat blurred together as we held each other in the darkness. And then later, when he asked if he could stay the night, I sank into the army cot and let him hold me in his arms.

I didn't know much, but I did know one thing. I didn't have anything to worry about as long as Ryder was by my side.

# CHAPTER TWENTY-SIX

The next morning at breakfast, I had to remind myself Ryder's and my night together wasn't a dream. Ryder had kissed my cheek and slipped out sometime around sunrise. Now I sat across from him as he laughed and showed Maria how to peel her hard-boiled eggs.

She had slept well. She proudly told everyone she'd happily pulled off her scratchy wool dress and tossed it in the nearest garbage bin. "I always hated those cheap bras and panties," she said, adjusting her new blouse. "You ladies know what I'm talking about?"

"You ladies" was, predictably, Jett and me. As Jett smiled and agreed they'd always bunched, I could tell from Cody, Trey and Adrian's dropped jaws that they were most likely picturing Maria without them.

Ryder was a different story. He gave me a fleeting eye roll when she detailed the way her new bra supported her breasts so much better, and he made a big show of yawning when Maria fumbled with her blouse ties, and giggled that she would have to work on keeping them secured.

But as soon as she stood to throw her garbage away, he jumped to his feet and snatched her tray from her hands. "For you, milady," he said, striding to the compost bin with a smile. "And do you want some company while you get your wristband fitted?"

I tried to tell myself I didn't care, and I didn't. Almost.

It wasn't until later – a few days later, really – that I began to regress into my own doubts. It was Thursday afternoon, and I was busy slacklining at Church Bowl with Trey and Adrian. When I heard the approaching footsteps, I assumed it must be Jett or Cody.

But it wasn't. It was Ryder, and he was strolling toward us with Maria by his side. She was laughing at something he was saying, and her hand was tucked neatly beneath his bicep.

I was so shocked to see her that I nearly lost my balance, but I forced myself to turn and stare straight ahead at the slackline. The webbing buckled beneath my feet, but I managed to take two more steps before she cried, "Autumn, you are *such* a badass!"

That was it. Concentration ruined, I sidestepped and jumped nimbly to the ground.

"You shouldn't have jumped off just because of me." Maria squeezed Ryder's arm and then hurried toward me. "That was *fantastic*; what are you doing, anyway? Tightrope-walking?"

I locked eyes with Ryder over her shoulder. Her very presence here, in this place that meant so much to us, felt like a betrayal. Never mind the fact that he allowed her to entwine her arm with his.

"Why don't you tell her what I'm doing, Ryder?" I asked, teeth clenched.

Ryder gave me a plaintive face and inclined his head toward Trey and Adrian – who sat surprised with their hands suspended over their drums. I'm here with her for them, his eyes seemed to say, but I didn't care.

Maria was at Church Bowl, and she didn't look the slightest bit interested in Trey or Adrian. She looked fully and squarely interested in *him*.

When I didn't answer, Ryder followed her and said, "She's slacklining, Ria. Kinda like tightrope-walking, but way harder. Most girls can't do it, but Red's tougher than most girls. One of the only girls I know who can walk seventy-five feet."

He smiled as he said this, but his compliment didn't calm me. Instead, I found myself clinging to one word: Ria. Apparently, Maria had a nickname now.

"Can I try?"

Maria seemed cocky, overly confident, so I stepped aside and motioned to the slackline. "Be my guest."

She pulled off her shoes, and her dark hair cascaded forward to cover her shoulders. Her blouse slipped a bit, and the sight of her tan breasts peeking through the top of her bra made my jaw clench even more than before.

"Don't worry; it's really easy," I said. I knew I was being horrible, but I couldn't help it. "All you have to do is put one foot forward and pull yourself to a standing position. Take a second to catch your breath, and then start walking."

I popped onto the line and took several quick steps to demonstrate. "See? Easy."

Maria nodded. She gathered her hair into a high bun and then placed her foot on the slackline. "Like this?"

"Yes. Exactly. And now straighten your leg."

I tried to hide my smirk when her knee collapsed beneath her, but I couldn't help my chuckle when the webbing jerked and bucked until she gave up.

I didn't feel bad until a few minutes later when she laughed and slipped back into her shoes. "You *are* hardcore, Autumn. That was actually really hard!"

She spent the rest of the afternoon cheering and clapping as Trey, Adrian, Ryder and I took turns walking. Her enthusiasm was so unbridled that I couldn't help but feel guilty for disliking her.

It wasn't even Maria I disliked, I realized with a sigh sometime around sunset. Trey and Adrian were busy playing their drums, and Ryder was balancing on one foot, just shy of the slackline's turn-around point.

Maria was looking pensive and rubbing the shiny surface of her Centrist pendant. "I was old enough to know better, you know? When my mom joined the Movement? But she believed in it so strongly that I let myself believe in it, too. You know how hard that is? When you just want to believe in something?"

I nodded. It had taken me weeks to finally take my pendant off, but it still sat on a ledge in my tent cabin. Its mantra seemed hollow now, but I couldn't bear to part with it. It was one of my only tokens from home.

As I studied her identical pendant, I realized the two of us weren't very different after all. Even though she was loud and overly flirtatious, she had no way of knowing she was stepping on my toes with Ryder.

She was just trying to fit in here, and none of this was her fault, anyway. It was Rex's fault for forbidding Ryder and me from dating, and it was about time I started remembering that.

"He's hot, isn't he?"

Her question jolted me from her pendant. Her eyes were far away now, and I could see from her dreamy, half-smile that she was focused on the slackline. Ryder was walking shirtless, and the muscles in his back flexed as he braced himself and swung into another turn.

"What?"

Maria giggled and twined a strand of hair around her finger. "I mean, I broke Centrist rules with guys before I got here, you know? But never with a guy that hot, and never without being nervous I'd get caught." She turned and beamed at me. "So, what's his deal, anyway? Is he available? He seems interested; do you think we'd make a good match?"

In an instant, my dislike was back. "No," I said, springing to my feet. "Sorry, Ria, I just don't see it."

"Why not?" Her voice was incredulous – so shocked by my audacity that she didn't even sound mad.

"I just... don't." I shrugged and glanced over my shoulder. "Ryder likes athletic girls; you just don't seem to fit his mold."

"But *I'm* athletic."

Her protest faded away as I approached the slackline. Ryder jumped from the webbing and whispered, "Heard that, Red. Not funny."

"I'm not trying to be funny." I climbed onto the slackline and took a moment to gain my balance. "I'm just telling her the truth. You two would be horrible together, because you're already dating me."

"I am at that." He nodded appreciatively as I began striding from one side of the webbing to the other. "And I'm quickly realizing it's gonna be hard to keep up with you."

That's how I found myself wedged in the crack between two cliffs the next day. It was early afternoon, and the spot was a

Church Bowl climbing route called the Parkay Squeeze. The name was apparently a word play on a twentieth-century brand of margarine, and my legs certainly felt liquid as I hovered in midair and clung, spiderlike, to the cracks.

The rock climbing harness dug into the skin of my thighs, and sweat poured into my eyes as I struggled to keep from feeling dizzy. All I apparently had to do was make my way through this cavelike crack and drop down on the other side. But no matter how hard I tried to concentrate on the end goal, I couldn't get past the idea that I may get crushed or fall to my death at any moment.

On a normal day, there's no way I would have ever even attempted this. But when Maria showed up at the slackline this morning, eyes focused and hair secured, I knew I had to step up my game.

When Trey suggested we take a break and try rock climbing for a while, how could I say no? Especially when Maria grinned and slipped on a pair of climbing shoes. Ryder insisted I didn't have to climb if I didn't want to, but I wanted to. Or at least I wanted to *have* climbed, so I pulled on another pair and approached the cliff myself.

Trey took a few moments to explain our gear and the mechanics of climbing, and he emphasized that it's your legs that give you the most lift, not your arms. I was starting to feel smug about my superior leg strength, but then Maria took to the wall, and she looked nothing short of a dark-haired jungle cat.

She was so long and lean that she reached handholds and toeholds I would have had to jump for. She was also stronger than I'd first imagined, and the muscles in her shoulders flexed as she braced herself and ascended the first climb with ease.

Then it was my turn, and I was sweating and cursing as I attempted to duplicate her movements. But she had a good three inches on me, and this made all the difference. Although I finally made it up the wall, I certainly didn't do it with the grace or poise she'd shown.

She noticed. She didn't say anything, but the little smirk at the corner of her lips was all the motivation I needed. When Trey suggested we step it up and try a slightly harder route, I knew I had to do better.

In my defense, I had no idea the Parkay Squeeze was classified as a "slightly harder" route. And again, Maria made it look so easy that I had no choice but to follow in her footsteps.

So here I was, wedged in the crack between two cliffs. As I struggled to keep my balance, I questioned why I'd ever let any of them talk me into taking my feet off the ground in the first place.

It wasn't even the height that scared me the most. It was the claustrophobia – the feeling of being crushed as the cold cliff walls closed in around me. My wobbly legs and the impossible toeholds didn't help, and my borrowed climbing shoes were at least two sizes too big.

When I finally emerged on the other side of the crack, I was a sweaty, breathless mess. My muscles felt like they were on fire, and the tiny scrapes that marred my skin burned with my sweat. I crumpled to the ground and struggled to catch my breath, and I questioned why I'd even bothered to attempt such a stupid, pointless feat. It wasn't like it changed anything or made any difference, anyway.

But then Ryder was there beside me, and he was pulling me into a wordless, secret kiss. That moment of togetherness, of being hidden by rocks and dappled with sunshine... That feeling made everything worth it.

# CHAPTER TWENTY-SEVEN

So that's how it began. The running around, I mean. Although Ryder and I weren't really *running around*, because that would imply we were doing something wrong. And we weren't. We were simply disregarding Rex's rules, and we had every intention of telling him when the time was right.

As for Maria... Well, here's the thing. I should have felt sorry for Maria – and I kind of actually did – but mostly, I just resented the fact that she had come here and put us in this position in the first place. We were perfectly happy without her. And even though Rex's decision hadn't been based on Maria's arrival, it coincided just closely enough that I began to lump the two together.

I know what Ryder and I were doing was secretive, but truthfully, I didn't even feel bad about it. Instead, I kind of enjoyed the secret, private knowledge that no matter what Maria did – no matter how beautiful or flirtatious she was, or how hard she tried to get Ryder to notice her – it would still be *my* hand he held on late-night meadow walks. It would be *my* lips he kissed by cover of moonlight.

Giving Maria a hard time actually became one of my favorite pastimes. I never said anything without being provoked, and I never said anything she could have pinned on me, but I made sure to let her know in an offhanded sort of way that she wasn't as amazing as she thought she was.

In my defense, she made it incredibly easy. After my comments at Church Bowl, she made a concerted effort to appear more athletic any time she was around Ryder. She also began wearing fewer and fewer clothes.

Hems became hitched, and she started taking in her blouses until they were nearly skintight. She looked great – she really did – but I would have never given her the satisfaction of hearing that. Instead, I simply rolled my eyes any time she approached, and I pushed myself even harder on the slackline.

Ryder noticed. Although he made it very clear that he didn't appreciate the unfriendly way I was treating her, he also marveled at my intense focus on the line.

By Thursday of the next week, I was easily crossing one hundred feet without falling. I didn't even lose my focus when Trey and Adrian moved our route to the base of Yosemite Falls. The churning, dark water below me didn't scare me any more than the soft grass of Church Bowl had.

Before we knew it, it was the beginning of July. The realization that Rex's first wave of research would be completed in less than a month sent a jolt of energy coursing through the Community. Everyone began buzzing, and everyone seemed on edge – electrified, maybe, by the thought that we would soon begin shifting focus.

Rex and Daniel assured everyone that the Community would continue to function as normal. "We are a family," he insisted during one of his Ahwahnee back-porch rallies. "Many of you will remain in Yosemite Valley after August, caring for our land and crops like always. The rest of you – primarily those who are no longer minors – may be drawn upon to help us with our endeavors in San Francisco."

Daniel added, "Once we have finished compiling our study's initial findings, we will call upon many of you to become prophets. You will be asked to return to the city, and you will be asked to dismantle the Centrist Movement's lies. But fear not, for although you will be faced with criticism, contention and even threats against your safety, you will carry something with you that is far stronger than anything Cedar can conceive. You will carry the truth."

Rex and Daniel's speech left me dizzy and elated – as always – but the thought that I might be asked to return to my family sent my mind into overdrive. I was obviously still a minor, so I probably wouldn't be in the first wave. But maybe after that... If I *were* called to become a prophet, what would it be like?

I had only been gone for a couple of months, but I had experienced so many changes – both internally and externally – that I felt like the Movement had been seven lifetimes ago. The realization that so little time had actually passed was staggering.

Was it really only mid-May when Jett and I charged off the train platform, traveling coats billowing behind us?

The granite walls of the Valley, the gushing water of Yosemite and Vernal Falls, and the carved faces of Half Dome and Church Bowl... These icons colored my reality now, and the shining metal high-rises and Centrist meditation robes seemed faded a little. They had swirled away somewhere to a place in my subconscious where it was easy to imagine they had ceased to exist. They were darkened slightly, and empty, like the broken-down carousels and crumbling buildings of Golden Gate Park.

I thought of Aunt Marie and my mother. I missed them – of course I missed them – but ever since I had settled into my routine here, I had barely thought of them. Gone were the nights where I rubbed my Centrist pendant and prayed that my mother would forgive me; gone were the mornings I glanced sideways out of my cot and expected to see Marie coming inside to greet me.

Marie would understand, I had told myself all those early mornings when I'd first arrived. She had practically told me to leave the Movement herself.

But she had also told me nothing mattered to her more than my mother and me, so I wondered if maybe she *did* resent my leaving. She understood I came here for Brady, right? Had she told my mother that?

Brady. The thought of my little brother sent crippling pain through me. I was here for Brady – was supposed to be, anyway – but I realized with a flash that I hadn't even thought of him as often lately.

I touched the pocket where I always kept his stuffed lion. This had to change. This was the month I was going to do everything possible to become the person I was supposed to be.

I would push myself as hard as possible, and I would be the first to volunteer to go home when Rex asked. When I got there, I would show my family Rex's findings, and they would understand I left because I wanted to prove they didn't need to live their lives in fear. No one did.

But… then what?

I realized the end of the Essence theory wasn't exactly straightforward. And even though Rex and Daniel assured us we would be armed with the truth when we returned to the city, the meditation masters would likely be angry. And Cedar might not appreciate our message one bit.

I was so worked up that I wasn't even asleep when someone rapped on my tent sometime around midnight. It was Ryder, but his face didn't have the sleepy, contented expression it usually did when he came for a late-night visit. Instead, he seemed wide awake, and his voice was energized when he said, "Get up, Red. We're going on an adventure."

"We are?"

"Yep. The boys are getting ready, and it's gonna be awesome. We're gonna zipline through the tunnel in the pitch black. No one's ever done it at night, so it's gonna be epic."

"Zipline through the tunnel? What tunnel? What are you talking about?"

"The Wawona Tunnel. A relic from the park's heyday. Just outside the Valley, on a broken-down road that used to lead to the giant sequoia trees. Almost a mile long, and half collapsed from the Great Quake. One end got lifted when the ground shifted, a sweet descent from one side to the other."

"What are we going to do in it?"

"The boys and I rigged up a zipline string through it last summer, but we've never done it in the dark before. Are you in?"

"I don't know. What's a zipline?"

He laughed. "A long line with a harness hung from it. You strap in, hold onto the handlebars and take off. Feels like flying, only faster."

I thought of the black claustrophobia I was sure I'd feel inside a tunnel, but Ryder cocked his head and said, "You know I'll always catch you, right?"

I nodded. And then we were off.

Cody, Jett, Adrian and I assembled near the Ahwahnee's back porch as Ryder paced, frantic and excited as usual. I was about to celebrate Maria's absence when she and Trey appeared from the darkness behind us.

"About time," Ryder said. "About to die of old age out here."

My heart swelled at the sight of Maria with Trey. They weren't holding hands or acting particularly romantic, but they were together, and that was definitely a good sign.

"So here's the deal," Ryder said, falling into step in front of us. "We need to stop by Camp Four first. My old man doesn't get pissed about much, but he would definitely get pissed about this, so you guys better be quiet once we get there." He glanced over his shoulder. "The gas shipment just arrived, so I think we should help ourselves to some."

My heart dropped as Trey whistled. "Jackpot," he said.

"You want to steal gas from Camp Four? But I thought no one was allowed inside." The voice was Maria's. As much as I hated to admit it, I was glad she'd asked.

"Most people aren't." He jangled a key. "But I'm not 'most people'. And my old man gave me a spare."

Maria swallowed. "But... You really want to sneak in and steal gas?"

"Yeah." He smiled. "A little. Just enough to get to the tunnel and back before sunrise."

"But isn't gas rationed? Won't Rex get pissed?"

"Not if we're sneaky about it," He lit a cigarette and winked. "You're not scared, are you, Ria?"

Her face colored. "Of course not."

I took the opportunity to speak up. "Sounds like a great plan, Ryder. I'm in."

"Knew I could count on you, Red." Ryder slipped an arm around my shoulder, and I risked a sideways glance at Maria. She was smoldering.

"I didn't say I wasn't in," she insisted, rushing forward to walk on his other side. "I was just asking. You know, I stole a car back in the city once. Made it all the way to Sausalito before Cedar's goons found me."

"Great. Maybe we can rely on your stealth at Camp Four, then."

I felt my eyebrows draw together, but I stopped my frown before Maria could notice. "Sounds good," I said. "Ria, you can make sure the coast is clear while Ryder and I get the gas."

"I can get the gas," she said. "I'd love to. Sounds fun, actually."

Ryder stopped us before we could get carried away. "Two beautiful girls fighting to spend time with me? Doesn't get much better than that, does it?" He squeezed my shoulder, and the pressure was just shy of uncomfortable. "Thank you, ladies; I know you're up for the challenge. But I actually think I'll take Trey and Adrian in with me, and Cody can stand watch around the wall's perimeter. You ladies shouldn't dirty up your hands."

I shrugged and played nonchalant, but I couldn't stop my smirk when I noticed Maria was still watching me. I hadn't won, but she certainly hadn't, either.

"You don't have to be such an asshole all the time."

The voice was Jett's. We were sitting side by side outside the high stone walls of Camp Four. I was flicking pine needles, and Maria was sitting twenty feet or so from us – all alone except for the bread she was tentatively eating while we waited for the boys' return.

"What are you talking about?"

Things between Jett and me had been tense ever since she'd returned from the city. Although we had never mentioned it, our shared history with Ryder now weighed down the air around us. It was thick and oppressive as smoke, and it constricted my lungs more and more the harder I tried to ignore it.

"Maria. You don't always have to be such an asshole to her. She's actually pretty nice if you'd just give her a chance."

"She's not." I flicked another pine needle. "She's *not* nice, and I don't want to give her a chance. I already know I don't like her."

"She can't help how she feels about Ryder, you know. She doesn't even know you guys are dating."

"I know that."

"So why don't you just tell her and get it over with? We all know; what's the difference if one more person finds out?"

"I…" The truth is, I had never considered the question. I had just taken Ryder's words at face value. "Ryder doesn't want Rex to know, OK? He says it will ruin everything."

"You really think Maria's gonna tattle to Rex?"

I frowned. Instead of answering her question, I posed another. "Why didn't you ever tell me you and Ryder dated? Don't you think that's something I should have known when I got here?"

Jett's eyes widened. She regarded me for a moment, and then she shrugged. "What's to tell? Ryder treated me like shit and then moved on and forgot about me. Didn't seem like a good conversation starter."

"Yeah, but… You saw me with him. You knew I liked him, and you probably thought he'd hurt me, too. Why didn't you warn me?"

"Autumn, I don't pretend to know what's going on in other people's lives. You seemed happy with Ryder, and he seemed like maybe he'd changed, too. Don't you think people deserve second chances?"

"Yeah, but do you feel that way now?"

"What?"

"Do you feel that way now? About Ryder? Do you feel like he's changed, or do you think this whole sneaking-around thing is just another of his tricks?"

Jett regarded me again, and the look of hopelessness that clouded her expression told me everything I needed to know. "You don't," I finished. "You don't think he's changed, and you think I'm an idiot for believing he has."

Her expression softened. "That's not what I'm saying, Autumn. I just wish he wouldn't make you feel like the 'other woman' all the time. If he likes you, he should act like it. He shouldn't make you watch him flirt with Maria, and he certainly shouldn't make you sneak around and meet him in the middle of the night."

She sighed. "And he should stand up to that asshole father of his. I don't know how you feel about Rex, Autumn, but I don't trust him. And I don't think he always has Ryder's best interests at heart. Or any of our best interests, really."

"What?"

She sighed. "I don't believe in Essence drain anymore. Haven't for a long time. But I *do* believe in responsible choices. And being here for two years has taught me that just because you *can* do something doesn't mean you should." She began tracing lines in the dirt with her finger. "Look at what happened to Shayla. I have no doubt her Essence was perfectly intact when she took that fall last month, but are you really surprised she fell? That's what happens when you decide to walk over a dangerous creek at night."

I swallowed. "But Shayla's… a legend."

Jett frowned. "You know what? Maybe you aren't ready to hear this yet. That's fine – it really is – but file it away somewhere, OK? In case you ever need it."

She glanced at Maria and then pulled herself to her feet. "I'm going to see if Ria wants some company." She started to leave, and then she added, "Autumn, truly, if I can give you one piece of advice: please don't lose yourself in all this. It's not worth it."

I wanted to brush her off, but I couldn't. Her words reminded me of *my* words – of those fervent nights at the very beginning when I was so terrified I was going to lose myself that I couldn't think about anything else. Had I really changed that much? Was I now the person *someone else* scolded for being too elevated?

I wanted to chase after her and demand an apology, but more than that, I wanted Ryder to reassure me that she was mistaken. I hadn't really lost myself in all this, had I?

I brushed the dirt off my pants and strode into Camp Four to find him.

# CHAPTER TWENTY-EIGHT

The metal door that led through the wall reminded me of a bomb shelter. It was thick and industrial, so heavy I had trouble moving it. As I stepped through, I surveyed it skeptically.

*Why in the world does it need to be reinforced so much?* I knew Rex and Daniel kept supplies in here – and I knew people sometimes got desperate after earthquakes – but without Ryder's key, it would have taken an army to get inside.

Past the doorway, Camp Four opened as a scattering of low buildings in the moonlight. They were ringed by the wall and arranged in a concentric circle, and each was as dark and nondescript as the next.

Except one. Just before the oil tank – the one that glinted charcoal-black in the distance – a wider, more open building gleamed with electric light. It was two stories tall and at least ten windows wide. Solar panels were slanted at an angle on its roof, and window shades obscured all but residual light from inside.

I glanced around for Ryder, but I couldn't see anyone in the blackness. I could barely even see my hand through the shadows of the pine canopy overhead, so I took a tentative step toward the light.

I would like to say I was searching for Ryder, but I don't think I was. I was just so overcome by the building – its light and size and presence – that I felt compelled to get a closer look. Like a moth to a flame, as they say.

I tiptoed across the grass and extended my hand toward the closed metal door.

And then I heard it.

A scream. A high-pitched wail from inside – so broken and full of anguish that it stopped me in my tracks. I felt the hairs on my arm prickling, and it took everything in me not to turn and run that very instant.

But that sounded like a human scream. And I didn't know much, but I knew humans weren't supposed to be screaming in here. So I couldn't help but finish climbing the front steps, and I couldn't help but reach for the doorknob.

But then the leaves crunched behind me, and Ryder said, "Red, what are you doing in here?"

"I heard a scream." I whirled in the darkness.

He stood behind me, flanked by Trey and Adrian, and he held a large, red gas can in his hand. "A scream?"

"Yeah. Inside." I jiggled the locked doorknob. "Ryder, what's in this building?"

He tried the door himself. "It's where my old man stores bio-meds and research equipment. Those lights – those are grow lights. But... There's no one in there, Red. Are you sure it wasn't an owl?"

"Or a mountain lion?" Adrian offered. "They scream sometimes; always scares the shit out of me."

I shook my head. "No, it came from inside. I'm sure of it."

Ryder shrugged. "Maybe it was an echo. From the walls? Noise does funny things in here; you can never tell exactly where sounds are coming from." He extended his hand. "Come on, Red, let's get out of here. If we don't get on the road soon, we'll miss our window."

Try as I might, I couldn't shake the memory of that scream. It was so haunted and piercing that it seemed stuck inside my ears. As I sat crammed in the backseat of a Jeep with Ryder at the wheel, it played on a loop the entire way to the Wawona Tunnel.

Trees clustered over our heads, and the moonlight that filtered through the branches left the road bathed in spooky blue light. Trey produced a flask of moonshine at some point, and we passed it around as we drove, relying on its burn to ward off the chill of the wind. Because that was the thing about Yosemite. No matter how hot the sun shone during the day, an icy chill pervaded the second it dipped below the horizon.

It took almost an hour to make it from the Valley to the Wawona Tunnel. When we finally reached the cliffside overlook, the remains of what must have once been a parking lot were evident. Cracks now laced across the concrete.

A deteriorated rock wall lined the edge of the clearing, and this is where Ryder parked the Jeep. "Wish you could see the view from here, Red and Ria," he said. "Best vantage spot in this entire place."

I followed his line of sight, but I could barely make out anything past the shrubs that dotted the hillside in front of us. "What are we looking at?"

"Entrance to the Valley." He popped to a standing position and rested his elbows on the Jeep's windshield. "Just like you saw the first day you got here. Only now we're farther away, and we can see the cliffs all the way to the top. Can even catch a glimpse of Half Dome behind them. Our world, from a distance."

He shook his head and jumped from the Jeep. "But it's black as shit out, so I guess we should get going."

Jett crawled from Cody's lap in the front seat, while Trey, Adrian, Maria and I took a minute to squeeze out of the backseat. The movement sent the moonshine swimming in my head, but I shook it off and followed the group away from the viewpoint.

Ryder led us up the hill to the yawning mouth of a wide, black tunnel. It was huge, and he said it had once held two lanes of traffic. "Lots of fender benders here," he explained, taking a step into the darkness. "People emerged from the tunnel to be hit with that view, and they slammed on their brakes and became a hazard to everyone behind them. If these walls could talk, you know?"

Maria cleared her throat. "So, what's the deal?" she asked. "There's a zipline on the other side?"

"Yeah, we're at the low side now, so we'll have to hike through and then slide back down to this point. Kind of a pain, but at least you get the work out of the way before the payoff."

He fished a flashlight from his pocket. Shining it toward the roof of the tunnel, he pointed to the rope suspended from the ceiling. "Here's our line, boys," he said. "Think it made it through the winter all right."

The rope was secured by a pulley system attached to a large, metal pipe and a tangled mess of harnessing, and a handlebar of some sort dangled from one end of the rope. Adrian reached for a thinner guide rope and gave the harness a good tug. The handlebar bounced and dropped to our eye level.

"Think everything's still here," Ryder said, reaching for the straps. "Pretty good condition, too. Wanna give it another tug to make sure it's still secure?"

Adrian pulled on the thinner rope again, and the entire contraption bounced and wobbled.

"Looks good to me," Cody said, reaching for another flashlight. "Wanna start the walk-through?"

The boys lit their torches, and the seven of us started into the tunnel. "Almost a mile's walk," Ryder warned, kicking aside a branch and motioning for us to follow. "So if you're scared of the dark, you better stay close."

I felt so distracted by my conversation with Jett, the scream and the moonshine swimming in my brain that it took me a minute to start walking. During that pause, Jett grabbed my arm and said, "Are you mad at me?"

"Yes." My answer was automatic. "I am. Kinda."

She frowned. "Why? Did I honestly say anything you weren't already thinking yourself?"

"I didn't realize you were so anti-Rex and -Ryder. Or so anti-me."

"Autumn." Her face fell. "I'm not anti-Rex and -Ryder. And I'm certainly not anti-you. You just asked me how I felt, so I told you."

"I know." I rushed into an answer I didn't even mean: "I guess I probably shouldn't have asked you, then."

The hurt that flashed in her eyes was quickly hidden behind a wall of irritation. "Yeah, guess you shouldn't have," she said, jutting her chin forward. "Lesson learned, huh?"

# CHAPTER TWENTY-NINE

The tunnel was eerily still – except for the creak of the harness as Adrian dragged it by the guide rope along the ceiling. Everything echoed, so even this small noise seemed magnified. It bounced off the walls and mixed with the shuffling of rocks and pebbles beneath our feet, and it lent me to reimagining that scream.

Had it really only been an owl or a mountain lion? I had never heard either scream before, so I didn't know if I'd really recognize the difference. And Ryder was right; the sounds in Camp Four echoed nearly as much as the sounds in this tunnel. My thoughts began to loosen around the idea that I'd actually heard a person, and soon I became preoccupied with the fact that I was inside a tunnel right now.

It is difficult to describe the crushing, claustrophobic weight I began to feel closing in around me. Where the blackness began, just on the edge of my skin, I began to sense the creep of a presence, like someone was standing right beside me, leering at me.

Only the presence didn't stop at my sides. It began to stretch over my head and around my back. I felt like I was being held in the giant hand of a monster, like I could be crushed or smothered at any moment.

I also began to feel eyes on me – like a thousand scaly creatures waited at the edge of our pathway. Was that really breathing on the back of my neck? Were they slowly surrounding us, waiting to close in when they thought we weren't looking?

I clung like a drowning man to the wavering light of the flashlights in front of me. Their reassuring beams shattered the darkness and reminded me that this tunnel had once been wide enough to hold two lanes of traffic.

It was a big tunnel, really. Huge. With a wide, curved ceiling and smooth, creature-free walls. But maybe the monsters were just sensitive to the light. Maybe they evaporated or scurried away when the beams came blasting toward them.

I initially walked in the back of the line, but I quickly made my way past Cody and Jett. There, in the middle of the group, the fear of the unknown wasn't quite as strong. Even if a monster showed up, I was sure it would go for Cody and Jett before it went for me.

A weird tension now simmered in the air between us. This made me feel a little better about my racing inner monologue – which told me I'd surely have enough time to run for the tunnel's exit if they were attacked first.

I could pull Maria down as I passed, and that would buy me some time, too. And if a monster really did appear, I was pretty sure Ryder would stop to wait for me. Maybe he'd even pull me with him. His legs were definitely stronger than mine, and he knew this place better than anyone.

Trey and Adrian knew it, too, so I made a concerted effort to make sure I was within arm's distance of both of them. They may not be quite as excited to pull me to freedom, but they couldn't say much if I was already attached to them.

As for the claustrophobia... I tried not to think about my shortness of breath, about what might happen if the ceiling collapsed in on us. If I were trapped beneath a pile of rocks, with a broken leg or maybe my shoulder pinned to the ground beneath me... Would I have enough strength to pull myself free? Or would I be able to cut my own arm off, like some of those crazy survivalists I'd heard about in Centrist classes?

They had all died early, I had been told. All those people who had cheated disaster. Brushes with death were enough to expend an entire lifetime's worth of Essence at once, so it wasn't uncommon for those people to drop dead a few weeks or months after wresting themselves free of tragedy.

But that was a Centrist story. And Centrist stories were mostly bullshit, so I wondered if maybe I'd survive if it happened to me. The only thing I couldn't survive would be the slow crush of oxygen as the rocks expelled the air from my lungs.

But I was thinking crazy things now. And I was wavering a little, waving my arms at my sides to make sure I still could. But then the night sky appeared – as a little blue dot on the far side of the tunnel – and it grew bigger and bigger the closer we walked.

I felt spellbound again, and I couldn't take my eyes off that glowing midnight orb as we trudged through the rocks and boulders. It was just in front of us, so big it nearly filled the tunnel, and then it surrounded us. We were free.

I inhaled enough night air to fill up my entire body. I would have collapsed to the pavement in relief, but Maria was beside me. She was catching her breath and talking about how she'd always wanted to go cave diving.

"Can you imagine?" she was saying. "A tunnel like that, but underwater? I once read about cave divers in a book... Can you imagine how incredible that must feel?"

I wanted to punch her, and I suddenly didn't feel bad about my secret plan to feed her to the tunnel's monsters. If I were forced to, 1 certainly would. Maybe I would even if I weren't forced to.

After a moment, the hammering in my heart settled. I was nearly free of my fear, and no one would ever have to know how heavily I'd felt it.

"Hey, Red, you got my lighter?"

The voice was Ryder's. He was watching me pointedly, and an unlit cigarette dangled from his lips.

"No," I stammered. A better answer: when have I *ever* had your lighter?

But he was insistent: "You *just* had it. Didn't drop it in the tunnel, did you?"

Before I could respond, he finished. "Well, you better come back and help me look for it. You're not getting off that easy." To Trey and Adrian: "Wanna get that rig set up? We'll be back in a flash."

It was only after he'd escorted me into the blackness that I realized he'd separated me from the group purposefully. I waited for him to turn on his flashlight, to tell me to be nice to Maria or ask what was wrong with Jett, but he didn't.

Instead, he reached for my hands. "You OK? Looked a little freaked out back there."

"I'm fine." My answer came out strained. "I wasn't freaked out."

"Red, you don't have to do this. I know you don't like tight spaces."

"Why can't we tell Maria we're dating? She wouldn't tell Rex."

My question startled him, and it took a moment for him to respond. "Where is this coming from?"

"I'm sick of fighting with her, Ryder, just like I'm sick of sneaking around and talking in tunnels because of her. It's not healthy, and I can't understand why-"

"Red, this thing with my old man... I don't think you understand how serious this is. If he found out we went behind his back..." He shook his head. "He has big plans for me. Wants me to lead his whole uprising. He'll understand where we're coming from once we've proved ourselves, but if he finds out before then..." He paused. "Let me ask you something, Red. Do you trust Maria?"

"No." My voice was firm. "I don't trust her, and I don't like her, either."

He snorted. "I know you don't. So listen to me. The last thing we need is Maria letting things slip to my old man. You can last a few more weeks, can't you? I know it sucks, but the end is in sight. You trust me, don't you?"

I sighed. "I do."

"Good." He began kissing my jawbone, and the goose bumps that prickled their way down my neck made it difficult to concentrate. "Less than a month," he said, "and then my old man won't have anything to say to anyone."

I nodded. He kissed my forehead, and then he added, "And you know what I was thinking we could do?"

"What?"

"Tomorrow. After we're done here. We should blow off chores and head up to Taft Point. Do some practicing with safety ropes. Think you're ready for it?"

I imagined myself dangling three thousand feet above the Valley floor, and a cold sweat began rising on my arms. But

Ryder was right. We only had a few weeks left, so it was about time I got used to the feeling.

"Think you're ready for it?" he asked again, and this time I nodded.

"I do. And I'm in. Let's show Taft Point what we're made of."

Despite Ryder's protests, I purposefully let myself look a little disheveled when we reemerged from the tunnel. Although Jett's disappointed frown hurt me more than I wanted to admit, Maria's look of outrage almost made up for it.

She was standing by the harness, handlebar in hand, and she quickly turned to Trey. "Let's do this," she said. "I'm ready to go first."

Trey shook his head and took the bar from her hands. "No way, sweetheart. Wouldn't risk your safety." He made eye contact with Ryder and added, "Looks good from this end. Only one way to find out."

Ryder nodded. "Hit it."

Without further ado, Trey strapped himself into the harness. Gripping the handlebar with both hands, he rocked backward and then rushed forward into the darkness. He picked his feet up as his body disappeared in the tunnel, and we heard his exhilarated cries long after he'd faded from sight.

After a few minutes – breathless, tentative stretches of waiting for something bad to happen – the line rocked and became slack. Two tugs signaled a safe arrival, and then Adrian pulled the harness back. He worked hand over hand and laughed in anticipation when the empty harness finally reappeared.

"Who's next?" he started, but Maria was already at his side. She took the harness without smiling, and then she was off, glancing over her shoulder and smirking as the handlebars carried her down the line.

Her cheers seemed forced – too high, maybe, and strained – but I quickly lost the energy to judge her, as each pulley return brought me one step closer to my own taste of blackness. Jett was next, and then Cody, and then I insisted Ryder take his turn so I could secretly build my courage in his absence. He seemed skeptical, but he finally harnessed up and promised he'd be waiting for me on the other side.

Finally, it was my turn. As Adrian held the handlebar steady, I fumbled with the security straps on my harness. My palms were sweaty, and my hands must have been shaking, because he finally nudged me and said, "You'll have a blast, Red. Just pick up your legs and remember not to let go."

"Let go?"

"Of the handlebars. The harness will hold you in place, but you'll flip sideways or upside down if you don't hold onto the handlebars." He smiled. "Don't worry; no one's ever dropped 'em before. Just remember that. In case you get scared."

"I won't get scared."

"I know you won't. But if you do, just remember not to let go. Trey and Ryder'll be waiting for you on the other side."

The second I entered the tunnel, I knew I had made a terrible mistake. There was no way I had tightened those straps nearly as snugly as I should have, and my hands were so slippery, I had trouble staying clamped to the handlebar.

I couldn't even really formulate these thoughts, because I was whooshing so blindly that it was hard to make sense of anything at all – anything except the frantic beating of my heart and the roar of the wind as it streamed past my ears.

The sound was deafening, and the air was freezing – so cold it cut like a knife through my clothes. I wanted to crumple in on myself and surrender, but I couldn't. I was too busy holding on for dear life.

Why did I ever think ziplining was something I could handle? I could barely make it through the Parkay Squeeze without panicking. Now here I was, racing through a half-collapsed passage with nothing to protect me but a ratty old rope hanging from the ceiling.

And the walls were closing in on me. I could feel them. I could sense the slow advance of rock and concrete as it splintered and constricted under the weight of the mountain. I could feel the rope pulling the ceiling down around me.

Monsters were everywhere – reaching out, slicing their claws through the air, screaming. They were *screaming* – just like someone had been screaming in Camp Four. Were they owls or mountain lions or monsters or people? Did it matter? What was the difference, anyway?

My breath was coming in gasps now, pushed from my lungs by the crush of the wind against my chest. And the ceiling was so low – so black and dark and unstable – that I could feel the ground advancing toward my feet. I tried to pick them up – to hold them high in the air like beacons – but my arms were already shaking from the pressure, and my legs were wobbly against the beating whip of the wind.

Tears streamed from my eyes, and panic knotted such a heavy weight in my chest that I couldn't decide if I was crying now or just hyperventilating. Either way, the slippery wetness of my palms wasn't relenting, and I was sure my legs were going to be ground like hamburgers into the pavement at any moment.

The tunnel walls were pinching against my sides, and I had the strange feeling I was falling into a hole. A hole that led to the center of the Earth, or maybe the North Pole – where snow and ice and hail would stone and freeze me to death. Leave me dead in a snowbank, with ground-up legs and no breath left in my lungs.

I tried to pull myself into a ball again. The smaller I was, the better chance I had to get out of here without being crushed by the mountain. So I twisted. And kicked. And somehow, my left hand slipped from the handlebar.

The last thing I remember is the glowing, midnight orb of the exit as it appeared in the distance. The color was blue and soft, and it promised an end to the careening, uncontrollable blackness.

But then the rock connected with my forehead. And everything faded to black.

# PART THREE:
# TAFT POINT

# CHAPTER THIRTY

There was blood everywhere. In my eyes, in my hair, across the front seat of the Jeep, where Ryder held me while Trey jammed the accelerator into gear.

I don't remember most of the ride back to the Valley. I don't remember anything at all, really, except the chill of the wind and the sticky, warm way my blood clotted against my clothes and skin.

Then the darkness of the Ahwahnee parking lot. The frantic way Trey and Adrian scrubbed blood from the vinyl as Ryder carried me up to his bedroom. The prick of the needle and the drip of a stolen IV bag. Or was that a stolen blood bag?

I remember hearing words I didn't recognize. Things like "intracranial bleeding" and "hematoma". And then I remember arguing.

Was that Jett pacing in front of the window, shouting about the emergency room? It was hard to make her out in the rising morning sunlight. But there was someone big beside her, and I guessed that had to be Cody.

Before I could be sure, they both disappeared. Or maybe I just blacked out from the pain. It's hard to tell. I remember Ryder holding me, kissing my forehead and saying he'd take me to Rex if I wanted him to. But I didn't want him to, and the look of relief that flooded his face when I said so showed me he was thankful for that.

I remember him saying I shouldn't fall asleep, but then I remember sleeping. Or not sleeping. Maybe just drifting aimlessly, like those gelatinous spots on the insides of your eyelids.

One time, I woke up – or didn't wake up – to find flowers by the bed. Another time, I felt a strange tightness tugging the skin of my forehead. That's when I realized Ryder – or someone – had stitched my wound closed. I could feel the parallel lines of sutures edging across my temple like train tracks.

I'm not sure how much time passed. Maybe hours. Maybe days. But at some point, Ryder told me I could sleep without fear of a concussion. So I did. For a long, dark, period of blackness – almost as horrible and constricting as the tunnel had been.

I awoke to a gentle rapping against Ryder's bedroom door.

I was hunched into such a tight ball that Javi almost didn't see me when he entered. There was a moment of him staring at the bed, eyes unfocused, as he tried to decide what I was. Then his gaze must have fallen on me, because his expression darkened, and he took a hurried step backward. His cleaning supplies banged with a clatter against the wall behind him.

He would have left completely, but I called out to him – so turned around and twisted up inside that I think I just needed a familiar face. Although Javi and I had stopped being friends, my heart still yearned for the easy, quiet support he'd offered those first few days after our arrival.

That's what I think my motivation was, anyway. Either way, he was sitting by my side before I knew it. His eyes were wide and filled with panic as he surveyed what I'd later find out were my blackened eye and swollen, rigid temple wound.

"Did he do this to you?"

The question was so absurd that I almost laughed, but there wasn't a trace of humor in Javi's eyes. Instead, he looked enraged, like lightning in a bottle.

"He did, didn't he? Motherfucker *hit* you."

Before I could stop him, he was on his feet. His fists were clenched, and he was about to destroy the black and white photograph of that shirtless man highlining when I finally managed to croak, "No, Javi. Stop. It wasn't Ryder."

"Then who was it? Trey? That little shit Adrian?"

"No. It wasn't anybody. It was a rock. I was ziplining, and… Javi, I'm fine. It's nothing, really."

"Nothing? Is that what Ryder calls the caved-in side of your face?"

"It's not caved in." I reached to inspect my cheekbone.

"When did this happen? What did Rex say?"

"Rex…" I tried to shake my head, but I didn't even have to. Javi already sensed my answer.

"Rex doesn't know. Can't know for some reason. Is that right?"

If I expected him to be angry, I was wrong. He didn't look mad at all; his features just crumbled until he looked more scared than I'd ever seen him. "Autumn," he whispered. "Why did Ryder tell you not to talk to Rex?"

My words seemed to have a mind of their own. "He didn't. But we stole gas from Camp Four. Snuck in late last night – or maybe two nights ago."

"You went inside Camp Four?" Javi's eyes widened. "No, actually, scratch that. I don't care if you went inside Camp Four or not. I just want to know why you think stealing gas means you shouldn't get medical treatment."

"I don't need medical treatment." I motioned to my temple. "Already got it. I should be back to normal in a few days."

"And then what? You're back on the Taft Point thing?"

"Yeah." I felt defiance creeping into my voice. "Back on the Taft Point thing. Gonna do it for my baby brother. What are you gonna do?"

He sensed my creeping distance. Rising from the bed, he said, "Not gonna do any dumb shit, if that's what you're asking. Not gonna risk my neck so Rex can tick my name off a little higher on his list. Don't really care what that man has to say about me, to tell you the truth."

He turned to go. "I'm not gonna tell Rex what happened to you, but I could. And I will if I don't see you getting better." He paused. "But this is bullshit, Autumn. Just so you know. I don't like who they've made you become."


Javi's words were off-putting, but he was obviously overreacting. So was Jett. After her initial visit to Ryder's bedroom, she didn't come back to see me once. Not to say "hi", not to visit, not even to make sure I was OK.

Cody lingered around some, but even he disappeared after the first couple of days. Said it was too hard to juggle what Jett needed and what I wanted.

I guess wanting company was too much for either of them to handle.

So I was left in Ryder's bedroom with the occasional company of Adrian or Trey. The boys read books and played board games with me, and they taught me twentieth-century staples like checkers and poker. Ryder preferred chess, but its endless rules and slow movements bored me, so he quickly gave up on playing games with me at all.

Instead, we sat and talked, took naps and looked at old picture books. Within a few days, I was even able to walk around the room a little. Although I was struck by a peculiar sense of vertigo any time I tried to stand for too long, Ryder assured me my dizziness and headaches would soon fade.

"You whacked your head pretty good," he said one afternoon. "Lucky you didn't get *really* hurt. But dizziness happens all the time after head injuries, and hey, your stitches look great."

I ran my fingers over the sutures, and I smiled when he playfully whacked my hand away. "Don't touch," he said. "Tomorrow will be a week. We should probably wait one more day, then we'll take them out on Sunday."

I realized with a pang that my next appointment with Rex was tomorrow, but Ryder stopped me with a smile. "Don't worry. You're covered. Ran into him this morning and told him you've been hiking the High Country near Half Dome all week. Won't expect you back down until Monday or Tuesday."

"And my head? How will we explain that?"

"Trail medicine. Slipped on a rock or something and had to bandage yourself up. Lucky for you, you sewed the quilts back home."

I touched my wound again. "Think he'll believe that?"

"Of course. If your readings plateau too much after the fall, you can always just say you holed yourself up and waited to feel better before you came back to the Valley."

His expression became serious as he came to sit beside me. "Hey, just so you know… I think you're amazing, Red. And I can't tell you how much I appreciate the fact that you're willing to cover our tracks like this." He smoothed a lock of hair from my forehead. "Your safety is the most important thing to me, so the fact that you trust me enough to take care of you..."

He frowned. "That's Jett's deal, you know. She thinks I should have taken you to my old man right away, but Jett doesn't get me like you do. She doesn't understand that I've been training under my father my entire life." He attempted a smile. "You want stitches? I'll give you stitches. Want medicine? I know exactly how much you should take. It's like having your own private doctor, you know?"

I nodded. "I trust you, Ryder."

"And I said I'd always catch you, right?" He grinned and leaned in to kiss my cheek. "Meant it, you know."

When I turned sideways to intercept his lips, he started. "Red," he said. "What are you doing? You don't feel well..."

But I did. Suddenly, the throbbing in my head was silenced by the thrumming of my heart. My pulse quickened, and an ache slid down my belly at the thought of him taking care of me. He'd been selfless, and he'd worried about my safety more than anything.

He wanted me now. Although his desire was tempered slightly by his hesitation, I could feel the wanting. It was just below the surface, coiled like a spring, and it sent his body shuddering when I ran my fingers along the edge of his collarbone.

"Ryder," I whispered. "I want..."

He nodded. Pinning my hands to the pillow, he murmured, "Yeah, I want that, too."

# CHAPTER THIRTY-ONE

I was back on my feet early the next week. The scabs from my stitches were nearly hidden by my hair, and my black eye had faded to a sickly, greenish yellow. The discoloration wasn't even noticeable if you didn't stare at it for too long.

That's what I told myself, anyway, as I strode toward my chores in the stables. Ryder told me Cody had picked up my slack, so I carried a handful of wildflowers as a token of my appreciation.

Ryder said bouquets were usually only given to girls, but I couldn't think of anything else Cody might want. And he liked flowers. At least I hoped he did. But really, I just wanted *something* to give him. Something to cut the tension he undoubtedly felt around me. Because Jett was pissed. Or so I heard. And I knew that must be awkward for him.

I had tried to find Jett that morning as well, but she was nowhere to be seen. Ryder told me she'd been spending time with Kadence lately, and I couldn't quite bring myself to approach the meditation tents. I was sure Javi had already told Kadence my story.

I kicked myself for letting Javi know about the gasoline and Camp Four. I blamed the painkillers and the stress, but that didn't take away the fact that I'd tattled. I hoped my indiscretion wouldn't come back to haunt me.

My headaches had faded, but I was still struck by occasional bouts of vertigo. The dizziness seemed to correspond with certain head positions – like if I bent down to fix my shoes or if I bolted too quickly from sitting to standing. I did my best to avoid these movements, and I religiously took the painkillers Ryder pilfered every afternoon from the clinic.

He'd done a beautiful job with my stitches. Each suture was perfectly aligned with the next, and they formed a tiny row of parallel ridges when he removed them. He said the lines would fade in time, but part of me wished they wouldn't. They were proof I'd faced my fear in the tunnel and emerged to fight another day.

The first of August now loomed less than three weeks away. I hadn't attempted to slackline again yet, so I knew I needed to push myself to make up for lost time.

Ryder, Trey and Adrian were already practicing with safety lines at Taft Point, and from what I heard, Maria wasn't far behind. She hadn't made the transition from slacklining to highlining just yet, but she supposedly hiked up there to support them every chance she got. Trey said she was really starting to conquer our route over the base of Yosemite Falls.

"Gets one hundred feet easily now," he reported to me one evening. "Even gets all the way back sometimes."

I like to think Maria's progress wasn't the catalyst that sent me back into the real world, but maybe it was. All my goals – proving myself for Brady, pleasing Ryder and Rex, disproving the Essence theory and preparing myself for my eventual return to the city… All these dreams had swirled together somehow, so now it was less about the why and more about the how.

My biggest concern this morning was how in the world I was going to walk Taft Point if I couldn't even make it to Ryder's window without fearing I'd fall down.

That's where the mental toughness came in. And that's why I'd refused Ryder's help and insisted on climbing to the Balcony by myself that morning. Although the rock approach had left me queasy, the unobstructed views of the Valley had been a welcome relief when I finally washed the filth from my skin.

Now it was nearing 9 o'clock, and the stables were crowded as I began looking for Cody. It took a while to pick him out in the corral, but I finally found him refilling a water trough and chewing on a blade of straw. He looked every bit the cowboy.

"Autumn!" He rushed to the split rail fence when he saw me. "How are you feeling? Your eye looks so much better."

I extended the bouquet. "Flowers," I said. "For you. For pulling my weight around here this week."

"Thank you." The flowers looked strange in his bear-sized hands, but his expression was soft as he took them. "How are you feeling? Any headaches?"

"No. They faded a few days ago."

I didn't mention the vertigo, because I was suddenly aware of a strange, humming tension. Before I could put my finger on it, he placed his arm on my shoulder. "Autumn, have you talked to Kadence lately?"

"No. Is Kadence mad at me, too?"

He shook his head. "No. Just worried. And she wants you to know…" He cleared his throat and leaned forward slightly. "She's leaving, Autumn. We all are."

"Leaving? What are you leaving?"

"This. Everything." He encompassed the Valley with one sweep of his hand. "We're leaving Yosemite. Me, Jett, Kadence, Javi. A few others, too. We don't like what's been going on around here lately."

"What are you talking about? You can't just *leave*."

"Yeah, we can. And we will. Soon. In the next few days. Jett got her hands on a map of the High Country; we're gonna take some horses and trek up to Tuolumne Meadows. Shayla's up there, you know. Once we have her..." He paused. "Autumn, there are tons of settlements on the East Side. Places like Mammoth Lakes and Bishop. We're gonna start a life out there, escape this whole uprising thing and put Rex's experiments behind us..."

"But, Cody..." I couldn't believe half my friends were actually going to abandon me. Abandon *us*. Abandon Ryder and Rex and everything we'd ever worked for.

"But you can't just leave," I said again. "We only have three weeks left."

"And then what? Strap on guns and charge back to the city? Or worse, strap on the *truth* and hope for the best?" He sighed. "I've had doubts about this uprising for a while. All of us have. But once we heard Rex's plan and saw how things started shaking out..."

His voice dropped. "We're just pawns, Autumn. All of us. We're foot soldiers and guinea pigs, and Rex has become so blinded that he doesn't even care if we get hurt. Instead, he sends us away to Tuolumne and hopes no one notices how screwed up we were when we left."

"But we're going to disprove the Essence theory! We're going to free the Movement's followers, and we're going to spread the truth..."

Cody shook his head. "Don't kid yourself, Autumn. This uprising isn't about freeing the Centrists. Not really. It's about punishing Cedar. It's *always* been about punishing Cedar."

"Well, Cedar's a bad guy…"

"And Rex fell in love with him just like everybody else did." Cody leaned closer. "Can't you see? Rex would have done anything for him, would have followed him *anywhere.* So after he saw what he saw that night in the meditation rooms… He's orchestrating this entire uprising to punish Cedar for turning his back on him fifteen years ago."

"No, Cody, you're wrong about that…"

"Am I? Then tell me, Autumn, where are all the Centrist spies Rex says are out to get him? Where's the political movement, the uprising to stop Rex from telling the world what he knows?" He spat. "There aren't spies, and there isn't an uprising, because Cedar doesn't give a shit about Rex. Never has. That's why Rex won't rest until he destroys him."

"Cody…" I took a step backward. "That's completely ridiculous. You… sound like a stiff right now. You sound like Kadence."

"Maybe there are worse things than sounding like Kadence." He reached for me across the split rail fence. "Autumn, can't you see? You're a pawn, too. Why else would Ryder have refused to take you to the clinic when you needed it? Ryder's blinded just as much as Rex is. Scared to stand up to his father, scared to do anything except what Rex says. Bet he would have left you in the tunnel if he thought that's what Rex wanted."

Suddenly furious, I smacked the flowers from his hands. "Think what you want, Cody, but I know the truth. Ryder would never put *anything* before my best interests, not even Rex's research." I turned to leave. "Don't think Rex would appreciate you stealing his horses, either. Maybe I should let him know what you're planning."

"Autumn, no." In one quick movement, Cody bolted over the fence and grabbed me by both shoulders. "Autumn, you can't say a word. Promise me you won't."

"No." I struggled, and the movement sent pain shooting through my temples. "No, I *don't* promise. Maybe you should have thought of that before you brought me into this."

"Autumn, we're leaving because we're pissed at the way Rex and Ryder are treating *you*. The way they're treating all of us. Don't you think you deserve better than this?"

"I'm fine, thank you. More than fine, and I can't believe you expect me to be OK with you walking out and abandoning everything we stand for..."

"Everything *who* stands for, Autumn? Ryder? Rex?"

"And me. And Trey. And Adrian. And everybody else. How can you be so ungrateful?"

"I'm not ungrateful. I'm just done with this."

"I'm done, too. Let go of me, Cody; I swear I'll scream if you don't."

"Autumn." I don't think I've ever seen panic cloud a person's eyes as quickly as they clouded Cody's. He glanced around frantically. "Autumn, I'm serious. I can't let you go unless you promise you won't tell..."

"Help! Help me!" I wrenched away from him. "Please, somebody help me! Somebody get him away from me!"

But then something twisted. And maybe that was Cody's arm sliding around my neck. Because suddenly, I wasn't screaming anymore. I was falling. And once again, I was surrounded by blackness.

# CHAPTER THIRTY-TWO

For a brief, horrifying second when I woke, I thought I was back in the tunnel. But I wasn't. I was lying in a makeshift bed inside some sort of cave.

The sky was dark, but even that couldn't camouflage the folded coat laid on the ground by my feet. I was covered by something – blankets? a sleeping bag? – and a canteen and foil-wrapped loaf of bread waited by my head.

So did this note, which I struggled to read by light of the moon: *Autumn, this isn't the way we wanted things to go. We want you, as soon as you've come to your senses. By the time the sleeping pills wear off, it will be too late to stop us. But remember the East Side. There's a place called Mono Lake.*

There was no signature, but the handwriting was easy enough to decipher. Kadence's.

I struggled to sit up, so furious I could barely contain myself. Had she actually left me in a cave? I pictured my so-called friends standing around me, carrying my lifeless body and dumping me here, where a bear or mountain lion could have easily eaten me.

Didn't think about that, did they?

Or *did* they? Maybe they didn't care. Things would be a lot easier for them if I were out of the picture. They'd demonstrated *that* clearly enough. If they were so worried about my health and safety, why didn't they just take me with them?

I wiped the leaves from my hair, thankful they hadn't. The depth of their deception ate at me, and I wondered how I'd been so easily duped. Were they planning on deserting all along? Soaking up Rex's hospitality with no intention of living up to their end of the bargain?

One thing was for sure: Rex must be pissed right now. And Ryder... Ryder was probably terrified something bad had happened to me. Or worse... Did he think I had deserted, too?

*I would never do that. He must know that.*

I struggled to my feet and fought a wave of dizziness as I approached the cave's entrance. How much time had passed? A day? More?

I wondered if Rex had sent a search party looking for me yet, but I quickly decided I wasn't going to wait around and find out. Just beyond the cave, I saw what looked like a trail. Dented with hoofprints, it led up and away from the cliffs and skirted the canyon walls to my left. In front of me was Half Dome, which meant North Dome must be behind me. The water babbling in front of me must be Snow Creek, and that meant Mirror Lake and the Valley must be down the trail to my right.

Only, how far? I couldn't imagine my so-called friends dumping me too far from civilization, but then again, I wouldn't have taken them for dumping types at all. Certainly not backstabber types or twist-your-neck-and-leave-you-unconscious types. So what did I really know about them, anyway?

I wondered if I should start walking in the middle of the night. My cave was remarkably sheltered, but the thought that Ryder might be mourning me for dead or thinking I'd abandoned him was enough to get me moving.

I took a swig of water, stowed the bread in my coat and wrapped the blanket around my shoulders. The air was heavy but expectant, and I wondered if we would finally see some rain. I crossed my fingers the deluge would wait until I'd made it to safety, and then I steadied myself and began walking.

It was nearly morning by the time I finally reached the Valley floor. Although the weather held off for the most part, a few scattered showers dampened my blanket and caused me to slip a little.

I probably looked ridiculous, like some kind of mud monster, but I wasn't thinking about what I looked like when I finally turned toward the Ahwahnee. I was staggering, off-balance and weak. But mostly, I was angry. At Kadence and Javi for spreading lies, at Cody and Jett for believing them. I couldn't believe they had the nerve to say they were mad *for* me but then care so little about me that they actually stashed me in a cave like a dead body.

How could they possibly think that was any more acceptable than the way Ryder had taken care of me after the Wawona Tunnel? Besides, he'd even suggested taking me to Rex himself. It was *me* who'd told him I didn't want to go. It was *me* who'd paved the way for him to nurse me back to health himself.

I blushed when I thought of the way caring for me had graduated into something more, but I couldn't waste much time dwelling on that. I had more pressing matters to attend to first.

I wondered if my so-called friends had made it to Tuolumne Meadows yet. Would Shayla have anything to do with them?

I secretly hoped she wouldn't. After all, she believed in Rex's research more than anyone here did. I smiled when I pictured her brushing them off, and I imagined with smug satisfaction the way they'd feel when they finally reached an East Side filled with Outsiders. Maybe then they'd realize how good they'd actually had it here.

I patted the piece of paper in my pocket. Mono Lake, that was where they said they were going. I wondered if Rex and Daniel could intercept them before they arrived. But then what? Would they drag them back here, force them to participate in our research?

What was the point?

I realized I wanted to find them – not to make them stay, but to tell them how wrong they were about me. To show them they had Ryder and Rex and this whole place misinterpreted.

But maybe there were more important things. Like walking Taft Point. And just like I'd ignored those Outsiders who waited outside the temple for us, maybe I should ignore my friends' absence as well. Maybe they weren't even worth my time.


Ryder was smoking on the Ahwahnee back porch when I arrived. It was just after dawn, and the sky was still lightening. The air swirled around him in soft shades of pink, but his eyes were focused on the ground in front of him.

He looked listless. And distracted. And defeated.

I rushed toward him without thinking, and the bewildered look in his eyes told me he hadn't been mourning me for dead at all. He'd been mourning me for a deserter.

"Red, what are you doing here?" He dropped his cigarette. "Are you OK? Where've you been?"

"I didn't leave." It was the most important thing to say, so I made sure I said it first. "I didn't desert or decide to abandon you. I've been walking all night to find you."

Now Ryder's arms were around me. Mud smeared his clothes, but he didn't seem to care. "Holy shit, I thought you left. I didn't think I was ever going to see you again. What happened to you?"

I sank into his embrace and allowed him to steady me. "Cody knocked me out or something. Then they drugged me and dumped me in a cave near Mirror Lake."

Ryder's eyes widened. "Did Cody hurt you? I swear I will kill him if he as much as laid a finger…"

"I'm fine." I leaned into him. "Just exhausted. How long have I been gone?"

"It's Wednesday morning now. Last we saw anyone was dinnertime on Monday. Seven people deserted. Do you know where they went?"

Before I could answer, I heard footsteps approaching. And then a deep, velvet voice: "Is that Autumn? Thank goodness you're safe, dear; do you need medical attention?"

It was Rex. Before I knew it, I was lifted into Ryder's arms, and the three of us were headed toward the empty Ahwahnee lobby.

A short time later, I sat curled in a battered leather chair in front of one of the Ahwahnee's many fireplaces. We were in a small sitting area called the Mural Room, and an intricate wall painting stretched above the room's rich wood panels.

Daniel pulled the French doors shut and came to sit beside Rex. It was clear he'd been in the woods all night. His dark camouflage pants were stained with mud, and he carried a rifle slung over his shoulder.

The rifle sat by the bookcase now, but its presence made me nervous. It reminded me how many wild animals actually prowled the Valley's woods, and I felt thankful all over again that I'd made it down from my cave without incident.

"So, start from the beginning," Rex said. The three of them were sitting in a row now, mismatched bumps on a long, leather log.

"Cody and Kadence drugged me. Jett, too, and Javi. They were afraid I was going to tell you they were leaving, so they knocked me out and hid me in a cave."

"And how did you know they were leaving?" Rex asked.

"Cody told me before chores on Monday. Said they were sick of the way you guys were treating us." I swallowed, self-conscious at the words. "I'm not, though. Sick, I mean. I don't agree with them or anything."

Rex nodded. "Very well. Please continue."

I cleared my throat. "They don't like the uprising. And they don't like how you handled Shayla's crossing over."

I opened my mouth to add another disclaimer, but Rex waved me on. "Did Cody say anything else?"

"No. Just that he didn't want to be part of the Community anymore. He wanted to start a new life somewhere."

"Where?" Daniel leaned forward. "Where were they going, Autumn?"

There was something unsettling about the hard look in Daniel's eyes. Something dark. And wild. Something I didn't like seeing.

I felt myself shrinking. Rex must have sensed it, because he put his hand on Daniel's shoulder. "It's been a long night, hasn't it, my friend? Why don't you head upstairs, and we'll finish up here?"

Daniel swallowed. Glancing at Rex and Ryder, he nodded. "I'm sorry, Autumn. I didn't mean to sound so forceful. I'm just... I need rest now."

With that, he slung the rifle back over his shoulder, and he was gone.

In his absence, something changed. The room became still, and Rex's eyes became eager. An ambiguous sense of unease filled me, and the walls seemed to close in a little. "I apologize, Autumn. You were saying?"

"Fresno. They're headed to Fresno." I don't know what came over me, but I decided I wasn't going to tell Rex anything. At least not until this reluctance left me.

"Fresno," he repeated. "Did he say what they wanted to do in Fresno?"

"Take a train south, I think. Head to Bakersfield or LA or something. Try to start over."

"Very well." He glanced at Ryder. "Horses can probably travel twenty, thirty miles in a day. That gives us a day or two to intercept them."

Ryder nodded. "Should we get going?"

"No." Rex shook his head. "We'll leave this one to Daniel and the entrance guards. Only two and a half weeks before our research anniversary; I'd think it would be more valuable for you and your friends to continue practicing for Taft Point." He made eye contact with me. "Does that sound all right, Autumn?"

When I nodded, he stood. "Thank you for your assistance in the matter, and I'm sorry you had to go through so many trials on our account. We will ensure that these seven are apprehended and appropriately reprimanded for their part in this incident. Your dedication will not go unnoticed."

Rex's words should have made me feel better, but they didn't As soon as he'd exited the Mural Room, I turned to Ryder. "What is Daniel going to do if he finds them?"

Ryder shrugged. "Not sure. No one's ever been quite so bold about leaving before."

"But people *leave*. You told me people leave all the time."

"Yeah. But not like that. Not with such a blatant disregard for what we're doing." He extended his hand. "Come on, babe, let me get you to my room. You need rest."

"But when he says they'll be apprehended and appropriately reprimanded... What does that mean? He wouldn't hurt them, would he?"

"Of course not. Probably won't even make them come back. Just wants them to know how important it is that no one knows we're out here." He shrugged. "And the fact that you helped... Well, that's huge, Red. Things would be a lot worse for them if you hadn't told him where they were going. Remember that."

Again, the words were meant to comfort me, but they didn't. They left a queasy feeling of guilt and uncertainty instead.

I wasn't quite sure why I hadn't told Rex the truth, but I knew it was too late to go back on that now. Rex would question my intentions, and maybe so would Ryder. Everything was so tremulous right now that I couldn't afford either.

So the best I could hope for would be that the intermittent rain showers had wiped out the hoof prints last night. And maybe Daniel would think the group had just gotten away – slipped off the trail somehow or decided to change course at the last minute.

I don't know why I cared so much, but something told me I should. And the weight of that was suddenly so heavy that I could barely manage a nod when Ryder suggested taking me to his room again.

My eyes closed almost as quickly as my head hit the pillow.

# CHAPTER THIRTY-THREE

Daniel returned four days later.

Ryder and I had taken the day off from slacklining, and we were sitting around an empty Ahwahnee porch table, idly playing cards before dinner. The clamor of the older-model truck was unmistakable, and it wasn't long before we dropped our cards and rushed to the parking lot.

If anyone was hoping to catch sight of the deserters, they were in for a disappointment. When it became clear that only Daniel, Rex and the white-blond guard Brian were in the truck, an audible murmur reverberated through the crowd.

But then Daniel stood up and held his hands in the air. "Intercepted!" he announced. "Caught up to the deserters just outside Oakhurst."

A cheer erupted, but I felt myself glued in place. *Intercepted?*

"They scattered when we arrived, but it was easy to round them back up. Unprepared for the weather, and one of them had already broken his leg."

My heart seized. *Javi? Cody?*

I caught myself as Daniel continued working through the group's list of mishaps and setbacks. *But Javi and Cody aren't in Oakhurst. Aren't even close. They're in Mono Lake. Headed north and east when Daniel went south and west.*

But had I gotten it wrong somehow? Or had they given me false directions, knowing I'd turn them in?

I felt color drain from my cheeks. Of course. They knew I'd tell Ryder, because I always told Ryder. And they knew Ryder would tell Rex. And if Rex and Daniel were busy looking for them on the East Side...

I swallowed. Did they really count on my betrayal?

I tuned back into Daniel's speech just in time to hear: "They are shamed by their actions, and they understand that their rashness has led to much strife here in the Valley. They begged my forgiveness, and they asked for our mercy." He paused. "They understand they will most likely be scorned here in the Valley, so we have agreed to provide a temporary home for them in Tuolumne Meadows until they feel fit to return."

A gasp rose, but Rex shushed it. "Now, brothers, sisters. Remember we are a family. Daniel briefed me on the situation a short time ago, and I agree that he has made a powerful choice. Tuolumne is sacred to us, but we mustn't turn our backs on our misguided brethren. It may take them a short time to return, or it may take them quite a while. But if they do feel fit to rejoin us, we must welcome them with open arms. This is the Community way."

I heard murmurings of dissent, but this quickly transformed into a quiet round of applause, and then a loud and deafening round of applause as everyone cheered the Community's sense of forgiveness and rebirth.

Everyone except me. And maybe, possibly Ryder. He stiffened at Daniel's words, and his applause was half-hearted at best. If anything, he looked pale, and maybe even a little stricken by the news.

My emotions were likewise out of whack. I understood why Cody and Kadence would have lied about their destination, but I didn't see them returning to the Community so easily. I certainly didn't see them clamoring for a chance to live in Tuolumne Meadows. If this is what they wanted, why hadn't they headed there in the first place?

I wanted to ask Ryder what he was thinking, but he rushed away when the crowd broke apart. Claiming a headache, he hurried to his father's side and disappeared in the truck with Rex and Daniel.

The only person left was Brian, but he was quickly pulled into the crowd. He was peppered with questions and finally ushered inside the Ahwahnee – carried away, no doubt, by the sense of celebrity bestowed on him.

Because he was there when it had happened. And he'd showed compassion.

An upright, outstanding member of the Community.

It was nearly ten o'clock by the time I made it to Ryder's bedroom that night. I figured he'd still be out, so I was surprised when the tangy scent of tobacco wafted through the door's entrance. There he was, hunched on his windowsill with one long leg propped at his side.

His windows were open, and his filmy curtains drifted on the night breeze, partially obscuring him from view. But I could tell even from a distance that his shoulders were knotted. By the light of his lanterns, I saw the ashtray next to him was filled to overflowing.

"Are you allowed to smoke in here?"

"Hey, Red." Ryder's eyes were bloodshot, and he looked like he hadn't slept in days.

"Where'd you go? I didn't see you at dinner." I pushed the door shut and took a few steps toward him.

He glanced at his ashtray. "Been here. Been smoking. Is dinner over already?"

I frowned. "Do you know what time it is?"

His answer was immediate. "Daniel didn't find Cody and the others in Oakhurst. He's lying."

"What?" I hadn't known what he would say, but I definitely wasn't expecting that. The world took an unexpected turn, and I fought the sweat I felt rising on my temples. "What do you mean, he's lying?"

"He's lying. So's my old man. They don't want morale to go down. But they didn't find Cody, and they didn't find shit. Have no idea where anyone is."

"Oh-kay?" I felt myself struggling through his words the way you struggle through mud or quicksand. *He didn't find them? Didn't rescue them and take them to Tuolumne Meadows? Does this mean they're really on the East Side? Does this mean they really told me the truth?*

Another thought: *why would Daniel lie about that?*

Ryder spoke again. "You know where they really are, don't you?"

Now I felt my foundation crumbling. As I stood there trying to figure out what to say, he gripped both my hands in his. "Don't. Tell. Anyone. OK? Don't tell me; don't tell them. Don't you tell a single soul where they are, do you hear me?"

"Ryder…" I recoiled. "What…?"

"I'm serious, Red. As if your life depended on it. Promise me."

"Ryder…"

He interrupted: "Did you see the look in Daniel's eyes in the Mural Room? Did you? Remember that look, Red. That was the look of a man you don't want to mess with. And if you know where the deserters are heading... You don't want a guy like Daniel on your bad side, OK?" He took a breath. "I need to hear you say it, Red. Say you promise."

"I..."

"Red, I'm not kidding. There's shit going on here that you don't want any part of. Do you understand?"

Before I could respond, someone knocked on his bedroom door. "Ryder?"

The voice was Rex's, and Ryder stiffened when he heard it. "Red, he can't see you in here. You need to hide."

As he hurried to the door, I slipped to the floor behind his bed. "Yes, sir?"

Ryder and Rex's conversation sounded discombobulated, with no visuals or expressions to guide me: "Are you smoking in here?"

"No, sir."

"You know you're not supposed to smoke in here. Could burn this whole place down."

"I wasn't smoking."

"Is that an ashtray by your window?"

"No, sir. Just a vase."

A pause. "Did Autumn tell you any more about the deserters' plans?"

"No, sir. Doesn't seem to know anything."

"I thought as much." Another pause. "Think we honestly missed them?"

"I do. Tracks could have easily been covered by rain."

"If they get to Fresno... We have to stop them before they get to Fresno."

"I know. Don't worry. Daniel will find them."

Silence. And then: "How's highlining?"

"Great. Coming along right on schedule."

"And Maria?"

"Doing fine."

"Spikes aren't as elevated as when she first got here. Work on that, will you?"

"Yes, sir."

"And there's another girl in the gardens. Lacy? Lindsey? Came in February or March. Have you been with her yet?"

"No, sir. Was dating a friend of mine."

"I think she's single now."

"I'll work on it."

The sound of contact – the patting of a shoulder; the exchange of a hug? – and then, "Goodnight, son. Better not catch you smoking in here."

"Yes, sir. Goodnight."

The creaking of the door. Footsteps across the bedroom. The flick of a lighter. And then: "Lucky I *don't* burn this place down."

Rex and Ryder's conversation left me unsettled in so many ways that I didn't know where to begin. So, of course, it was the most trivial detail that worked its way out first: "Rex asks you to sleep with girls for him?"

Ryder took a drag of his cigarette. "Guess so."

"Has he always done that?"

He exhaled out the open window. "Asks me to do a lot of shit I don't want to do."

"Do you do it?"

"What? Sleep with girls for him?"

"Anything. Anything he asks?"

He took another drag. "Guess so. Most of the time. Not since I met you, though."

"You don't do what he asks anymore?"

"I don't sleep with girls anymore." He rubbed his temples. "This shit's giving me a headache, Red. Can we go to bed?"

"What about Fresno? Why does Daniel need to stop the deserters before they reach it?"

We made eye contact. The cigarette wavered in Ryder's hands, and my stomach dropped to the floor. I knew the answer. Right there, with a sinking certainty more powerful than anything I'd ever felt in my entire life.

I knew it, just like I'd sensed it the moment I saw Daniel's eyes. It had been there, in the nervous energy of the Mural Room, in the easy set of his rifle and in the way he'd slung it over his shoulder on his way out the door. He wasn't concerned about bears or mountain lions.

"He needs to kill them first."

It took a moment for Ryder to respond. In that pause, I saw the truth hovering in his eyes. I saw it wavering and darkening and spreading like a virus through his limbs. It was all encompassing, heavy as the sea, and it covered him so completely there was almost nothing left.

"You just found out." It wasn't a question. It was a truth I knew with the same weighted certainty I knew my own name. Ryder hadn't known before. And he knew now. And things would never, ever be the same.

Realization smacked me so hard, it left me breathless. If Daniel found our friends, he would kill them. He would shoot them and leave them rotting in the wilderness, and no one would ever know the truth.

I almost felt too stunned to speak. "When did you find out?"

"Just now. Before dinner."

"And Rex knows?"

"Think it was his idea."

There was a hollowness to Ryder's expression now. His foundation had just been ripped out from under him, and I could see he was reeling. Slowly filling with the realization. Poisoned by it. Drowning.

"How did you find out?"

He met my eyes. The weight of his stare was unnerving, and I suddenly felt like I might drown, too. He wasn't finished.

"You need to sit down, Red. You're not gonna like this."

# CHAPTER THIRTY-FOUR

"What do you mean, I'm not going to like this?"

I felt all my muscles tensing, like every cell in my body was preparing itself for a blow, but Ryder just sighed and snubbed his cigarette in the ashtray. "It was the Tuolumne comment that did it."

"The Tuolumne comment?"

"Yeah. Cause here's the thing. Tuolumne's bullshit, too."

My fingers clenched. "What do you mean, bullshit?"

"Bullshit. A lie. A complete and total fabrication. Nothing more than a windswept piece of land – about as wild and unkempt as the moon. There's no such thing as crossing over."

I couldn't help it; I bolted to my feet. My elbow struck a nearby vase, and it dropped like a stone and shattered between us. The sound was loud and no doubt explosive, but I didn't even hear it. I couldn't process a word he was saying.

"But... What about Shayla? And everyone else?"

"Shayla's not dead. Don't worry, Red; she's not dead."

"Then where is she?"

"She's OK. She's here. In Camp Four."

*Camp Four?* My mind returned to the fortified walls and impossible stone doors, to the oil tanks and low buildings. "But Camp Four's for supplies…"

But there it was. The answer was right in front of me – inside the building with the low lights, in the place with the locked door and the high-pitched scream. The wail so tortured and fearful it sent my blood shooting into ice.

That scream was Shayla's.

"You knew." Again, it wasn't a question. Ryder hadn't known about Daniel, but he had known about Camp Four. The truth was written all over his face.

"Why?" My voice was rising now, and strength was returning to my limbs. I didn't feel off-balance anymore, just deceived. And furious. "Why did you leave her? Why didn't you *do* something?"

He held his hands up to placate me. "Red, wait. You don't understand. Shayla's in there because she needs to be in there. Needs treatment. Needs help."

"Inside Camp Four? Inside a secret building no one knows about where no one can hear her scream?"

"She's safe in there. Protected. It's where she can receive the best medical care."

"*Why?* Why is she locked away in there? Why does everyone think she's in Tuolumne Meadows?"

"It's… it's for morale. So no one has to worry about her." Ryder swallowed. "Did you see that head wound? There's no way she could have ever bounced back from that. It scrambled her, changed her into something different than what she was." His voice dropped into a whisper. "Camp Four's where my old man sends the ones who aren't going to get better."

"Why didn't you tell me? Why doesn't anyone else know?"

He snorted, but it was a dark noise. The sound of a man collapsing. "Isn't the best public relations idea, is it? Letting people know there are consequences to our actions? Better to let everyone think we'll be rewarded for our sacrifices if anything ever goes wrong."

"But… What about Essence drain? Does this mean…?"

"No. Essence drain's still bullshit. Probably. But just because you don't have a time bomb ticking in your chest… Your actions still have consequences, you know?"

I thought of Jett's words, of the way she'd warned me about being elevated all the time. *Just because you can do something doesn't mean you should,* she'd said. She was right.

They were all right.

The knowledge infected me, and I suddenly wanted nothing more than to be as far away from Ryder as I could. "You knew, and you didn't say anything. Didn't warn anyone. Didn't tell me when you picked me off the streets in San Francisco. 'Abundance is the key to longevity'; isn't that right, Ryder? The harder I push myself, the more alive I feel?"

Instead of fighting me, he just sighed. "That's right. I let you believe this place was paradise. Let Jett and Cody and everyone else believe it, too. Joke's on me; looks like we don't stop at just institutionalizing people."

The reminder tempered my anger some. I glanced around the room and realized I'd never felt so overwhelmed in my entire life. *What am I going to do now?*

I steadied myself on the dresser. "I think you need to start from the beginning."

"A guy named Will Serrano was the first. To be 'sent away'." Ryder's words were flowing fast now, and his eyes were unfocused. He spoke like a person with nothing left to lose.

"Parachute malfunctioned off El Cap; broke nearly every bone in his body."

I shuddered, but Ryder didn't notice. "I must have been eleven or twelve at the time," he continued. "Daniel stabilized him, but he was never able to walk again. Was different, too, you know? Confused. Bitter. So angry he started bringing down everyone around him."

He cleared his throat. "Rex tried to rehabilitate him, but it was no use. Everyone's readings started slipping, and people stopped BASE jumping and climbing and doing anything on El Cap. The Community fell into a rut, so…"

"Rex put him away. For the good of the Community."

Ryder looked like he might protest, but then he simply nodded. "Yeah. Maybe. Took him to Camp Four. Told everyone he'd left for treatment in Fresno."

"Why *didn't* he leave for treatment in Fresno? Someone there could have maybe actually helped him…"

"Couldn't risk it. That's what my old man said, anyway." He shrugged. "The authorities might have found out what we were up to, might have locked us away for kidnapping or child endangerment or something. Would have ruined everything he was trying to do out here."

He paused. "Look, Red, I'm not saying it was the right thing to do. But a funny thing happened. The moment Will was out of sight, everyone's readings began to soar again. People started climbing El Cap, and they were BASE jumping again. Everyone's morale went through the roof, so…"

"Out of sight, out of mind."

"Yeah. That."

I looked at Ryder, at the boy I'd once thought I knew, and I realized I didn't know a damn thing about him. If he really *was* the type of person who could let his father lock people away in the name of research… It was intolerable – inhuman, even. How do you push your friends and loved ones into taking risks when you know better than anyone what's actually waiting for them if they fail?

The tunnel. My thoughts returned to it with an aching sense of dread. What would have happened if I'd hit my head any harder? Would Ryder have driven me back to Camp Four? Dropped me in a cot beside Shayla and kissed my forehead for good luck?

He seemed to sense my thoughts. "You can go, you know," he said. "Get out of here. You don't have to stay with me anymore."

"Go?" The thought was laughable. "Go *where*, Ryder? Daniel's apparently prowling the borders with a hunting rifle. Where the hell am I gonna go?"

"I don't know." His eyes lost focus again. "I don't know anything anymore."

I fought the urge to comfort him. The realization that we'd built our entire relationship around a lie was enough to prevent me from ever reaching for him again.

"I *am* going to go," I finally said. "Back to my tent – where I'm going to figure out a way to get the hell out of here without getting killed in the process." I strode toward the door. "Yosemite was a mistake, Ryder. *You* were a mistake. I should have never believed you were anything more than a fake and a liar."

Standing up to Ryder should have felt like a triumph. But it didn't.

The truth is, I could barely see the trail below my feet for all the tears streaming down my cheeks. I felt duped and betrayed. But worse than that, I felt sickened by the way Ryder collapsed the moment I reached for his doorknob. He looked stricken and terrified, and the realization that I was leaving him in the midst of his pain was almost more than I could bear.

But this whole thing was his fault. He'd lied to me. He'd lied to *everyone*, and he had stood idly by while his father ordered us to do things he knew could kill us. *He'd* ordered us to do things he knew could kill us.

Truthfully, we knew those things could kill us, too. But the *expectations* Rex and Ryder set for us – the way they encouraged us to push ourselves... They'd promised us a crossing-over celebration and a peaceful retirement in Tuolumne Meadows...

I stopped myself. They'd pushed us, but they hadn't ordered us. Hadn't threatened us or tortured us or forced us at gunpoint. So what did that say about *us?*

I reached for my pendant necklace and was actually surprised to find it wasn't there. *Neutrality is the key to longevity, neutrality is the key to longevity...*

But it wasn't. Neither was abundance. So what was? I realized I didn't have time to think about it; I needed to escape Yosemite before anyone learned I knew the truth.

But... then what? Return to the city? Go to the East Side? What about Shayla? I couldn't just leave her stranded in Camp Four, but how could I take her with me?

Through the pine trees, I glimpsed the silhouettes of two people strolling by the light of the moon. A tall, dark-skinned person with dreadlocks, and a shorter person with silky hair.

Trey and Maria. They looked like they were holding hands, like Maria had finally given up on Ryder and decided to give Trey a chance. I swallowed. I couldn't leave them, either.

Footsteps shuffled on the trail behind me. I swirled, expecting to see Ryder, but it wasn't Ryder. It was Rex, and he was heading right for me.

"Autumn." The line of his jaw was firm, and his steps were purposeful. "Do you have a moment?"

I froze. For a fleeting instant, I thought he hadn't seen me exit Ryder's bedroom, but this hope died the moment he reached my side. His grip was hard around my bicep, and his eyes shone without a trace of warmth.

"Been spending quite a bit of time with my son lately, haven't you?" Before I could answer, he pulled me away from my tent cabin. "Been spending almost every single night with him, isn't that right?"

I struggled in his grasp, but it was no use. His hands were powerful, and they rippled with definition from the countless surgeries he had performed.

"Oh, come on," he said, hauling me down the trail. "It isn't a big surprise. Both of your readings have been nearly identical for the last four weeks."

We bypassed the Ahwahnee and began walking toward the parking lot. "You know why we have rules, don't you, Autumn? It's not for me; it's for the good of the Community."

Brambles tore at my pants as I struggled to stay on my feet. My arm was beginning to feel tingly, and fear crippled me so deeply it didn't even occur to me to cry out.

"I have forbidden Ryder from dating, because Ryder has a higher calling."

We were walking toward the cars now. I glanced over my shoulder, hoping to catch a glimpse of Ryder on his windowsill, but his lanterns were darkened. His curtains flapped idly in the breeze.

Rex continued. "Ryder will lead our uprising in San Francisco, will take my place if anything ever happens to me. Because the world needs to know the truth about the Centrist Movement. There's no room for distractions."

He opened the door to a Jeep and flung me inside. "You're a good girl, Autumn, but you're just a girl. Remember that. Ryder will forget about you as soon as you're gone."

*Gone?* The way Shayla was gone, or the way Daniel hoped my friends were gone?

He slid into the driver's seat. "I hope you don't think I enjoy this, just like I don't enjoy patrolling our borders or tending to cripples in our ward. Because Ryder told you about these things, didn't he?"

I tried to protest, but it was no use. We made eye contact, and Rex's eyes became steely. "I was afraid of that."

He paused, and then his voice became measured. "You must understand where I'm coming from, Autumn. I can't let anyone leave this place. If Cedar's spies find out where we are, there will never be an uprising. We will never get the chance to free the Movement's followers from his abuse, and we will never–"

Before he could finish, someone banged hard on the hood of the Jeep. "Stop! Where do you think you're taking her?"

"Ryder." Rex's voice was pinched. "This is none of your concern. Go inside; I need you to rest."

"Let her go! She doesn't mean anything to you."

"She doesn't mean anything to you, either. Or shouldn't."

Ryder blocked the road in front of us, and the Jeep's headlights spotlighted him. He looked more wiry than usual, and sweat soaked the curls of his hair. "She does, OK? But that doesn't mean I've stopped caring about this, or us, or you. I'm just as committed to this as I was the day we started…"

"Then why did you tell her about our borders? About Camp Four?" Rex's voice cracked. "Do you think I enjoy doing this, son? Do you think it makes me happy? This isn't what I want, but you've left me no choice. She *can't* know; she'll tell everyone here."

"She won't." Ryder made eye contact with me. "Right? You won't, will you, Red?"

"I won't." I kept my eyes focused on him. "I won't. I swear I won't."

"She will. You know it as well as I do. Maybe not today, maybe not tomorrow, but someday it will come out. And when it does, it will ruin us."

Ryder's expression fell. He was silent for a moment, and then he said, "So let her leave. Let her disappear and never return. She doesn't want any part of this; she's harmless."

"But she knows where we are."

"She'll forget. Isn't that right, Red? Won't you forget about us when you leave?"

I don't know why, but a pit formed in my stomach at the thought that I'd never see him again. It was misplaced and ill-timed, and it was so unexpected that it seemed almost comical. But it wasn't. It was real, and there was no way to undo it.

"Yes," I finally stammered. "I'll forget. I'll forget everything, and I'll never come back. I'll never tell anyone what I saw here…"

"Father, please, I'm begging you." Ryder's eyes were pleading now. "I love her. I've never loved anyone before, but I love her. I don't know what I'll do if you don't let her go."

Rex's expression hardened. "Ryder, listen to me. You aren't thinking clearly right now…"

"I am!" Ryder smacked the hood with so much force that Rex and I both flinched. "I'm serious. Let her go, or I'm done."

"Done?" Rex stifled a laugh. "You're done?"

"Yeah. Done with your experiments, done with your recruiting. See how well this place runs without me."

"Ryder, listen to me. You're overreacting about this. We can talk tomorrow–"

"No!" Ryder smacked the hood again. "I have done *nothing* but bust my ass for you ever since we got here. I've never asked questions, never protested. I've always done everything you've wanted me to do." He glanced at the Ahwahnee and then back at his father. "I'm serious. I know a lot of secrets that would upset a lot of people around here. You probably don't want to blow me off right now."

Rex's eyes narrowed. "Are you threatening me, son?"

"Yes." Ryder's voice sounded strained at first, but he quickly gained conviction. "Yes, I am. Let her go, or everyone here will know the truth."

For a moment, Rex seemed to falter. His jaw fell open, and his long fingers began clenching and un-clenching around his steering wheel. Then, just as quickly, his expression hardened. "Fine," he said. "You win. I'll let her leave, but she walks Taft Point first."

"What does Taft Point have to do with this?"

"I refuse to compromise her final readings, son. She may only leave after she has done her part here."

Ryder scoffed. "That's ridiculous. There's no way I'm going to agree to something as pointless as—"

Rex cut him off. "Don't forget *your* delicate situation, son." His eyes were penetrating. "You may have information, but I have Autumn. And I have you, your friends, everything you've ever built or believed in. I would encourage you to very carefully consider your options before you rush into a decision you are going to regret." He cleared his throat. "Autumn walks, or Autumn doesn't leave."

Ryder's eyes narrowed. "Are you threatening *me*, Father?"

"I'll walk." My words were out of my mouth before I could stop them. I took a breath and then repeated, "I'll walk. It's fine; I can do it."

I swallowed. If I walked Taft Point, I could leave. It was the only way I ever would.

# CHAPTER THIRTY-FIVE

Wind whipped through my hair as Rex, Ryder and I bounced along a trail that bypassed the collapsed Wawona Tunnel. We were headed straight for Taft Point, along the twisting south side of the park's road system, and the night was so black, I could barely see the sky above our heads.

"She's not walking at night, you know. She needs to rest. Not taking a step until dawn." Ryder sat crouched in the seat behind me. Through the cracks between the seats, he secretly gripped my hand.

My thoughts were such a cacophony of dissonance that I couldn't make sense of them. Rex had planned to kill me. Or drug me and send me to Camp Four. But now he was going to make me walk Taft Point instead. And Ryder loved me.

I couldn't decide how I felt about that, but I knew I wouldn't be sitting here without Ryder's intervention. And I knew the warmth of his hand settled me some. He hadn't told me about Camp Four, but he'd stood up for me, too.

This was as far as I allowed myself to get, because I had bigger concerns: I had never walked Taft Point before. Not even with a safety line.

Although my vertigo had begun to lessen, it still came and went without warning. And those bouts of it – those swirling, dizzy moments where I couldn't even stay on my feet... Those were absolutely crippling.

My fear of heights didn't help. There were times when even sitting near the edge of the Taft Point cliff became too much for me. It had become a bit of a running joke – those instances when I had to stop cheering for the boys and move away from the highline – but the reality was anything but reassuring.

*Rex will let me use a safety line, right? He can't possibly expect me to walk without one.*

Two days ago, I would have answered that question without hesitation. But now... Now I wasn't sure about anything. Particularly not Rex's sense of forgiveness.

The sky was still dark when we finally made it to Taft Point. It was a few hours before dawn, so Rex informed me I could nap if I liked. He even procured a military blanket from the back of the Jeep for me.

I was struck by the inconsistency of this generosity. *He'll give me a blanket when I'm cold, but he'll also drug me or shoot me if he needs to?*

I wandered away from the parked Jeep and laid my blanket out beside a boulder. I considered tearing away into the wilderness or starting down the trail to the Valley, but what good would that do? Rex would find me – probably within a few minutes   and I had a feeling I was never going to get a better deal than the one he was already offering me.

Ryder initially stayed with his father, but I heard him approach an hour or so later. His footsteps were soft, and his voice was tentative when he whispered, "Red?"

I considered pretending to be asleep, but I knew Ryder was the only ally I had. So even though my feelings toward him were confusing, I only hesitated for a moment before answering, "I'm here."

"I brought you something." He extended his hand. "Money. Nicked it from my old man. Enough to get you started when you get back to civilization. And this." He pressed a silver locket into my hand. "I couldn't get back to your room – couldn't get your pendant – but I know it reminds you of your family. So take mine. And pretend it's yours, OK?"

I turned the locket in my hands. The Centrist motto was carved on the outside, but a photograph of a woman and a little baby was tucked inside. A blond woman. Ryder's mother.

"I didn't know you had this."

"No one does." He shrugged. "I used to follow her around sometimes, but I never talked to her. Rex forbade it – said she'd blow the cover on our whole operation. So I stayed away. And I watched her. One day, she dropped this."

"Is that you?"

"Not sure." He studied it. "Could be me. Could be one of her other kids. But that's definitely her, and I probably look at this thing ten times a day."

"Why didn't you ever talk to her?"

Ryder sighed. "Rex made a choice when he brought me out here. And I made a choice when I came with him."

"But Ryder, you were *two years old* when he took you from the city. How could you have possibly protested?"

"Doesn't matter. Nothing matters, 'cept the loyalties you choose." He paused. "I screwed up, Red. I should have never brought you here. I get that now, but I swear I didn't know Daniel was killing people on our borders. I didn't know you weren't allowed to leave."

"But you knew about Camp Four."

"I did." He sighed. "But when my old man explained it to me, it made sense. He wasn't purposefully hurting anyone, you know? He was just treating people there, was just letting everyone believe the thing they wanted to believe anyway: we're all invincible out here."

"But we aren't."

"I know. And it's wrong. I see that now, but it's too late."

I closed the locket. "You could leave too, you know."

He shook his head. "I can't. What kind of person would I be if I did?"

"What kind of father would expect you to stay?"

Ryder lowered his eyes. "Rex... has noble intentions. Wants to do the right thing out here."

"But what good is that if he's doing the wrong thing to get there?"

Ryder's expression became pained. "This is so messed up right now, Red. I know it is, and I can't tell you how sorry I am about it." He shook his head. "That doesn't mean shit – I know it doesn't – but I promise I'll get you a safety line. So even if you fall... My old man just wants your readings – wants to scare you a little, I think – but I swear on my life I'll make this safe for you. It'll be just like the Yosemite Falls walk."

I nodded.

"And... I love you. What I said back there... I want you to know I meant it."

"Then come away with me." Before I knew it, tears were clouding my eyes. "If you love me, you'll leave this place and come with me."

His eyes clouded as well. "I can't," he said, pulling me into his arms. "I'm sorry, Red, but I just can't."

"Why not?" I wanted to be mad at him, but there was no time for that. Instead, I found myself sobbing against his chest. "But I love you, too. I don't want to have to forget about you."

My ache was immense. It spread from my heart down through my limbs, and it sank so deep inside me that I couldn't imagine my life without Ryder in it. His arms tightened around me, and I think he may have been crying, too. It was impossible to tell, because my body was so wracked with sobs that it took everything in him to hold me steady.

"I don't know where I'm gonna go," I finally said.

The reality of this crippled me, but even more than that, I realized I needed to tell him something. "Mono Lake. They went to Mono Lake."

"Then that's where you need to go." Ryder picked up a stick and began sketching a map in the dirt. "It's hard to get there from here. You should turn around and head back to the Valley. I'll make sure you get a horse, maybe even a car. Supplies – a few days' worth, at least." He paused. "And I'll make sure Daniel doesn't follow you; I'll escort you out myself. Make sure you're safe, make sure you find them..."

Tears began rolling down my cheeks again. "But Ryder... I don't want to lose you."

As he pulled me to his chest, his answer was strangled. "I don't want to lose you, either."

I slept fitfully. My dreams were haunted by gunshots and vertigo, and even Ryder's arms couldn't comfort me. Instead of sleeping, I found myself memorizing every single detail about him. The feeling of his warmth as he lay behind me, the sound of his breathing, his suntanned skin and the freckles that spread across his forearms.

I thought of his laugh, of the sleepy way he always stole the blankets, and I was overcome by so much grief that it was hard to stop myself from breaking down again. It was only the pressure of his hand against my ribcage that kept me from losing it.

He chewed his fingernails right down to the quick, and a scar stretched around the curl of his right thumb. A tree-climbing accident, he'd told me one day while we sunned like lizards on the banks of the Merced.

Everything had seemed so hopeful then, so sunny and innocent that even my memories were clouded by golden light. But he'd known about Camp Four then, and Daniel was already killing deserters on our borders.

If I'd known then what I knew now, would I still have come away from the city? Would I still have left my family and the Movement and everything I'd ever known? Would I still have taken risks, conquered fears and slept under the stars? Would I still have fallen in love with him?

I didn't have much time to think about it. Just as I began to finally sink into sleep, wisps of gray began lightening the eastern horizon. Before I knew it, it was a chilly, early dawn.

Rex woke us by tapping Ryder's boot. Ryder started and rolled backward, and Rex must have still thought I was still sleeping, because he said, "Did she tell you where the deserters are?"

I froze, but Ryder's response was immediate: "Yes, sir. Confirmed they went to Fresno."

A pause. "Think you can trust her?"

"With my life, sir."

"Very well. If she tells anyone what we're doing out here…"

"She won't. Knows how much we have to lose."

"That's what worries me." Rex's footsteps crunched as he paced around the clearing. "How soon can she walk?"

"Soon. But just so you know, we're using a safety line today."

"We are?"

"She's never made this walk before."

A pause. "Very well. I just need some strong readings from her. I won't let her slip away without doing her part."

Ryder nodded. "You'll get them."


The highline looked like a string stretched across the top of the world. As Ryder double-checked the straps of my climbing harness, I realized I had grossly underestimated my fear of heights.

How could anyone possibly walk this without a safety line?

The Taft Point route stretched in the gap between two cliffs – a horseshoe of space that allowed Ryder to very quickly hike back and forth between sides, inspecting gear. The cliffs were gaping, and they opened to a narrow stretch of nothingness that was more than three thousand feet from top to bottom. The height was dizzying – incomprehensible even without a head injury – and the expanse of sky below us made my eyes play tricks on me. The dim stillness of the Valley floor seemed to be moving away from me, and the cliff walls stretched and bent as the sun worked its way over the horizon.

I imagined the granite shifting under my feet, and I was struck by the similarities between this and the way I'd felt inside the Wawona Tunnel. Neither extreme was healthy – too much space had the same effect on me as too little. Both made me feel small and insignificant, as vulnerable and defenseless as a child.

"See this ring?" Ryder pointed to the large steel ring attached to the other end of my safety line. The webbing ran through its opening, and it slid back and forth when he touched it. "Step over it when you start walking, and your line will drag it along the webbing behind you."

I nodded.

"The most dangerous place to fall is right at the beginning or the end, because you could swing around and smack into the cliffs. But if you fall in the middle, you'll have nothing to hit but air."

He tried to look reassuring. "If you feel yourself falling, try to catch the line with your hands. Otherwise, you'll bounce around and it may be harder to reach. But if you can't grab the line, don't fight it. The harness'll catch you, and you can sort out your balance once you stop bouncing."

I nodded. What I really wanted to do was turn around and run, but it was too late to leave now. Rex was waiting just behind me, and he had already double-checked my heart monitor to make sure it wouldn't malfunction during my walk.

"You understand why I need you to do this, don't you?" Rex had said. "We have worked too hard to simply let you walk away."

I didn't bother to respond. I had glimpsed into his soul – deep beneath his handsome face and cool, blue eyes – and all I had seen was greed.

Unlike Ryder, I didn't believe in greed for the right reasons.

What I saw in Ryder's eyes was harder to quantify. Grief, fear and remorse, mostly. These emotions were tempered by resignation, but they were sometimes overpowering – like when he tightened my safety line and whispered, "I'll be waiting for you on the other side, Red. You can do this. And even if you can't, I'll still be there to catch you. OK?"

Catch me. The idea sounded hollow now – its promise marred by its reality. But I knew Ryder was doing everything he could for me, so I simply squeezed his hands and waited for him to take his place on the far side of the cliff.

As he walked away, I felt Rex creep up behind me. "Godspeed," he whispered, laying his hand on my shoulder.

His presence startled me. I could feel the heat of his hand as it burned into my skin, but it wasn't comforting heat. It was too strong, like a flame, and I felt it creeping inside me and attaching itself to my fear.

I shrugged myself free and took a step toward the cliff. *Here goes nothing.*

# CHAPTER THIRTY-SIX

The webbing began to quiver the second my foot made contact. The sky below me twisted and wavered, and I felt perspiration rising on my temples. I took a moment to steady myself. *Get yourself together, Autumn.*

The horizon seemed to spin a little, and the breeze that kicked up below me sent the cliffs bending inward like the rocks inside the tunnel. I had the sense that I was poised over the edge of the world, that I would never stop falling if I lost my balance. Instead, I would keep tumbling and tumbling, head over foot over head over foot. For the rest of eternity.

My thoughts returned to Ken, to the only person who'd ever died on this highline, and I wondered what his body looked like when it had finally hit the ground. Did it liquefy? Splatter? Explode in so many directions that there wasn't anything left?

I shook my head and remembered what Ryder had said the first day I ever tried slacklining: *You gotta feel the webbing, Red. Every tiny vibration; every little inconsistency and flicker. You gotta know that webbing better than you've ever known anything in your entire life. Can't fake it, or you'll fall.*

I took a breath and felt my foot connect with the line. The spinning of the horizon lessened, and my shoulders began unknotting.

*See how I'm not just popping up to stand? Taking a moment to feel the webbing, and taking a moment to gather my thoughts before I start. Gotta clear all that shit out before you get up. Just... whoosh. You know?*

I closed my eyes. My eyes twitched this way and that, but I remembered Ryder's words, and I willed them to be still. I relived the way I'd felt that first afternoon at Church Bowl, the way Ryder's lessons left me amplified and present and centered.

*I will walk Taft Point.*

This was my last conscious thought before I began.

And then: just... whoosh.

From the moment I stepped off the edge, my eyes didn't leave Ryder's. He was standing on the other side of the cliff, still as a stone, and he held me in his gaze like an anchor.

He *was* an anchor. He was my anchor.

I placed one foot forward, and then another. The webbing jerked and bucked, but I swung my hands to the side and willed myself not to fall. I could feel the emptiness below me, the dizzying expanse of sky that opened into nothing. It left me sweaty and light-headed; it swirled and tugged at me like the claws of a monster.

I took another step, and I began to imagine that Ryder and I were connected in more ways than just our eye contact. I willed myself to see our Essences, to see a bridge between us, and I held onto it.

Slowly, step by step by step, I began to see strands of light. They twisted and shifted and spanned the distance between us. I think Ryder must have seen the strands, too, or maybe he just sensed them, because his eyes widened, and his intensity raced toward me. Strong arms wrapped around my shoulders, and I felt his promise: *I will always be here to catch you.*

Confidence infused my steps as I took one step forward, and then another, and then another. My feet stuck like glue to the webbing, and my arms became loose. The breeze began rippling through my hair, but I let the wind pass through me. In and out. In and out. Measured and controlled as my breathing.

Before I knew it, I was more than a quarter of the way across the gap. I could sense the drop below me, the crumbling of boulders and the slow tilting of the world on its axis, but these realities didn't scare me anymore.

I was walking Taft Point. And I was going to finish this.

The sun was getting higher now, and I could feel the warmth of its rays as they settled on my shoulders. A hawk keened somewhere in the distance, and then I passed the halfway mark.

Ryder was getting bigger now. His eyes were wide, and I was reminded of the first night we'd shared at Squaw Caves. I had glimpsed his soul then – had been so spellbound by its beauty that I'd completely lost my senses and given everything to him.

I realized here, walking across this chasm, that I didn't regret that night. I didn't regret a single thing about him, because I had been right about him. The depth of his soul wasn't simply an aftereffect of that little white pill. It was as real as the webbing below my feet, as the sun on my skin and the wind in my hair. It was real because I'd seen it then. And right now, I saw it again.

More than that, I meant what I'd said: I loved him.

I loved the tilt of his smile, the warmth of his eyes, the way he dreamt of being a doctor and leading the Community into the future. He wasn't perfect – not by a long shot – but he wanted more than anything to be a good person.

He wanted to make his father proud. And he wanted to make me proud. And he was going to help me get out of here.

When I passed the three-quarters mark, something in Ryder's expression changed. His entire body tensed, and I felt fear spread through his limbs and paralyze him in place. His eyes didn't waver from mine, but his jaw set, and a trickle of perspiration dripped down the line of his cheekbone.

*What just happened?* I could feel the disturbance. The air around me changed as fear and hesitation raced through his Essence. The feelings twisted and collided and ignited, and then the arms that steadied me wavered.

I became acutely aware of the distance between us, of the remaining twenty-five feet of webbing that stretched like a wire across the vastness below me.

I was standing on a highline. Between two cliffs. With three thousand feet of air between my body and the ground.

Terror shuddered through me, and the line began to shake. Gently at first, and then more violently – side to side to side like the coils of a spring. I wavered and rocked my hands as I felt my body twisting. The horizon was moving again, and my heartbeat echoed between my ears: boom, boom, boom, boom, BOOM.

My eyes flicked from Ryder's and began dropping to the highline below me. *If you feel yourself falling, try to catch the line with your hands.*

But there was something imploring about the look in Ryder's eyes. His headshake was slight – almost imperceptible – but it was there, and it was pleading: Don't look away from me. Don't look down.

Why? The highline stretched securely, and I could feel the snugness of my climbing harness against my waist. I was far enough from both cliffs that I didn't need to worry about crashing into them, but Ryder's expression was beseeching – even more powerful than my desire to end this. I took a breath and answered him with a nod of my own.

*Ryder thinks I can do this. So I can.*

The webbing didn't stop shaking until I refocused on Ryder's eyes. The fear lessened, and I heard his words again. *Just... whoosh.*

One step, and then another, and then another – until there were twenty feet between us... and then fifteen... and then ten.

I almost lost my footing when I passed the eight-foot mark. A breeze picked up and blew me off balance, and I had to swing my arms so violently, I almost overcorrected and pitched sideways.

My body was slick with sweat, but I was close to the end now. The cliff walls were bending toward me, the webbing was pulling me near and the world was spinning around me. Ryder was reaching for me, and I was striding, striding, striding – racing forward and collapsing into his arms.

His arms clamped around my back, and his entire body shuddered as he dragged me from the edge. Adrenaline and relief flooded me as we collapsed to the ground, and the smile that split my face was unlike anything I'd ever felt before. *I did it,* I thought. *I walked Taft Point, and you were here to catch me.*

His grip didn't loosen. I didn't realize he was crying until I felt his tears smear against my cheeks. But he wasn't just crying. He was sobbing – strangled, violent shakes that racked his entire body.

His sobs were so intense that after a few moments, I pulled back. We made eye contact, and I realized he wasn't simply relieved. He was furious.

"You son of a bitch!" Now he was on his feet. He was storming down the trail toward Rex, and his fists were clenched. "What the hell is wrong with you? Do you have any idea what could have happened to her?"

I rolled to my side and watched Rex's approach in bewilderment. The older man strode toward us cautiously, but it was no use. The moment he was within striking distance, Ryder threw a punch.

I gasped as Rex blocked him. "Son, you don't understand. It was for your own good..."

"My own good? How could that have possibly been for my own good?"

Ryder swung again, and Rex tried to dodge his blows as dust rose at their feet. The cliff edge loomed dangerously near, and a pit formed in my stomach as Rex swung Ryder into a headlock and insisted, "Son, trust me! It was for your own good!"

More punches. Shuffling. Rocks and dust and twigs rising and tumbling off the edge of the cliff. "You're a *monster*. Everyone was right about you." Ryder was out of breath now, and a trickle of blood oozed from a wound on Rex's cheekbone.

My mind reeled, and I struggled to figure out what I'd missed. I climbed to my knees, and I steadied myself for the safety line's tug as it strained against the highline behind me.

But there was no tug. No strain. No pressure from the climbing harness as it reached the end of its slack.

And then it hit me. The feeling of Rex's hand as it pressed against my shoulder. The uncomfortable heat. The nearness of his presence.

"What kind of psychopath would even *think* to unclip her?"

There it was. The fear and paralysis in Ryder's eyes, the disturbance in the air. The pleading, terrified expression that had told me not to look down. Not to fall. Not to trust the safety line that held me.

Because there had never been a safety line.

Rex had pulled it free before I even started walking.

# CHAPTER THIRTY-SEVEN

I couldn't react. Couldn't do anything except cling to the boulder below me as a wave of vertigo struck me so violently I feared I'd be flung to my death.

I hadn't had a safety line. Hadn't had anything between my body and the valley floor except an inch-wide strip of webbing that bobbed and shook and threatened to drop me at any moment.

I hadn't had a safety line, and Rex *had known* it. Realized as he held onto my shoulder that he was most likely sending me to my death. Counted on that. Planned it all along.

Ryder didn't share my paralysis. His reaction was all rage, but even in his anger, it was clear he was outmatched. Rex outweighed him by at least twenty pounds, and he easily blocked the majority of Ryder's blows.

Worse, it was clear he was getting angry himself. "Will you listen to me, goddammit?" he said, twisting Ryder's arm around his back. "I won't tolerate this insubordination from you much longer, son."

Ryder cried out and gritted his teeth. Mud and dust streaked his cheeks, and his breathing became uneven.

Rex hissed, "Ryder, I know what's best for you. I always have. And I know you think Autumn is the answer right now, but you're wrong. She's a distraction; she's taking you away from your purpose."

"Then let her go! Let her go like you said you would."

"I *can't*. You must understand that. She's a liability, and she'll destroy everything we've ever built together."

"Then why did you bring her here?" His voice became strangled. "Why make her walk if you had no intention of letting her go?"

Rex loosened his grip slightly. "I'm sorry, son. I just thought if she made the mistake herself…"

"You thought *what*?" Ryder whipped his arm free and turned to advance again on his father. "You thought there wouldn't be any hard feelings between us if it wasn't your fault?"

"Ryder…" Rex dodged another blow, and a cascade of pebbles skittered off the cliff by his feet. "You don't get it. You won't now – not for a while – but you have to trust me. Autumn is a distraction, and you'll thank me for getting rid of her someday when you look back and realize I'm doing this for you."

Ryder laughed. "*For me*? You honestly expect me to believe you're doing this for *me*?"

"I am." Rex's voice became defiant. "For the past fifteen years, I've done nothing but work every single minute of every single day. And do you know why? It's for *you,* son, to create a better world for you. Is this the gratitude you show me?"

"You expect *gratitude*? You lead us up here, pull a stunt like that, and you honestly expect me to *thank* you for it?"

"I expect you to show me some respect." Now, Rex began to falter. His voice lost its velvet edges, and he wiped a trickle of sweat from his brow. "I expect you not to blow everything I've built for you!"

Ryder surveyed the Valley floor and spit. "Didn't build this for me. Didn't even ask if this is what I wanted." He turned his back. "Come on, Autumn; let's get out of here."

I opened my mouth to speak, but I couldn't. Ryder couldn't see the transformation on Rex's face, but I could. Rex's eyes darkened, and his expression twisted so quickly that he became almost unrecognizable. Heartbreak and bewilderment flashed through his expression, and then his jaw set.

He hardened. I could sense the determination filling him – spreading through his insides and wrapping around him until he wasn't even Rex anymore. He was a soldier. A machine. A man with a purpose. And right now, only two things stood between him and his purpose.

Ryder and me.

"No!" From somewhere deep down, I found the strength to pull myself off my rock. I staggered to my feet, and then I ran – bypassing Ryder and vaulting into Rex as he marched forward to reach for Ryder's neck.

"Stay away from him!"

Rex was off-balance now, and I was punching – wailing into him with what little strength I had left. All the lies, the prodding, the cover-ups... I took my fear and my heartbreak, and I projected it into every punch I threw.

But it was no use. Rex was twice my size, and it wasn't long before he twisted me into a chokehold and pushed me toward the cliff edge. "Stay where you are, Ryder," he demanded. "I'm serious. Stay where you are, or she's gone."

Ryder met my eyes and clenched his fists. "Let her go."

"I'm not going to do that. I'm going to wait for you to get into the Jeep, and then the three of us are going to head back to the

Valley together. Autumn is going to get a nice setup in Camp Four, and you are going to lead my uprising. Or…" He shoved me toward the edge, and he held my neck as I faltered and tried to claw my way free.

The Valley floor dipped and sprawled before me, and I could feel my larynx closing as Rex pinched the air from my throat. Bright spots of color burst in my vision, and my legs wobbled as I struggled to stay on my feet.

"You'll forget about her in a month. Forget about everything except our victory when we prove to the world that the Essence theory is a lie."

I tried to glance sideways, to see Ryder's reaction, but Rex's grip was too tight. So Ryder's voice sounded strange and disconnected when he finally answered, "Fine. You win. OK? Just don't let her fall."

Rex's grip around my neck tightened. "I expect you to cooperate, son. She'll be safe as long as you follow my directions. Right now, I need you to walk to the Jeep."

The sound of shuffling. "Fine. I'm leaving. Get her away from the edge."

Rex waited until Ryder was out of range, and then he slowly pulled me from the cliff. We began walking, and he kept a tight grip on the back of my neck to prod me forward.

As I stumbled along the trail, I felt something heavy in my pocket. It took a few moments to place it, and then I remembered: Ryder's locket. It had a long chain, was reasonably heavy. He wouldn't expect me to have it; could I swing it around and hit him with it somehow?

The irony that I was turning to a Centrist pendant for salvation didn't escape me. I faked a stumble, dug into my pocket and dragged it free. Ryder and I made eye contact across the parking lot, and I could tell he saw it. His nod was almost unnoticeable, but it was all the encouragement I needed.

I dropped the locket and waited until the chain was fully extended, and then I wheeled and swung the pendant wide and fast until it arced through the air and struck Rex against the eye socket. The chain left a long slash across his cheek, and he cried out in surprise. Dropping my neck, he cradled his bleeding face with both hands.

Then Ryder was beside me. He gripped Rex's neck with both his hands and began pushing him back to the cliff. "You can't control everything. Don't you get it?"

Rex wiped at the blood in his eye as Ryder dangled him over the drop. "It's scary, right – to feel powerless? To have to trust that someone's looking out for you? Because what if he's not? What if he's just using you, letting you believe he cares about you so he can manipulate you?"

"Son, it's not like that. I care about you–"

Ryder shook him again. "Do you, Father? Do you?"

"I do!" Rex's voice was wild now. "I do, Ryder, I do! I'm sorry... I didn't mean..."

"What *didn't* you mean to do? Unclip Autumn's harness? Threaten to shove her off a cliff?" He snarled. "Tell me, Father, what *didn't* you mean to do?"

"I'm sorry, son... Please forgive me; please don't let me fall..."

"You don't want to fall?" Ryder pushed him farther into the emptiness. "Tell me, if it's OK for Autumn, why isn't it OK for you?"

"Ryder..." Rex was blubbering now. He held Ryder's arm with both hands and sobbed, "Please, son. I'm sorry. I'm so, so sorry... I'll let her go... I'll let you both go..."

"I could kill you right now." Ryder leaned closer. "I could. You know that, right?" He wrenched his father away from the edge and dragged him toward the beginning of the highline.

My heart dropped. I knew I should feel vindicated, but I didn't. I just felt... sad. And defeated. If we forced Rex to walk the highline, were we any better than he was?

Ryder forced Rex to the edge, but instead of making him walk, he simply reached for the safety line. "I could kill you right now," he repeated, wrapping the cord tight around Rex's arms and shoulders, "but I won't. You know why? Because you don't kill people unless you're truly a monster."

He left Rex lying in the dirt and turned to go. "Let's get out of here, Red. Think I've seen enough."

# CHAPTER THIRTY-EIGHT

Ryder didn't begin to crumble until he had driven us a few miles away from Taft Point. Pulling to the side of the road, he motioned to the steering wheel and said, "Can you drive, Red?"

I nodded. I had never sat in the driver's seat before, but the challenge seemed remarkably straightforward compared to everything we had just overcome.

"What the hell just happened?"

His eyes were wild as he slid into the passenger seat beside me. We made eye contact, and I realized it was my turn to carry him. Climbing into the driver's seat, I reached sideways and grabbed his hand. "We did the right thing. Now we're getting out of here."

He nodded and took a shaky breath. "Daniel should have left for Fresno by now," he managed. "The Valley will be unguarded, but what…?"

"We need to unlock Camp Four," I said. "Tell everyone what's really been happening in there. Let the Community dissolve if it wants to."

"And then what?"

"I have no idea." My words hovered between us. In that pause, I felt the full weight of our situation. It drifted on the wind and settled on our shoulders – as thick and heavy as it was devastating: we had both built our realities around truths that didn't exist.

Neutrality wasn't the key to longevity, but abundance wasn't, either. Both mantras were just words. They were as hollow and meaningless as the heart rate monitors that still clinked on both of our wrists.

I looked down at my wristband, and I tried to remember how nervous and excited I'd felt when I first arrived here. The Community was supposed to be the answer, and Rex was supposed to be our savior. He was going to overthrow Cedar and the Centrist Movement, and he was going to justify Brady's death with a truth that actually made sense.

But what was the truth, anyway? What had happened to Brady had been a terrible accident, but overthrowing Cedar wouldn't stop the pain that sank in my chest every time I thought about him. Nothing would ever stop that. It was now part of my truth – just as the Movement was part of Cedar's truth and the overthrow was part of Rex's truth.

"Maybe the truth isn't a reality like we think it is," I finally said. "Maybe it's just a choice – something you make up for yourself to give your life some meaning. Isn't right or wrong; just is."

Ryder closed his eyes. "So if the truth isn't a reality, what is?"

I pictured the twisting strands of light I'd seen spanning the distance between us. "This is true," I said, placing my hand on his chest. "Essences are true. That feeling you get, when you think your heart is going to burst through your chest?"

His expression softened. "Yeah. That's true."

"And so is this." I pressed my lips against his, and I felt energy ignite between us. He wrapped his arms around me, and I was enveloped by the taste of him, by the scent of his skin, and by the overpowering sense of *rightness* I felt when he was with me.

"Love is true," he finally said. "This is true."

"It is." I tightened my fingers around his. The future didn't seem quite so frightening with him by my side.

"So, where to?" he asked. "San Francisco? The East Side? Where should we head first?"

I touched Brady's stuffed lion in my pocket. I thought of Aunt Marie and my mother, of our friends waiting for us on the East Side, and I shrugged. "I'm not really sure yet."

I cast one last look at the Valley, and then I stomped the gas pedal. The Jeep jerked forward, and Ryder laughed. "Don't worry, Red. You'll get it. We'll figure it out together."

I smiled as we accelerated down the road. These things were true: the sunshine on my skin, the warmth of Ryder's hand in mine and the breeze that twisted through the tendrils of my no longer jagged hair.

I didn't know where the future would take us, but I did know one thing: as imperfect and flawed as we were, we were in this together.

Maybe that's the only truth we needed.

# ACKNOWLEDGMENTS

First and foremost, I would like to thank my parents, Kevin and Tammy O'Kane, my sister, Shana Laflin, and my grandmother, Ethel Odom, for always being my biggest fans. Same goes for Allen Walker, the best darn friend and critique partner a girl could ever ask for. This book would not exist without your unwavering support and encouragement.

Hannah Bowman, my literary agent extraordinaire, deserves five pages of acknowledgements for all the time and dedication she has put into this project. Suffice it to say ESSENCE has grown tremendously under her guidance, and I will be forever in her debt for always inspiring me to become a better writer. Many thanks for believing in me even when I wasn't sure I believed in myself.

I would also like to thank the rest of my family, particularly Jamie Watson, whose first draft feedback was spot-on and very much appreciated. My Colorado writers group—Beth Christopher, Christina McCarthy, Eugene Scott, Sean McAfee, Joe Kovacs and Rene Zimbelman—contributed immensely to my first fifty pages. I'm also so appreciative of Keith Wood for the fabulous brainstorming sessions and Mark Stevens for taking me under his wing during my very first writers' conference.

Molly Horner and Theresa Ho served as my resident Yosemite National Park fact-checkers, and they patiently answered many of my most inane questions, like, "Could you really climb a Pacific dogwood tree?" and "How probable is that Tunnelview zipline?" Many of the events in this book were inspired by the actual summer I spent living and working in Yosemite, so a special shout-out to all my 2004 Boystown partners-in-crime and all the real adrenaline junkies whose Camp Four antics and death-defying stunts never ceased to amaze me. I would especially like to acknowledge Mary Siner, who inspired the character of Kadence and who has always been the yin to my yang. Mary, I would live in Tent #44 with you again in an instant!

Erik Cobb and Anita Hunter are the two English teachers whose life lessons have left the biggest footprints in my heart. I am also incredibly grateful to Michael, Darlene and Larry Chickos for sharing in my excitement and joy while I wrote this book.

Special thanks to all the writerly friends I have met along the way, particularly the Goat Posse, the WIPMADNESS crew, and my QT Forum peeps. Also an immeasurable thank you to all the amazing soulmate friends who have inspired me through the years. You have shown me love, compassion, loyalty and adventure, and I wouldn't be able to write about any of these things if you hadn't taught me how to feel things with my soul.

My life is richer because you are part of it.

## ABOUT THE AUTHOR

Lisa Ann O'Kane is a young adult author and former vagabond who once camped out in Yosemite National Park for an entire summer, an experience that inspired her debut novel *Essence.*

Her background is in zookeeping and environmental education, and she has been kicked, cornered, bitten and chased by nearly every animal she has ever loved. She currently resides in Florida, and she is now a huge fan of shooting stars, indoor plumbing and keeping both her feet planted firmly on the trail.

*lisaannokane.com*
*twitter.com/lisaannokane*

16072396R00182

Made in the USA
Middletown, DE
03 December 2014